MATTHEW RIEF

GOLD IN THE KEYS
A LOGAN DODGE ADVENTURE

FLORIDA KEYS ADVENTURE SERIES
VOLUME 1

2nd Edition

D1524096

Press

Originally Edited by Eliza Dee, Clio Editing Services
Second Edition Edited by Sarah Flores of Write Down the Line
Proofread by Donna Rich and Nancy Brown (Redline Proofreading and Editing)

LOGAN DODGE ADVENTURES

Gold in the Keys
Hunted in the Keys
Revenge in the Keys
Betrayed in the Keys
Redemption in the Keys
Corruption in the Keys
Predator in the Keys
Legend in the Keys
Abducted in the Keys
Showdown in the Keys
Avenged in the Keys
Broken in the Keys
Payback in the Keys

JASON WAKE NOVELS

Caribbean Wake
Surging Wake
Relentless Wake

Join the Adventure!
Sign up for my newsletter to receive updates on
upcoming books on my website:

matthewrief.com

MAPS

This book is dedicated to my beautiful, amazing wife, Jenny.

PROLOGUE

Tenochtitlan, Mexico
1521

The thundering crack of gunpowder roared, and hot lead shot through Xuacal's left arm. The blow knocked the air from his lungs and twisted his body, forcing him to drop to his knees. Blood flowed out from the gash at the base of his left shoulder. Sharp pain burned through his body, but Xuacal ignored it as a large conquistador, dressed in full Spanish armor, marched toward him. The Spaniard eyed Xuacal with a grotesque gaze as he reached for the rapier sheathed to his waist.

Using his right hand, Xuacal grabbed his macuahuitl and jumped to his feet. Lunging toward his attacker, he reared back the wooden club and lodged its obsidian blades hard into the Spaniard's neck, just below his helmet. The Spaniard gave a shrill, anguished cry before collapsing to the ground. His body was motionless as Xuacal ripped his club free.

With blood still dripping from the blades, he swung his macuahuitl at another conquistador, stabbing through his breastplate with a sharp screech. The Spaniard howled, then ripped the club from Xuacal's grasp. He lunged at Xuacal, tackling him to the ground and sending both of their bodies tumbling down the stone steps before coming to rest on a small plateau.

Shaking himself free from the haze and dizziness, Xuacal jumped to his feet and reached for a broken spear under the bloody body of one of his brothers. Turning back toward the Spaniard, he saw that the man was taking aim at him with his firearm. With his shoulder burning from the lodged bullet, Xuacal dove to the ground just as the Spaniard pulled the trigger. There was a bright flash followed by a deafening explosion and a plume of white smoke bursting into the air.

The bullet had soared just inches away from Xuacal, who charged at the Spaniard with his spear. Using all of his strength, Xuacal slammed the stone tip with enough force to slice right through the Spaniard's breastplate. Blood dripped out as Xuacal ripped his spear free and kicked the dying man to the ground.

Xuacal trudged to the end of the plateau and peered down at the mass of white men forming at the base of the temple's steps. The Spaniards turned and fired off a volley from their matchlocks, causing a wave of hot lead to cut through the Aztec soldiers' lines and sending nearly an entire unit to the ground. Clouds of dark smoke blanketed the streets in the shadow of the Huey Teocalli, a structure that rose nearly two hundred feet into the air. On most days, it was a beacon that towered over the great capital city, its brilliant dyed stones visible for hundreds of miles around. Xuacal gazed up at the structure, then took a deep breath, feeling the sting of smoke crawl into his nostrils.

"Force them out of the city!" Xuacal yelled to his men. He pulled up his macuahuitl and pointed it at the conquistadors. Rushing down the stone steps toward the base of the temple, he rallied his warriors with a resounding battle cry and charged right into the heart of the fray.

Aztec warriors swarmed the Spaniards, forcing them to fall back toward the lakeshore. They attacked relentlessly with their clubs and rained spears down from their atlatls. The Aztecs fell by the hundreds, but thousands more took their place as the armies of the most powerful empire in the Americas closed in on their foreign enemies. Xuacal watched as the Spaniards were surrounded. There was only one hope for Cortés and his men. Sitting on his white horse, surrounded by hundreds of his countrymen, Xuacal heard the leader of the Conquistadors give the order for his army to retreat.

"They're on the run, Xuacal," an Aztec warrior said.

Xuacal held his hand against his shoulder, feeling the bullet lodged inside as he tried to stop the bleeding.

"Keep it that way, Zolin," Xuacal replied. "Force

them back to whatever abysmal land they came from, and let no pale demons enter the city again."

The young, promising warrior stared into his elder's fiery brown eyes. Summoning all of his willpower, he turned and ran after the fleeing Spaniards, leading a charge of thousands of fearsome warriors. Xuacal ordered his men to flank their enemies and strike them with spears as they fled onto the main causeway that connected the island city to the mainland.

Seeing that the battle was soon to be over, Xuacal returned his gaze to the holy Huey Teocalli. He walked to its base and looked up at the brightly dyed cloths that hung from the two steeples at the top of the temple. With his eyes narrowed and his heart thumping in his chest, he watched as they were engulfed in an inferno of yellow flames and black smoke.

Xuacal reached beneath his outer garments and felt a rolled-up parchment still tied by a thin piece of cloth, then heaved a sigh of relief. Gritting his teeth, he tackled the first few steps, trekking past the magnificent balustrades that flanked the broad staircase on both sides. He ignored the pain throbbing from his shoulder, forced his body onward, and eventually reached the plateau at the top of the staircase.

Rotating his body around, he gazed out over the vast horizon and quickly focused on the horde of warhorses and glistening armor being pushed back by Aztec warriors. Men tackled each other in the shallows near the causeway. Screams filled the air, coming from both the battle and the city around him.

Cracks of thunder and flashes of lighting from their enemies' weapons erupted across the air like a passing storm. Puffs of smoke combined to cover the fleeing soldiers in a haze of white.

Turning back to face the steeples, Xuacal gripped his macuahuitl and stumbled toward the structure's main façade. Blood dripped from his shoulder, splattering dark red across the smooth tezontle floor as he advanced through the towering entryway. Fire flickered from the lamps set around the edges of an immense space filled with statues and ceremonial objects, the walls covered with paintings depicting images from the Aztecs' past.

Xuacal, moving with labored steps toward the main chamber of the structure, noticed two Aztec warriors lying dead on the floor. Pools of blood surrounded them, and as Xuacal rolled one of the men over, he instantly recognized the warrior's face. It was one of his oldest and most trusted friends, a man who'd been chosen by Montezuma himself to be one of his personal guards. Xuacal pushed back his emotions and pressed onward, taking a few more steps before reaching the opening to the main chamber. His body froze in an instant as he heard the distinct sounds of footsteps and the rattling of metal echoing from inside. He gripped his macuahuitl as hard as he could and fought to control his shaky breathing.

The source of the sounds soon materialized as a conquistador stormed out from the chamber with heavy steps. The large man wore a full set of Spanish battle armor, including a gorget that offered protection for his neck. His hands were full of gold ornaments and heirlooms.

The conquistador grunted and adjusted his morion, his steel helmet with sweeping sides that came to a point. He took a step back as he noticed Xuacal staring at him and blocking off his escape. Glaring at Xuacal, he opened his arms, allowing each and every gold piece to rattle to the ground at his feet. He reached for the rapier sheathed to his waist and slid out the fine Toledian blade in one crisp motion, then pointed its tip straight at Xuacal.

The conquistador's armor and weaponry were vastly superior to Xuacal's, and the bullet lodged in his shoulder would hold him back, but he didn't care. He'd seen thousands of his warriors die at the hands of the white demons, and he vowed that this last conquistador would never make it out of the temple alive.

The conquistador gave a loud grunt, then charged at Xuacal. Rearing back his rapier, the Spaniard swung it swiftly toward Xuacal's chest. Xuacal dropped to the ground at the last second, narrowly escaping the blade as it sliced through the air just inches from his head. The conquistador brought his sword around, then swung it downward, forcing Xuacal to roll to the side to avoid having his body chopped into pieces. Just as Xuacal regained his balance, the Spaniard slammed his boot into the Aztec's forehead, driving his head back and knocking the air from his lungs.

Placing his hand on the ground to steady himself, Xuacal felt a sharp pain explode from his leg as his adversaries' rapier cut a gash across his exposed thigh. He rolled backward, ignoring the pain, and avoided two more swift attacks from the conquistador before painfully rising to his feet. Blood dripped down his leg, pooling on the ground beneath him. He kept his gaze drawn to the Spaniard, not allowing himself to wince for a second.

With flared nostrils, Xuacal lunged at the conquistador, dodging a swing of his rapier before rearing back his macuahuitl. Before the Spaniard could react, Xuacal launched the obsidian blades through the air, stabbing them into the back of his enemy's breastplate. There was a loud screech as the rows of razor-sharp blades pierced through the armor, penetrating the conquistador's flesh. He wailed, then slammed the handle of his rapier onto the top of Xuacal's head.

With Xuacal dazed, the conquistador ripped the macuahuitl from his hands and grimaced as he pried the weapon free from his breastplate. He tossed the Aztec club to the other side of the chamber, then turned and swung his rapier, slicing a gash across Xuacal's chest and forcing him to fall backward as blood flowed out. Xuacal felt his life slipping away as the conquistador gripped his long black hair with a tight fist. The man stared deep into Xuacal's eyes, watching him as he brought his rapier back, preparing to strike a final blow. His intense eyes bulged, and he snarled like a wild animal as he forced the rapier toward Xuacal's neck.

Just as the blade was about to sever Xuacal's head from the rest of his body, the Aztec warrior ripped his hair free of the conquistador's grasp and reached for the dagger latched to his enemy's ankle. Summoning all of the strength he had left, he tackled the man to the ground, and in one quick motion, stabbed the dagger into the side of his face. The conquistador gave out a final, labored breath, then his body went limp.

Xuacal ripped out the blood-covered dagger and dropped it to the floor. Unable to stand, he crawled toward the main chamber, moving over the gold pieces the conquistador had dropped. Easing his body down two stone steps, he soon reached his destination, a chamber filled floor to ceiling with gold artifacts, bars, and jewelry. Xuacal let out a sigh and fell to his side. He heard footsteps approach but didn't move, let alone reach for a weapon. He was dead now regardless, and he knew it wouldn't take long. Blood pooled around him as the footsteps got louder, soon materializing into a figure he recognized as one of his own.

"Chieftain Xuacal," a young Aztec warrior said as he ran over to the dying man. He dropped to his knees beside his leader, grabbing hold of a nearby cloth to try and stop the bleeding. The young warrior's clothing was plain, not like the colorful, adorned garments of a seasoned Aztec warrior. He wore a simple red loincloth with matching feathers that formed bracelets around both wrists. Xuacal noticed a large jaguar tattoo across the side of his chest, indicating that he, too, was a member of the jaguar militant group.

Xuacal shoved the young warrior's hands aside.

"But Chieftain, you'll die," the warrior said.

Xuacal sighed and waved a trembling hand. "Nothing can stop that now." He took a good look at the warrior, staring into his youthful, almond-shaped brown eyes. "You are a jaguar. Tell me, what is your name?"

"Acalan. From the House of the Pelts."

Xuacal nodded as best as he could. "Acalan. I knew your father and knew him to be a good man. Your eyes tell me you are as well, and you will need to be to complete the task I have for you." Xuacal coughed up blood, then pressed his hand against the gash across his abdomen.

"What will you have me do, Chieftain?"

Xuacal took in a deep breath and let it out. He reached for the young warrior, bringing him in closer, then stared into Acalan's eyes with a fierce gaze. "These white men from across the great waters will return."

"But Chieftain, we have them on the run. Their beasts carry them across the causeway toward the mainland as we speak. Their dead bodies fill our streets."

Xuacal shook his head. "As the wave draws back—only to regain its strength and strike once more—so, too, will the white men return."

"And then what will happen, Chieftain?"

"I don't know. But the king's treasure must be taken away from this place. It must be kept safe." Xuacal reached his shaking arm behind a cloth tied around his colorful armor and pulled out a rolled-up parchment. Handing it to Acalan, he said, "Take this. It was given to me by our beloved emperor. He tasked me with it just before he died. Now, you must do as it says, Acalan."

Acalan unraveled the parchment and examined it briefly, his eyes widening as he realized what it was.

"But Chieftain, how will I complete this task? No one will follow my orders."

Xuacal reached for a leather pouch pendant hanging from one of his necklaces and pulled out a stone crest. After soaking it in the blood oozing from his chest, Xuacal then pressed the object against the top of Acalan's hand. He removed it, revealing a marking imprinted on Acalan's skin.

"That is my crest," Xuacal said. "Show that to Zolin, along with the parchment, and he will help you." Xuacal's eyes began to close, and his head fell softly to the ground.

Tears filled Acalan's eyes.

Before taking his last breath, Xuacal whispered, "The Aztec treasure must be kept safe." His body went motionless, and the young warrior knew he was gone.

Acalan rose to his feet and moved into the main chamber, freezing as he focused on a pile of gold that filled the room and adjoining spaces. He'd never seen anything like it before. Still gripping the parchment in his hands, he held it up to his eyes and read the instructions at the top of the page. The lower half of the page was a detailed map describing the location where the treasure was to be taken.

Looking back up at the treasure, Acalan whispered to himself, "May the gods bless our journey."

ONE

Curacao, Southern Caribbean
Spring 2008

I held the long metal spear out in front of me as I finned through the clear tropical water, moving closer and closer to my prey. Rays of sunlight snuck down through the blue overhead, reflecting off the colorful corals and tropical fish surrounding me. My body glided smoothly over a patch of dark green seagrass, then around an edge of jutting limestone.

Looking ahead, I watched as the large grouper I was following swam toward an opening under a rock. It had olive-colored scales with lighter splotches across its sides, and I estimated its stout, oblong body weighed over fifty pounds. Kicking my fins harder, I shot my body toward it, moving in for the kill. Taking aim, I let go of the spear, and the rubber tubing snapped forward, launching the spear through the water like a torpedo. The tip pierced the center of the grouper's head, causing its body to go lifeless in an instant.

I grabbed hold of my spear with one hand and my kill with the other and kicked for the surface, letting out the rest of my air just before breaking through. The sun beat down on me from the west, and I glanced at my dive watch. It was already well past four. I'd lost track of time and had spent over three hours in the water. Not that it mattered. I had nowhere I needed to be and no schedule I had to keep.

I locked the two prongs at the end of the tip back into place, slid the spear out of the grouper's body, and clipped its mouth onto a black mesh bag I'd filled with lobster. Feeling the weight of the fish in my hands, I estimated that it was even larger than I'd originally suspected.

After making sure everything was secure, I swam the quarter mile back to shore. When I was able to stand, I slid my mask down and slipped out of my fins, carrying them by their straps in one hand as I sloshed toward the beach.

A young Jamaican boy ran through the shallows of the crashing waves, meeting me before I could reach the shoreline. His lean body jumped wildly when he laid eyes on the grouper I was now holding in my hand. "Mista Dodge! Mista Dodge! You have caught a great fish today. My papa will be pleased to cook it for you."

I held the grouper out, offering it to the boy. "Give my regards to your father, Jethro."

"I will." He grabbed hold of the fish, carrying it as best as his tiny frame could. "He'll have it cooked in no time. Thank you, Mista Dodge."

"You know where I'll be." I patted him on the back, and he smiled at me before running the fish proudly toward the shore.

A few other kids came out from the palm trees lining the beach to help him carry it to his father's restaurant. One of them ran over to me, and I handed him the bag of lobsters that hung over my shoulder.

Moving up the beach fifty yards, I made my way down a stone path lined on both sides with palm trees and a manicured lawn. I rinsed down my gear and took a quick shower using an outdoor spigot, then toweled off and walked barefoot to my favorite place on the island. Right where the green grass met the white sand, a hammock was strapped between two palms, overlooking the turquoise water of Santa Martha Bay. I grabbed hold of the fabric, plopped down, and let out a long, satisfied sigh as the warm breeze blew against my face.

After a few minutes, one of the resort's waiters approached me, returning soon after with two mojitos. I grabbed one from the bamboo table beside the hammock and brought the cold glass to my mouth for a sip as I watched the waves crash over the shore. After three months of work in the hills of Colombia, this was just what I needed: fresh Caribbean air, blue skies above crystal-clear ocean, and a chilled drink in my hand. It would be nice to be away from the action for a while. To kick back and relax and catch up on some diving.

I gazed out over the water, observing the boats cruising in and out of the bay. I watched as they sailed into the horizon and vanished into the endless blue, carried by the same breeze that played the palm fronds over my head.

There's something about the ocean and crashing waves that causes my mind to drift off with the current.

The Colombia job had been a dangerous one, filled with unexpected attacks sparked by loose alliances. I'd known of the potential dangers before accepting, but it had paid well. Eight years in Naval Special Operations, and another five as a gun for hire, had given me a set of skills unique among the general population—skills that governments and organizations were willing to pay substantially for.

I'd never shied away from danger before, and I liked the freedom that being a private contractor offered. Truth was, I wouldn't mind this life forever. But at thirty-one, I guessed it might be time to settle down soon. To get out of the mercenary game and get a normal job. I'd been tempted to before, but I always ended up missing what I do too much to leave it all behind. No matter what I do, I always find the action, and I always end up in the water. It's just the way my life's been since I was young.

I first went scuba diving with my dad when I was seven. He was stationed in the Middle East and took me to see a shipwreck in the Red Sea. I remember everything about that day. I was nervous at first. The BCD was constricting, and the tank strapped onto my back was heavy, making it difficult to stand. But once I dropped back into the water, all the jitters washed away.

My heart raced as I broke through the surface and took a hesitant breath. Breathing underwater for the first time is a life-changing experience—or at least it was for me. Being able to roam free in the world beneath the waves, admiring the sea life, and exploring the shipwreck without having to resurface for over an hour was the greatest thing I'd ever known at seven years old. Needless to say, I was hooked.

I dove with my dad every chance I got. We explored sites all over the world together—exotic places like Iceland, Greece, Australia, Indonesia, and of course, the Caribbean. I was PADI Open Water certified at ten and certified as a Master Diver during my senior year of high school. Whatever I've done, wherever I've traveled, I've always tried to get below the water and explore as much as I can.

Curacao has great diving and a good nightlife, but it also has places like Pearl Beach, where I can have an entire waterfront almost completely to myself and still be close enough to town. I visited here often to see my dad after he retired and bought a condo, and now that he's gone, I stop by a few times a year to check on the place and enjoy the scenery. He told me in his will to sell it, but I don't think I'll ever be able to bring myself to.

"Finally back, huh?" a familiar voice said.

Turning my head, I watched as Angelina approached my hammock. She was a sight to behold. At five ten, and with brilliant blonde hair and vibrant blue eyes, Angelina Fox looked more like a supermodel than a mercenary. She'd come with me to Curacao to get away from the fighting and relax, if only for a little while.

"If it were anyone else, I'd have sent a search party," she continued in her faint Swedish accent.

I gave her my best smile as she stood beside me, dark aviator sunglasses covering most of her face. Unlike every other time I'd seen her since we'd arrived three days earlier, she wasn't dressed in a bikini or short shorts, but pants and a long shirt.

"Ange . . . Aren't you a sight for sore eyes? What's with the clothes? Heading back into the mix already?"

She nodded. "Got a job offer I couldn't pass up. You gonna be okay here without me?"

"You know I won't. But if you must go, I guess I'll just have to enjoy this view alone. Where are you off to so soon?"

"Cuba."

"Cuba? What kind of job is it?"

"It's a security gig."

"Personal?" I grinned. "You're going back to babysitting, huh?"

She threw her palms in the air. "I go where the money is. Highest bidder. You know that."

Angelina and I first met when I left the Navy and started out as a gun for hire. We'd been hired for the same jobs multiple times since and had saved each other on more than one occasion. She'd been with the Brazilian Special Operations Command and was one of the deadliest snipers in the world—the kind of person you want watching your back in a nasty situation. She kept her body in incredible shape, and despite her innocent looks, she could—and would— kick your ass if given a reason. We'd tried dating before, but our lifestyles didn't exactly allow it to work out well. Afterward, we became friends with occasional benefits and had been that way ever since.

Grabbing hold of my second mojito, I held it up to her. "At least stay for a drink. I have fresh fish on the way. What's one more night of fun gonna hurt?"

She laughed, then shook her head. "I wish I could, Logan, but I have a flight to catch." Leaning over my hammock, she ran her hand through my short brown hair and pressed her soft red lips against my cheek.

"Your Colt's in the back of my rental. Keys are on the counter."

"Already grabbed it while you were swimming."

I gave a soft laugh. "Of course you did."

She smiled, then grabbed the mojito and slammed it back, leaving only the ice cubes behind as she set the glass on the table beside my hammock. "Try and stay out of trouble."

"Trouble? I've got nothing but beaching on my mind for at least a month."

She chuckled. "Heard that before. I bet you don't last a week."

I rolled my legs over, sat up, and slid my sunglasses down to look into her eyes. "Good luck, Ange."

"You too, Logan." She grinned and walked inland, back toward the resort.

I pushed my sunglasses up over my eyes and fell back into the hammock. A few minutes later, Jethro appeared with a plateful of some of the grouper I'd caught, blackened to perfection over an open flame. I ate the fresh fish while lounging in the hammock and looking out over the horizon, savoring every bite and thinking the entire time that nothing beat fresh seafood.

When I finished, I washed it all down with a

coconut water, then dropped my head back and closed my eyes. I took in a deep breath of the fresh air, then let it all out, my body relaxing as I swayed in the tropical breeze.

Having fallen asleep, I woke up just as the sun was dropping below the horizon, fading from view in infinite variations of reds and yellows. Reaching toward the table beside me, I bumped my smartphone, which illuminated to life, revealing that I'd received a message. It was strange because I'd synchronized my phone to my laptop, a habit I'd formed to better enjoy myself whenever I didn't want to be disturbed. The only way I could receive a message directly to my phone was if one of my contacts sent it, and I didn't have very many contacts. I grabbed the phone and shielded my eyes from the sun so I could read it.

Heard your job's up and you're off the grid. It's been too long since we've caught up. I'll be in Argentina for a few more days. There's great diving here, as you know, and we could go to the Khyber for dinner. Hope to see you, old friend.

The message caught me off guard for more than one reason. The first being that it was from Scott Cooper, someone I hadn't seen or heard from in a while. Back in the Navy, he'd been the division officer for years before I showed up to the team. We'd butted heads at first, but our friendship had come about due to our common love of the ocean. We even took a few trips to The Bahamas, and one to his home state of Florida, where we spent three days diving off Key West. But it had been over a year since I'd seen him.

The other reason the message caught me off guard

was its contents. I had to read it over a few times, but the message was clear. Years ago we'd been on an undercover mission in Kuwait. Knowing that our phones were tapped, we'd lied about our location, saying that we were hiding out in a restaurant called Khyber. That was a long time ago, but seeing Scott's message took me back there in an instant. I didn't know what Scott was up to, but I did know that he sure as hell wasn't in Argentina and that he was up to something bigger than just sightseeing. It was clear that wherever he really was and whatever he was doing, he felt his phone might've been compromised.

I replied, letting him know that I would fly out as soon as I could and that I was looking forward to seeing him. A moment later, my phone vibrated to life.

Flight to Buenos Aires at 0900. Saddle up.

Saddle up was what we used to say in the SEALs while we gathered our gear for a mission. Scott must have expected some kind of trouble. I checked the clock on my phone and saw that it was just after seven in the evening. It looked like my relaxing tropical getaway would have to end prematurely. I smiled as I thought about Ange and how she'd been right about me not being able to last a week here. Though, in my defense, it wasn't exactly my fault.

Another hour passed, and I sat swaying in the Caribbean breeze, wondering what Scott might be up to. I'd thought he no longer did this kind of thing. He'd been out of the Navy for a while, but instead of going into contracting, he'd put his degrees to work and started a career in politics. He'd risen fast and had been elected as a US senator representing Florida two years prior. I didn't understand what kind of problem he could possibly have that he would need me for.

When the sun completely vanished, I debated spending the evening in the hammock. It was warm and incredibly comfortable, but I'd made that mistake before, and my body had felt the wrath of the bugs for days. Instead, I stumbled back to my room just up the beach. I opened the sliding glass door, then shut it behind me and collapsed onto the king-sized bed.

TWO

I woke up naturally at zero six hundred, slipped into my shorts, and took a run down the beach, watching the sunrise over the water. Being my last day on the island, I wanted to enjoy one final taste of it before having to leave. I made it the three miles to Rocky Point, then turned around and kicked into high gear for the run back to Pearl Beach.

When I made it back, my lungs were screaming, my heart was pounding, and a layer of sweat covered my body. I'd always loved the way I felt after a nice long run, especially in the morning. To cool down, I splashed into the ocean and dove headfirst into the crashing waves.

I toweled off, then grabbed a quick breakfast of toast, eggs, and fresh pineapple as I headed back to the condo. I took a quick shower, got dressed, and packed up my things. I didn't need much—just a duffle I could throw over my shoulder. The rest of my stuff, including my guns, would stay there. If I needed weapons, I knew I could get them wherever it was I was going. The last thing I needed was to get arrested for bringing a firearm into a country illegally.

I drove to Curacao International as fast as the Camaro I was driving could take me. I parked the car at the rental place and strode toward one of only three ticket counters in the airport. Grabbing my ID from my wallet, I handed it to the woman behind the desk.

"Will you be checking your bag, sir?"

"No, thanks."

She gave me my boarding pass, then pointed to the security checkpoint. "Your flight has already begun boarding."

I thanked her and went through security. As I approached the gate, I peeked at my watch and saw that it was eight fifty-two. The airline staff ushered me onto the terminal, closing the doors just a few minutes after I went through. Looking at my boarding pass, I saw that Scott had booked me first class.

The view from the window at takeoff was beautiful, and the clear sky allowed me to see Bonaire before we reached five thousand feet. I settled in and enjoyed a screwdriver after takeoff, thinking that it was never too early in the day for orange juice. Before I put in my headphones to take a nap, I checked my boarding pass again, this time looking at the destination for the first time. Mexico City.

I guess the Khyber will just have to wait.

The flight from Curacao to the Mexican capital took four hours, and after exiting the plane, I went straight to the departure drop-off location, as it generally had far less traffic, and I knew that that was

28

where Scott would look for me. Yellow cabs lined one side of the road, intermixed with buses and shuttle vans. Mexico City International is a vast conglomerate of vehicles, people, and bright buildings intermixed with the sounds of car horns, police whistles, and the distant taking off and landing of jumbo jets.

I stood alongside the busy road, taking intermittent swigs from my chilled bottled water and wiping the thin layer of sweat forming on my brow. A moment later, a four-door black Jeep Rubicon with off-road tires and a winch covered in mud drove up and idled next to the curb beside me. The driver's door swung open, and Scott stepped out.

It was difficult to imagine more badass crammed into one man than Scott Cooper. He could be doing anything. Like myself, he had the guts and combat ability to be hired by any contractor in the world. But *unlike* me, he had the intelligence to be a Rhodes scholar and hold a major political office.

He wore jeans and a long-sleeved shirt rolled up to his elbows. Smiling behind his dark-rimmed sunglasses, he strode over and threw an arm around me. "Logan!" he said, pulling me in tight.

He was just shorter than me at six foot one, and I had about twenty pounds on him. But despite his new career behind a desk, I knew he was still the same man he had always been: Scott Cooper, the guy you didn't want to compete against, whether it be in a gunfight or a game of chess.

"It's good to see you, Scottie."

"You too," he said, then loosened his hold. "I'm glad you could come. It's been a long time."

"Over a year."

"That long?"

"Back in Madrid," I reminded him. "Time flies when you're running a district."

He smiled. "Or fighting rebels in Colombia."

I shook my head. "Never a dull moment with that one. Got close to biting it a few times."

Scott opened the back door of the Jeep and threw my duffle bag inside.

"I doubt that," he said. "Climb in, and tell me all about it. We've got a long drive ahead of us."

I opened the passenger door and hopped in. I noticed a pistol lodged in its holster resting on the center console and a rifle case on the backseat. Glancing in the rearview mirror, I spotted two black bags half-covered by a Mexican-style blanket. "Where are we going?"

"Sierra Gorda," he said as he sat in the driver's seat and started the engine. "It's up in the mountains, a few hours north of here. I'll tell you more about it once we get out of the city."

He drove the Jeep out of the airport and onto Mexico 57D, an eight-lane superhighway that connects Mexico City to the northern parts of Mexico and the United States.

We spent the next hour catching up. He told me about life as a senator and how his wife and daughter were doing, and I told him about all the jobs I'd had since we last spoke. But our conversation soon turned to the old days in the Navy, like our conversations usually did. We talked about our missions and the people we'd fought with. He was better at keeping tabs on them than I was, and I was glad to hear that most of them were doing well.

After another two hours, we exited the highway and took a back road. The landscape shifted quickly from buildings and houses to sporadic farmland and dense jungle. The old two-lane road soon gained elevation, weaving up into the mountains of Queretaro as we blared Grand Funk Railroad's "We're an American Band " through the speakers.

After a few minutes, Scott turned down the volume and glanced at me. "Do you remember that time in the Keys?"

"Of course," I said, knowing exactly which trip he was referring to. "Three days of raising hell in Key West. Diving and fishing all day and hitting the bars and clubs at night. We were living the dream."

We were driving slower now with the windows rolled down and the top collapsed behind us, both relishing the warm air.

"Have you talked to Jack lately?"

"Yeah, just before I went to Colombia. He's doing good. Still running the charter out of Key West."

Jack Rubio had been a friend of mine since I was young, back when my dad was stationed at Naval Station, Key West. Years later, I introduced him to Scott when we traveled to the Keys, and the two hit it off as good as Jack and I first had.

"Can't imagine him doing anything else. You ever think about that day near the Marquesas Keys? What you found wedged against the reef?"

My eyes grew wide with his words. "Yeah, sometimes. . . ."

Of course I'd thought about it. It would've been impossible not to. I had just grabbed hold of a spiny-tailed lobster when I spotted something shiny beneath the shifting sand. I swam closer and realized it was a gold coin, but it was stuck between a ledge and a large growth of coral. I let go of the lobster and grabbed my dive knife from the sheath strapped to my leg. My heart racing with excitement, I jammed the blade under the coin and pried it free, examining it for a moment, and then closing my hand around it.

Running out of air, I looked up and kicked for the surface. Scott saw me on the way up and raised his hands, wondering what had happened, but I kept kicking and held the coin tight, not wanting it to slip free. When I broke the surface, Jack was sitting at the bow of the boat with his feet hanging in the water.

"What happened?" he'd asked. "I thought you had that one."

I slipped my mask down around my neck and caught my breath. Lifting my fist up to my face, I opened my fingers and watched the gold glisten in the Florida sun.

"What's that?" Jack said.

Scott splashed out of the water ten feet away from me.

"What the hell, Dodge?" he said. "That was a beauty."

"Not as beautiful as this," I said, showing him the coin.

His jaw dropped, and he swam toward me. When I handed it to him, he rubbed it with his fingertips as if he couldn't believe it was real.

We set it on the boat and examined it for a few minutes. The large coin with strange markings around its edges was unlike any I'd ever seen. A person's image was etched craftily into the middle, though none of us had any clue as to who it might've been.

We'd spent the rest of the day swimming all around that ledge, searching for more gold. We spent hours looking around every corner, every crevice in the ledge, and every space in the coral, but by the time the sun was setting, we hadn't found anything else. A few days later, we took it to a dealer in Miami. Unfortunately, he didn't know what it was or where it could've come from, but he did verify that it was gold, and he offered us fifteen thousand dollars for it. It was difficult to see it go, but that was a lot of money for me at the time, even after splitting it three ways.

Since that day in the Keys, we'd never been able to find anything about it, despite hundreds of online searches and numerous trips back to the place where we found it.

Scott was silent for a moment as we drove down a dirt road that was getting worse with every mile. We maneuvered over potholes, through sharp turns, and up steep hills surrounded by thick green jungle.

"What made you think about that?" I said, curious as to why he'd brought up an incident that had taken place so long ago.

He glanced at the GPS open on his phone, then set it on his lap.

"I was in Dubai a few months back and had dinner at a mansion owned by Arian Nazari," he said. "You know, the billionaire oil tycoon?"

I nodded. I'd seen him in the news more than once and knew that along with being incredibly wealthy, he was also very controversial.

"Well, turns out Nazari is an avid antique collector. He's got one of the biggest collections in the world. I was strolling about after dinner with a few other representatives when I saw your coin resting alongside a trove of other artifacts."

"Are you sure it was the one we found?"

He slid his hand into his pocket and pulled out a coin, then handed it to me nonchalantly. As soon as I grabbed it, I knew it was the one. It was the same size, had the same markings, and it had the same person's image engraved in the middle. Also, it had the distinct patterns of coral on one of its sides from being pressed against the reef for so many years. I stared in awe at the incredible piece of treasure that I'd doubted I'd ever see again.

"How'd you get Nazari to part with it?"

Scott grinned. "Long story, but it involved a wager."

"Did he know anything about it? Had he found out where it came from?"

"Turns out that's not a coin." Scott paused, clearly enjoying the surprised look on my face. "Believe it or not, that's an Aztec medallion dated back to the fifteenth century. The image is believed to be Axayacatl, the father of Montezuma the Second. It's incredibly rare. That's why we couldn't find anything about it. In fact, it's the only artifact like it ever found—or at least it was up until a few days ago."

"Someone found another one?"

"That's why we're here," he said. "In 1519, when the Spanish first entered Tenochtitlan, Cortés was amazed by how much gold they found. He wrote that never in human history had so much treasure been in one place—that not even Solomon's troves could compare. We're talking chambers filled from floor to ceiling with gold bars, statues, and all kinds of jewelry. And Cortés wanted all of it." Scott avoided a cluster of potholes, then dialed down the music. "Montezuma offered gifts, but they weren't enough to get the conquistadors out of their hair. In 1520, Cortés and his men held Montezuma hostage in exchange for the city's treasures. But when the king was killed, the whole city attacked the Spaniards. Cortés barely made it out alive, then returned the following year to finish the job with a wave of attacks that eventually led to the city's fall. But legend says that Montezuma had handpicked eight thousand soldiers—the greatest warriors in his army—to take control of the gold and defend it with their lives if anything ever happened. They supposedly took it out of the city and hid it in a secret location where it would be safe from Spanish explorers. The eight thousand men then killed themselves so they could defend the treasure as ghosts for eternity . . . or so the story goes."

"And you think they hid it in Sierra Gorda?"

"Well, the legend says the men hid the gold underground. Then they drained a lake, dug through the earth up to a cave, hid the treasure, and filled the lake again, making the gold inaccessible." Scott opened the Jeep's center console and removed a manila folder. He pulled out a photograph and handed it to me. It was a picture of a round gold artifact. "*That* was found by a goat farmer three days ago."

I stared at it in awe. Holding the Aztec medallion in my other hand, I compared them. They were an exact match, down to the smallest details. The only difference was the coral marks on the one I'd found.

"Imagine, Logan, the greatest treasure in the history of mankind. And it could all be just a few miles away from us."

"Do you really think this is the best use of your time, Senator?" I asked with a grin.

"Do you have any idea how far a treasure like that could go in helping the people here in Mexico? I'd say it's a perfect use of my time."

"Fair enough . . . as long as it gets into the right hands when we find it. But who else knows about it? There's no way something like this could be kept a secret."

"A collector friend of mine in the city called me as soon as he saw it. It was the same collector I'd spoken to before when I came here in search of answers a few months ago. He told me about it when he saw the medallion yesterday."

"Who else did he tell? We can't be the only ones going for this."

"That's why I was in such a hurry to get here. It's also why I used the code in my message. I'm not certain, but I think someone might be following me."

"Any idea who?"

He shook his head. "No clue. There were a few different cars yesterday, but I haven't seen them at all today. But it's strange since I never told anyone where I was going. Searching for gold in Mexico isn't exactly typical politician behavior."

I smiled, knowing that Scott was anything but a typical politician. He'd even run on the premise of fighting against the power that career politicians had abused for years.

"There's one major piece to this puzzle that doesn't seem to fit anywhere, Scottie," I said, rubbing my chin. "If the treasure was from the Aztec capital in Mexico and hidden away in an underwater cave in Sierra Gorda, how did this medallion end up in the Florida Keys?" I held up the gold artifact, still just as enchanted by it as I'd been the day I pried it from the reef.

THREE

Scott eyed the gold medallion, then focused his gaze forward, thundering the off-road vehicle through the rural landscape. He let my question linger for a good minute before offering a reply.

"I don't know. No Aztec treasure has ever been found in the Caribbean before. At least, none that I'm aware of. But perhaps it was one of the many artifacts Cortés looted from the city in his rushed escape."

It was far from a strong theory, but it was possible. I thought it over as we cruised between two hills covered in green shrubs and trees, then eased our way over an old rickety bridge with a white-water river below.

We rounded a sharp corner at the base of a hill and saw two trucks a half mile ahead of us, parked in the middle of the road. Aside from a few locals walking along the shoulder and the occasional ox cart, we really hadn't seen anyone else over the last thirty minutes of driving. Scott pulled the Jeep over at a spot that offered a good vantage point but was still far enough away to go unnoticed. We both stepped out, and Scott grabbed a Leica Monovid eight-times-magnification monocular from the back seat.

"The road's closed," he said as he stared into the monocular. He pulled it from his eye and handed it to me.

I held it up and quickly realized why we'd reached the end of the line. The two trucks were parked end to end, blocking the road. In front of the trucks stood two guys holding AK-47s, and three more were sitting in chairs—smoking and listening to a radio.

"I don't like the look of this," I said.

"There's five in all. I'd rather not start any trouble with these guys."

"Is there another way?" I said, lowering the monocular.

Scott opened the back of the Jeep and pulled out a tourist map of Sierra Gorda. Unfolding it, he pointed to where we were on the map.

"This road is the only route to this side of the lake," Scott said. "If we drive back to the other side or just park here, we're looking at a six-mile trek to where the farmer found the medallion. That's too far to carry all the gear."

I examined the map and noticed a thin line that branched off the road about a quarter mile back. "This could be a service road of some kind."

Scott squinted at the map. "Possibly. If it is, I'm sure it's severely overgrown. But it's worth a shot."

"That's what the winch is for," I said, patting it with my hand.

We turned around and drove back to where the service road was on the map. It took us a few surveys to find it, but when we did, we realized that *overgrown* was an understatement. It was little more than a footpath, really, but Scott drove the Jeep over it anyway, bouncing our way through drooping branches, muddy creeks, and over rough boulders. Using the winch a few times, we managed to reach the other side of the hill, and we stopped when we found a good vantage point.

"There's more by the lake," Scott said, staring into his monocular. "It's a good thing we didn't go all the way back and try the other side. We would've been met with a roadblock that way, too."

We searched the area as best as we could and formulated our plan to stealthily reach the location where the farmer had discovered the artifact. The lake was much larger than I'd expected, stretching at least two miles at the base of the hill, and I couldn't see the other end as it wrapped around a steep mountainside. The roads to the lake were blocked, and there were two boats—one near the edge of the lake and another in the middle—both carrying armed men.

"That's where we need to go," Scott said, pointing toward a waterfall a mile away. "That's where he found the medallion."

The area appeared to be surrounded by men.

"Any idea who these guys are?" Scott asked.

"They're definitely not Mexican military, that's for sure. My bet would be one of the many drug cartels here got a whiff of the treasure and are looking to bring their operation to a whole other level."

After taking another minute to scan over the lake

and the rest of the landscape, we got an idea. We drove the Jeep down the hillside and parked it close to the main road, hidden behind the thick brush, and almost impossible to spot while passing by.

Scott opened the back door and pulled out two bags. "Saddle up," he said. He opened both bags, revealing two full sets of Draeger rebreather dive gear, including weights, masks, fins, and wetsuits. I couldn't count the number of times I'd utilized the closed-circuit breathing apparatuses over the years. Once during a particularly daring mission in Nigeria, the lack of noisy bubbles from the specialty equipment allowed me to take down a high-valued target before he even knew we were there. It was a good thing Scott brought them along, as I knew they'd be necessary if we were going to reach the base of the waterfall undetected.

He handed me a dry bag, and I filled it with two flares and an extra set of clothes and boots before zipping it up and stashing it alongside the rest of the gear. Scott removed a pair of Subgear Prolight flashlights and two Cressi dive knives from a rucksack. I checked the flashlight, then threw it and one of the knives into the front pocket of my pack and zipped it up. He also brought a satellite phone, which he stashed in his dry bag.

I grabbed the pistol and holster from under the passenger seat. The Sig Sauer P226, complete with a gold trident—the SEALs insignia—engraved on the slide, had been standard-issue and the Navy SEALs' handgun of choice for years. I removed the magazine, making sure all fifteen rounds had been loaded, then put the gun back into its holster, strapped it to my leg, and threw my gear bag over my shoulder.

Scott slid the gun case from the back seat and pulled out an HK MP5N with a silencer, scope, and flashlight. He checked it over, making sure the chamber and sights were good and that the mag was full. After handing me two extra mags, he slung the submachine gun over his shoulder, strapped a Glock 19 to his leg, and clutched his gear bag. "Ready to roll," he said, shutting the doors and locking the Jeep.

We moved quickly but quietly down the hillside and across the road, keeping our distance from the men forming the roadblock. The jungle was thick, and the ground was rocky and covered in moss with occasional steep drops. It wasn't the easiest terrain I'd ever lugged gear through, but also not the hardest.

We stopped just above the lake to catch our breath and have a look around. I checked my watch and saw that it was almost fifteen hundred and the temperature was eighty-two degrees. Scott surveyed the area around us through the scope of his submachine gun. One of the boats was in view. It was a center-console, appeared to be about twenty feet long, and had twin Honda 150s pushing it through the water. The three men standing in the boat wore camouflage battle vests and surveyed the area surrounding the lake.

"They haven't found it yet," Scott said, smiling.

"How can you be sure?"

He pointed to the boats and the trucks blocking the road on the other side of the lake. "They're not hauling anything out. If they'd found it, they'd be running trucks back and forth."

"Or maybe they're loading it up now."

Scott grabbed his bag and threw it over his

shoulder. He motioned for us to move down closer to the water. "Only one way to find out."

We reached a spot near the water's edge, where overhanging branches and thick shrubs provided sufficient cover. Once in our wetsuits, we performed the pre-dive inspection of our rebreathers, starting with a full integrity check. After warming up and testing both units, we did buddy checks. Though rebreathers have advantages over scuba, they are much more complex and therefore require a higher level of knowledge to operate correctly.

We stowed our clothes and boots in dry bags and sealed them up, clipping them to our BCDs using carabiners. I strapped my dive flashlight to my wrist and holstered my Sig around my leg, making sure it was snug, while Scott slung his submachine gun across his chest.

When both boats were out of sight, we strapped on our masks, waded out into the lake, and slipped into our fins. The visibility was about forty feet, making it easy for us to navigate underwater. Using our compasses, we quickly found our bearings and kicked our fins smoothly, gliding our way toward the waterfall.

We kept our eyes peeled and our heads on a swivel, looking out for passing boats and other divers, then we leveled off our buoyancy at thirty feet down, and soon the lake floor disappeared beneath us. The lake was filled with brown trout, rainbow trout, and bass that swam close enough to make me want to come back with a speargun someday.

After we swam a few more minutes, the rocky bottom of the lake became visible again, and we could see the water getting shallower. Once we were at a depth of twenty feet, Scott motioned for us to search the area since we were close to where the medallion had been discovered. We heard the distant rumble of the waterfall as we approached it, then saw the hazy mist and sloshing water on the surface a hundred yards ahead.

I searched the bottom, hoping to spot something shiny, while also hoping we were the only ones in the water. From the surface, there had been no signs of cartel divers, and no dive flags or tanks on the boats or with the men onshore.

I kept finning along the bottom, and then something caught my eye. There was a deep pool just beneath where the waterfall crashed into the lake. I pointed it out to Scott, then swam for it, fighting against the swirling currents that raged in all directions around me. The waterfall was booming now, a constant roar that thundered overhead. When I reached the pool, I saw that it was much deeper than I'd originally suspected. I adjusted my position and kicked straight down where the water was much calmer, then turned on the flashlight strapped to my wrist. The pool narrowed and appeared to end about fifty feet down. It looked like a dead end.

We finned to the bottom of the pool to survey the lake floor. As we scanned our flashlights along the rocks, we illuminated what appeared to be the narrow opening of a cave. I glanced at Scott and knew that he, too, was smiling behind his mouthpiece. We pointed our flashlights into the opening but couldn't see where it led. I stabbed a finger at myself, then at the opening, and then gestured for Scott to follow me.

He gave the "okay" signal, and I finned into the cave.

The dark cave lined with jagged rocks cut into the earth, the narrow, gloomy passageway zigging and zagging before arcing skyward. Gradually, the cave opened wider, and I could see what looked like the surface. I unholstered my Sig and held it in one hand and my flashlight in the other as I slowly broke free of the lake and scanned the area around me. The cavern was roughly twenty feet tall and thirty feet wide, with impressive stalactites jutting down from its roof. I pushed my mask down to rest around my neck and took a better look at the cave as Scott surfaced beside me and removed his mouthpiece.

"Any sign of cartel?" he said.

I shook my head, then swam for the water's edge. The rocks were slippery, but after removing our fins, we were able to climb up a crevice and slog onto a flat surface large enough for us to change out of our gear.

Scott, though focused and alert, couldn't stop smiling. "We found it. An underwater cave. Just as the legend said."

I couldn't stop grinning myself, and my heart raced at the prospect of finding such a treasure. I'd been in dangerous situations time and time again and had learned how to stay calm under pressure, but there's something about searching for lost treasure that can make a grown man feel like a kid again.

We slid out of our rebreather gear and stowed it behind a boulder, then slipped our wetsuits off and got dressed, our clothes still dry as a bone. Leaving everything behind except for our guns, flashlights, and the satellite phone, we trudged deeper into the cave.

We didn't make it five paces in before we both froze in our tracks.

"We're not alone in here," I said as I shined my flashlight on three sets of scuba gear on the ground ahead of us.

Scott and I stood still for a moment, listening intently to the silence before looking at each other and then stepping closer.

"They're still wet," Scott said, examining the gear. We searched them for clues but found only the standard scuba gear, with nothing but weights in the pockets.

While Scott searched the area around the gear, I did a full scan of the cave ahead of us, then crept a few steps deeper inside.

"Over here," I said, aiming the beam of my flashlight at a passageway fifty feet ahead. The limestone rocks split, revealing a space just wide enough for us to fit through.

"It looks man-made," Scott said. "And look over here." He pointed to markings on the stone—distinct shapes from a language used centuries ago.

We pressed on through the opening, which soon revealed a vast open space. It was completely dark and roughly forty feet high with openings along the sides, probably leading to other caves. The giant web was a series of tunnels sprouting out from the main one. The glows from our flashlights scanned the space, and a cluster of small, shiny specks of light reflected back at us. I locked eyes with Scott, then we moved in closer.

We neared the unknown object, then paused upon

realizing what it was: faded metal in the distinct shape of a morion—a helmet worn primarily by the Spanish in the sixteenth and seventeenth centuries. The helmet was round, with a perpendicular rim around the edges and a fin that stuck out from front to back like a Mohawk. Resting beside it was an engraved stone that had been sculpted in the shape of a cross.

We searched the rest of the cave, making sure we were alone, then Scott turned to me. "How's your Spanish?"

Many of my jobs had brought me to South America over the years, which resulted in me learning the language almost fluently.

I knelt down beside the cross and read the old carved words. "May we be blessed on our voyage to the motherland, as our beloved captain is blessed on his journey to Heaven." The name "Francisco de Cavallos" was carved into the top of the cross. "It's a grave site," I said.

After exploring the rest of the cave and finding nothing, I turned to Scott. "Looks like we're a few hundred years too late."

I shined my flashlight in Scott's direction and saw indentations in one of the walls—strange grooves that twisted the light from my flashlight.

"Hey, look at this," Scott said as I moved closer.

My jaw dropped as I realized what the indentations were. The entire rock face was covered with human skulls stacked on top of each other.

"Montezuma's warriors," I gasped.

"Must be. You find anything else out about the grave site?"

47

"Nothing. But it sure looks like the Spaniards cleaned house."

Scott shined his flashlight down the nearest passageway, which extended away from the cavern we were standing in. "Only one way to find out."

We advanced through the tunnel, watching our step and keeping a lookout for any movement or foreign features. Hundreds more skulls lined the walls beside us as we strode through the narrow cave. Up ahead, it opened up again, this time revealing an even larger space, easily a hundred feet to the top and more than double that in length. We moved in, hopeful we might find something, but the cavern appeared to be empty.

After taking a minute to search the cave, I shrugged. "The treasure isn't here, Scottie."

Before he could reply, a loud explosion echoed through the cave and violently shook the earth.

FOUR

We both took cover in an instant, dropping to the ground as rocks tumbled all around us. A boulder broke free, falling toward me as I rolled out of the way, narrowly escaping certain death. When the blast and shaking subsided, I shined my flashlight toward Scott but was unable to see him through the layer of dust in the air.

I weaved in and out of the debris and found him taking cover near the entrance to the cave. "Are you all right?"

He rose to his feet and took a look around. "Yeah. You?"

"Never better," I replied, trying to regain my bearings.

"They must be trying to blow their way out of here," he said.

He was right, and I knew that soon they'd succeed and that the cave would be swarming with men.

"All right. Let's get the hell out of here before this whole place caves in on us."

I moved past Scott toward the passageway we came in from, but he held up his hand to stop me.

"It's too late for that," he said, his eyes wide.

He shined his flashlight into the cave, and I saw that it was blocked off with large rocks. There was no way we'd be able to fit through.

I sighed. "We better hope they blow a way out of here. Otherwise, we may join that Cavallos guy and become permanent residents of this cave."

I'd been spelunking before and knew firsthand how easy it was to get turned around or delirious, or fall and break something. Although following a marked path is well and good, venturing out into unknown portions of a cave is one of the most dangerous things you can do. I'd read many stories of adventurers getting lost in caves, their flashlights dying on them, and their bodies being found weeks later.

We moved to the other side of the cavern and into another passageway, heading in the direction the explosion came from. The cave was silent again, the only sounds being the occasional drip of water from the stalactites above and the soft echo of our boots shuffling against the rocks with every step.

After five minutes of trekking through the darkness, taking notes with every turn to remember our way back, Scott held his right hand in the air. "Do you hear that?"

We froze and listened as footsteps echoed down the narrow space.

"Yeah. There's at least two of them."

The distinct sounds of boots stomping on the rocky surface grew louder and louder, and we knew they would reach us soon. We took a quick glance at the walls around us, then switched off our flashlights. To our right, ten feet overhead, the rocks turned sharply, jutting out to form a narrow plateau.

"I'm climbing up," I whispered as I wrapped my hands around a large stalactite, gripping it with my fingertips as I heaved myself up. I stretched my leg up and over the ledge, then leveraged the rest of my body, sliding between the damp and slippery grooves in the rocks. Peering down, I saw that Scott had vanished into the shadows.

Lying completely still, I waited in the darkness as the men approached our position. When streaks of light appeared from down the cave, I peeked over a rock and saw two men stomping toward me. The first wore a cutoff shirt and had a brown bandana tied around his head. Tattoos covered his arms, shoulders, and neck up to his shaved head. The second man had long hair, wore a black T-shirt, and had to weigh at least two hundred pounds. Both of the muscular men carried themselves like they'd been in the military before.

As they moved closer, I could hear most of what they were saying to each other. I'd hoped to get an idea of who they were and who they were working for, but their conversation revolved around the previous night's trip to a nearby strip club. They walked right past me, unable to see me as I pressed my body against the cold rock. They took a few steps, then jolted back in surprise as Scott appeared from the black in an instant and lunged for the first guy.

Scott wrapped his arm around Tattoo's back and held him from behind, his right arm flexing around the guy's throat. The man gagged and struggled, but in one quick motion, Scott knocked him out, and his body fell limp to the cave floor.

This was my cue. The guy with the long hair reached for the pistol on his hip just as I pounced from my position high above, and using all of my body weight, I lodged my elbow into the back of his head. The guy grunted and collapsed as I fell on top of him, his body going limp as he lost consciousness. I grabbed the pistol from his holster and searched his pockets, finding a radio, a pair of brass knuckles, and a switchblade, but no identification.

I glanced over at Scott, who was crouching beside the other guy. "You find anything?" I asked.

"Nothing," he replied, standing and walking toward me.

I slid the magazine out of the guy's pistol, and just as I was about to throw it aside, I noticed something strange etched into the handle: a custom symbol—two black snakes slithering in a circle. I dropped down beside the man on the ground and grabbed his left hand. The same two snakes were tattooed around his wrist.

"What is it?" Scott said. "You look like you've just seen a ghost."

"Holy shit," I whispered, blinking to make sure I wasn't seeing things. "These guys are Black Venom."

Scott knelt beside me, and I handed him the pistol. He examined it briefly, then threw it to the ground.

Black Venom, one of the most powerful and deadly drug cartels in the world, work primarily out of Mexico, but over the last few years, they'd expanded immensely, and I'd even encountered some of them while working in Colombia. They're notorious for hiring and training only the best fighters, which means that an encounter with them is never an easy one.

"Looks like we were right about them being cartel," Scott said.

"We've got to get the hell out of here," I said. "These guys had radios, and when they don't reply to any communications, you can bet that this cave will be crawling with more men."

Scott shined his light forward, then down at the two unconscious men at our feet.

"There's no time to hide them," I added. "We're just gonna have to risk the third guy stumbling in here. We need to get out of this cave."

Scott reached for the waterproof satellite phone in his pocket and thumbed a button on the home screen. "Damn," he said. "Even *this* can't get a signal in here."

We continued quickly down the passageway, still heading in the direction the explosion had come from, figuring it was our best chance, if we had one, at getting out. Our only other option would've been finding a way back to the water and working our way down alternate passageways in an intricate and elaborate maze of tunnels. In a cave that size, we could've been wandering for hours, perhaps days, and eventually, our lights would've gone out.

"Looks like it opens up ahead," Scott said.

We both stopped, turned off our flashlights, and listened. It was quiet, and after a few breaths, we gave ourselves the all-clear and moved in.

Light was coming from what we realized was another large cavern. Rocks and boulders littered the ground, and a wide beam of sunlight streamed down from above.

We glanced at each other, then scanned the space as best as we could before slowly moving in. I held my pistol at shoulder height, ready to take aim and pull the trigger at a moment's notice. Being there with Scott by my side felt like old times—just like hundreds of situations we'd found ourselves in before.

"Do you hear that?" Scott said as we reached the middle of the cavern.

I nodded. It sounded like the clattering of a diesel engine, and it was coming from just outside the cave. The opening was right over our heads, and the good news was that it was plenty large enough to fit through. The bad news was there was no way for us to get out. From the burn marks on the ground, it looked like whoever was trying to blow out of there had accidentally caused the ceiling of the cave to collapse into itself, leaving a massive opening with no means of escape.

The edge was thirty feet above us, with grass and vines hanging over the side. We kept an eye out for cartel but saw no movement above us or inside the cave.

"Where the hell is everyone?" I asked, looking around.

Scott shrugged. "Who knows? You think you could give me a boost up to that vine, though?"

It was a liana vine, a common plant in South

America, characterized by its thick, woody stems and astonishing lengths, sometimes in excess of three thousand feet. Aside from the broken end that hung freely roughly ten feet overhead, the vine appeared to be intact and secure in its position.

I slid my Sig into my leg holster, moved just below the vine, and patted Scott on his shoulder. "Let me do it. We don't know how secure this is, and Susan would kill me if you broke your neck." I wanted to add that I was in better shape than he was, as well, but as good as Scott was at swallowing his pride, I knew he'd never back down if a fellow SEAL questioned his physical prowess.

Though not happy about it, he relented, and I climbed onto his shoulders and grabbed hold of the vine. I gave it a couple of hard tugs, just to test it out before trusting it with all of my body weight. The vine tensed but felt strong, not making any creaking sounds or loosening at all. Hand over hand, I climbed, trying to be as quiet as possible and keeping my senses constantly on the alert for any movement above. I soon reached a patch of overhanging green vegetation, and just as I did, I heard the sound of another diesel engine, this one quickly approaching our position. By the loud rumble and vibration of the earth, I knew it had to be a large truck.

Hanging in the open with no cover, I had to move. As fast as I could, I climbed the remaining length of vine, hoisted my body over the rim of the opening, and crawled under a patch of Caquib plants with large green leaves that provided ample cover. I turned around and watched as an army-green off-road Ford Raptor approached and stopped just on the other side of the cave opening, less than a hundred feet away from me. The truck looked new, but its exterior was covered in dirt and mud. Surveying the area around me, I saw that we were in the middle of the dense tropical jungle with no roads in sight.

The truck's engine died, the driver's-side door opened, and a man stepped out wearing a black cutoff shirt and camouflage cargo pants. I kept still as he slammed the door and then walked to the edge of the opening. After taking a moment to examine the cave, he said something into his radio that I couldn't hear, took one final puff of his cigarette, then flicked it into the hole and turned around. He walked back to the bed of his truck, removed the cloth canopy, and pulled out a rope ladder. Tying one end to the tow hitch, he threw the rest over the edge, shaking it a few times to get all of the rungs to unravel.

The guy stood at the edge of the opening and gazed down toward the base of the rope ladder. "Juan! Miguel! Carlos! Get your asses up here!" he said in Spanish. "Marco wants to know what the hell's going on down there."

He stood there for a moment, but there was no reply from below. Irritated, he grabbed the radio from his hip and yelled into it, ordering the three men to leave the cave and give a report. When no answer came, he grabbed a nearby rock, wedged it under one of the truck's back tires, then flung himself over the ledge while holding on to the rope ladder. Before he took two steps down, he froze and listened as the sound of scuffling bodies echoed from the cave below. The sounds stopped in an instant as a gunshot went off.

The man climbed to the top of the ladder and ran to the back of his truck. He reached beneath the green canvas, pulled out an AK-47, and darted back over to the edge. Trying to get a better angle, he skirted around the rim of the opening, sidestepping his way toward my position. As he came closer, I saw that he was much bigger than he'd looked from afar. He was at least my height and probably had twenty pounds of bulging muscle on me. I debated using my Sig but decided against it, knowing how far the sound would travel and how many cartel members it would inevitably alert. The gunshot below had been partially muffled by the cave, but a shot up here in the open would be heard for miles.

The man stood in front of me and raised his rifle to chest height. The blacked-out stockless Draco AK-47 he was holding would be difficult to shoot at a target so far away, but I wasn't about to give him a chance. Just as he looked like he was about to fire, I sprang from my cover behind the shrub. Grabbing the top of his shoulders for leverage, I kicked the sole of my boot against the back of his right knee, forcing his lower body to collapse. He groaned as I whipped his body around, slamming his head into the ground and holding his left arm twisted behind him. The rifle flew from his hands as he fell and tumbled just beside us, partly hanging over the edge of the opening.

"What the fuck!" he yelled, his face buried in the dirt.

I pulled on his arm tighter, making sure he couldn't move, then peered over the edge and into the cave.

"What's your status, Charlie?" I said, my voice

echoing down into the cavity below.

After a brief silence, I heard, "All clear, Delta. Heading up the ladder now."

"Get off me, asshole!" the man said. "We have a hundred men in these mountains. You two will never escape. Marco will track you down and kill you like dogs!"

"Shut up!" I said, pulling even harder on his shoulder. He was strong and difficult to hold in place, even with his arm twisted behind his back and my boot pressed against his pelvis.

Scott reached the top of the ladder, and I motioned for him to check the truck. While striding to it, he grabbed the satellite phone from his pants pocket and made a quick call, informing local authorities what was happening in Sierra Gorda. When he was done, he slid it back into his pocket, opened the driver's-side door, and leaned in to check the ignition and the driver and passenger seats.

He glanced back at me and shook his head. "Must be on that guy."

"Give me the damn keys," I said, forcing my boot down harder.

The man grunted, then spat dirt from his mouth. He reached into his pocket, and when I heard the jingle of metal, I snatched the keys from him.

"Here," I said, tossing them to Scott.

He caught them and fired up the truck.

"Now," I said, grabbing the radio from the man's hip, "you're going to tell the rest of your goons that you're under attack on the western shore of the lake."

I figured that could draw the trucks as well as the boats away from our current position near the eastern shore. But before he had a chance to speak into the radio, gunshots erupted from behind me.

FIVE

I turned around and saw a man crouching at the edge of the jungle, peppering rounds into the side of the truck as Scott put it into gear and floored it toward me. I zeroed in on our attacker with my Sig and fired off two shots, the first one hitting him in the shoulder and the second one going straight through his chest. He fell back, firing bullets from his Uzi into the air until he landed hard on the ground.

The large man suddenly broke free of my grasp, proving to be much stronger than I'd thought. In an instant, I aimed my pistol toward him, but he was already lunging at me. He tackled me to the ground, and we rolled twice before I broke free and got him with a hard kick to the ribs. The man tried to stop himself, but his momentum drove him over the edge of the opening, and he howled as he flew out of my sight. He slammed into the ground at the bottom of the cave, the sounds of his shattering bones echoing from below. I peeked over the edge for just a moment and saw him lying motionless on his back, blood spilling from his mouth.

"Get in!" Scott yelled as he spun the truck to a stop beside me and shoved opened the passenger door. There were bullet holes all over the side of the truck from the guy with the Uzi, and the back windows were shattered.

I grabbed my pistol and radio from the ground, then jumped in and slammed the door shut. Just as we were deciding where to go next, an ATV appeared from the jungle on the other side of the clearing, followed closely by another truck. A skinny guy riding the ATV wore tinted riding goggles and a black bandana over his mouth. He raised his arm and pointed at Scott and me, shouting while looking back at the truck.

"We gotta go!" I yelled.

Scott was swiftly examining the jungle around us. We were boxed in by steep hills and a sharp cliff, and the only flat surface was behind us, where the ATV and truck were.

Scott revved the engine, then floored the gas pedal, forcing the wheels to spin freely through the ground and shoot back mud for a second before getting their grip and propelling us forward into the dense jungle. He drove right up the hill, weaving around tree trunks and forcing branches and bushes out of our way. Looking back, I saw the ATV closing in behind us, its driver holding a pistol over his head.

"Hold on!" Scott said before turning sharply and driving up a steeper section of the hillside.

When we reached a clearing, I climbed into the

back seat and took aim through the broken window. The guy on the ATV saw me and fired off a few rounds, which hit the tailgate and the frame just over my head. I ducked down, then rose up and let loose a rapid succession of 9mm rounds. One bullet struck home, exploding his front right tire and causing him to spin out of control and crash into a tree.

Scott drove through another patch of jungle toward a clearing ahead—a patch of grass on the windward side of a hill—and as we reached the crest of the slope, I saw the truck still on our tail two hundred feet behind us. Its engines roared, and a guy leaned out the passenger-side window, aiming a rifle in our direction. He disappeared from view, along with the truck, as we drove down the other side of the hill. Looking forward through the glass, I gasped as I realized we were heading straight for a cliff that dropped down over a hundred feet to the lake below.

"Holy shit!" Scott yelled.

He swerved the truck hard to the right. The tires tore through the brush, and the hefty, off-road vehicle almost flipped over as Scott steadied the wheel. He drove along the top of the cliff, bouncing over boulders and swerving in and out of trees. Bullets pounded the back of the truck, and we both took cover while watching the way ahead as best as we could.

"Keep her straight," I said, dropping the clip from my Sig and loading in a fresh one as I peeked over the window. The truck behind us was closing in.

"Use this!" Scott yelled, throwing his MP5N on the seat beside me.

I slid my Sig into my leg holster, grabbed the

submachine gun, and popped up through the broken window. Just as I did, a storm of bullets rained down on the truck, and I dropped back down. When the shots stopped, I promptly rose, took aim, and opened fire on the truck behind us. I hit the guy in the passenger seat twice before he slid back into the truck through the open window. He fell out of sight, and I knew he was done for, but there was still the driver and a guy I hadn't seen before in the bed of the truck.

I kept firing at the truck, trying my best to aim as Scott drove over large rocks, bouncing us up and down, but none of my rounds penetrated inside the truck.

"Windshield's bulletproof!" I yelled, then ducked back down to reload.

As I grabbed a magazine from the belt next to Scott, out of the corner of my eye, I noticed a large moving object in the direction of the lake. It was one of the center-consoles from before, flying across the water by its twin 150-hp engines, and it was right alongside us but about a hundred feet below. One of the guys was wearing a camouflage tactical vest and aiming his AK-47 in our direction.

"We've got a problem, Scottie!" I yelled, pointing down toward the lake.

He eyed the boat, then focused back on the rough landscape ahead. A moment later, bullets rattled against the side of the truck from the guy in the boat. Scott swerved and braked hard, trying to avoid the projectiles as best as he could.

"Hell yeah, we do!" Scott yelled back, pointing ahead of us.

I looked forward and saw that the side of the

mountain was about to get a lot steeper and then drop off completely. It was clear that there was nowhere for us to go. We were trapped.

I fired off a few quick shots at the boat, forcing the guy with the AK-47 to drop to the deck for cover, then took aim at the truck behind us.

"I'll try to take out the truck!" I yelled, then fired off another series of rounds. "If I can stop it, we might be able to turn around and find a way off this rock!"

I continued firing at the truck and even took out its two front tires, but it kept gaining ground. I knew it had to have been armor-plated in addition to the bulletproof windshield and that it probably had even more upgrades than the beast we were driving.

"Already found a way, Dodge!" Scott yelled. "Remember that time in Nigeria? That was much higher than this!"

The cliff was getting closer every second. Nearly ten years earlier, Scott and I had been in a similar situation. After performing a routine reconnaissance mission in the northeast region of Nigeria near the border of Cameroon, we'd been forced to leave a compound in the mountains in a hurry, along with the other six men from our platoon. In order to escape from a trail of vehicles heading our way, we'd split up, and Scott and I ended up driving a van over a cliff into a river below.

We took cover again as more bullets slammed into the truck, this time coming from both sides at the same time. With that kind of beating, I knew the truck wouldn't last much longer. There was already smoke billowing out from the engine, and at least one of the tires was flat.

I patted Scott on the back. "Just tell me when we're about to go over so I can climb out of here!"

"Roger that!" Scott yelled, then floored the gas pedal.

Focusing on the truck behind us, I saw the guy in the bed leaning over the top of the truck and holding on to what I instantly realized was a rocket-propelled grenade launcher.

The guy yelled at the driver, telling him to move in closer. As quickly as I could, I rose from my position behind the back seat and held the submachine gun up against my shoulder. Aiming through the broken glass, I fired off a cycle of automatic rounds at the cartel. He flew back but managed to pull the trigger on the RPG. The rocket exploded from the launcher hissing toward us, and I dropped back behind the seat, yelling for Scott to brace for impact. Before I could grab on to anything, the rocket exploded, shaking the truck violently out of control. My back slammed into the front passenger seat, and for a moment, I thought I'd lost consciousness. My ears rang from the explosion, which had apparently just missed the truck.

"Time to ditch!" I heard Scott yell over the ringing in my ears.

Scott and I climbed through the back window and into the bed of the truck, which was half-missing from the explosion. We knelt down and held on as the truck flew over the cliff, its momentum driving it forward for an instant before nosediving toward the water below. We jumped over the side of the truck before it did a front flip, launching ourselves as far away from it as we could. Thrown into an uncontrollable spin, I fought to straighten my body and barely managed to splash feet first into the lake. A jarring pain shot up my legs as I broke the surface, slicing through the clear water before being forced to a stop.

Ignoring the discomfort from my sub-optimal smack of a landing, I quickly got my bearings and watched as the truck sank to the bottom front-first, bubbles slithering out of all its open spaces and racing toward the surface. Scott, who'd jumped out of the bed on the other side of the truck, was only forty feet away from me. He looked my way, then gave me a thumbs-up. I repeated the gesture, then surveyed the surface of the water for any sign of the boat. After seeing none, I held my right hand out in a fist with my thumb pointed down, letting Scott know I wanted us to get deeper. With the cartel boat nearby, I wanted to put some distance between us and the surface before our enemies spotted us. I held my hands out to my sides, cupped them, then pushed up, letting my body sink down. When we reached roughly twenty-five feet, I stopped and resumed my search of the surface.

Before hitting the water, I'd taken in a deep breath and knew Scott had done the same. During our time in the Navy, and whenever we'd gone freediving together to spearfish or catch lobster, we'd always challenged each other to stay down longer or go deeper. I could hold my breath for a little over five minutes and knew Scott could do the same. However, we'd been in a car chase and been shot at. Despite our years of training to keep calm under pressure, our hearts were beating abnormally. I figured we'd been under about thirty seconds and that I could go another minute max before having to surface.

Looking at Scott, I could tell he was thinking about just swimming for it. If we swam along the shore, we could try and get out of sight of the cartel and escape into the jungle unnoticed. I considered it but knew they would be sweeping the area with both the boat and the truck, and that more would no doubt be arriving soon. Our best shot was to hijack the boat and go full throttle across the lake back to the Jeep.

After a minute underwater, we saw the hull of the boat appear quickly, then slow to a stop right above us. Occasional bubbles still trickled up from the truck, letting the cartel know exactly where we'd crashed. We watched as one of the guys above shot a few rounds into the lake. Even hitting the water straight on at a ninety-degree angle, the large-caliber rounds of the AK-47 were only able to penetrate about three feet before breaking apart and stopping.

When the shooting stopped, I signaled to Scott to ascend. We kicked our way up through the water, and when we were about ten feet from the hull, I pointed at myself, then at the bow. Scott nodded and pointed at himself and then at the stern. We would take them out by rising at different ends of the boat. I reached the hull just under the bow and eased my way up, making sure not to come into contact with the boat. A small center-console will rock slightly, even with just a bit of force applied against it.

I rose stealthily, barely breaking the surface, and took a quick look around. The first thing I saw was the other truck idling on the edge of the cliff overhead, but there was no sign of the driver. I listened to the two guys on the boat.

"Where the fuck did they go?" one of the men said.

"They couldn't have stayed down this long," another man replied. His voice was high-pitched, and he sounded young. "They must be dead."

"They're not dead," the other man barked. His voice was low and raspy, like the voice of a man who'd smoked a pack a day for ten years. "Unless you see their bodies, they're not dead. You got that, Danny Boy? You go telling Marco that your targets are dead when they aren't, and you'll end up at the bottom of this lake with a tow chain strapped around your ankles. Now keep looking, dammit!"

The young man didn't reply, but I heard him walk toward me at the bow. His footsteps were light, and I saw his shadow as he leaned over the edge of the boat.

This was my chance.

In one quick motion, I grabbed the corner of the bow, hoisted myself up, then wrapped an arm around the young man and flipped him over the railing. I held him tight as we splashed into the water, his legs kicking and his arms flailing as he tried to break free from my grasp. I pushed down, swimming as hard as I could until we were about fifteen feet under, then I ripped the rifle from his shoulder and dropped it into the darkness below.

He tried to fight back but was much smaller than I, and although it was clear he'd had hand-to-hand combat training before, he was no match for me. His body began to shake, and I knew he was running out of air. His long hair parted away from his face, and I realized he was even younger than I'd first suspected. I pegged him to be no older than eighteen, and he was terrified as I held him beneath the surface, his lungs screaming for air. Examining his desperate body, I saw that he had no other weapon, so I swam us both up toward the surface.

Just before we broke out from the water, I pushed him aside, then grabbed my Sig from my leg holster. Reaching for the side of the boat with my left hand, I hoisted myself up and scanned the shoreline, gripping my pistol with my right—ready to fire at a moment's notice.

I caught a glimpse of movement behind the truck parked on the edge of the cliff. A moment later, the driver appeared, holding an Uzi. As soon as I saw him, I took aim, ready for him to try something stupid. He scanned around the lake and then turned rigid as his eyes locked on me. He began to move the Uzi toward my direction, and I fired off three shots, two of the three rounds hitting him square in the chest. He swayed a little, then fell over the cliff, doing two front flips before splashing into the lake below.

SIX

Seeing the shoreline was clear, I made my way onto the boat, pistol at the ready. Scott was at the stern, standing over the body of the other cartel member, who appeared to be unconscious. He stripped the man of his weapons as I bounded toward him. The young man I'd let go was struggling to stay afloat on the surface beside the boat. He coughed a few times before calling out for help. I reached into a space just below the helm, grabbed a life ring, and chucked it out onto the water. He grabbed it eagerly.

"Time to get the hell out of here," I said, stepping around the console behind the helm.

I quickly scanned the horizon. The only other boat in view was probably a quarter of a mile away and sat idling near a dock on the northern shore of the lake.

"Wait one," Scott said. He grabbed a life jacket and wrapped it around the unconscious man at his feet. "Help me put him in the water."

Scott grabbed his shoulders, and I grabbed his feet. Together we lifted him up, then lowered him into the water beside the boat. The young man didn't swim over to help him but instead just treaded water and stared at us. He was clearly still in shock. I hoped he would live but knew that the drug runners he worked for wouldn't be too happy with him for letting us get away.

I stood behind the helm, grabbed the throttles, and shoved them forward. The dual 150-hp engines roared to life and shot the small boat through the water with ease. Within a few seconds, I had her up on plane and doing forty knots. I didn't care about appearing suspicious to the other boat, I just wanted to put distance between us and the cartel. So, I piloted the little craft to the western side of the lake, keeping as far away from the other boats as I could and cruising as fast as the boat would let me. When we reached a cove ten minutes later, I pulled in and eased back on the throttle.

"Do you still have that phone?" I asked.

Scott pulled out his satellite phone from his pants pocket, dialed a few numbers, and was routed to an emergency point of contact in Mexico City. He relayed the new information and gave the dispatcher the coordinates for the entrance into the cave. When he finished, the dispatcher asked for his information, but Scott quickly told her that he preferred to remain anonymous and hung up the phone.

"ETA five minutes for the first responders," Scott said. "They sent a platoon of armored trucks from the military base just south of here. The government isn't messing around with these drug lords anymore.

They've launched an all-out war on the drug trade."

"Must be why they've grown desperate enough to go after ancient treasure." I grinned. "Damn, I would've loved to see the looks on their faces when they discovered the treasure was all gone."

Scott grinned back. "Probably looked something like ours when we realized it."

With the scope, I looked out over the lake and watched as a trail of trucks appeared from the main road leading to the entrance. They were far away, and all I could see was their green canopy tops flapping in the wind, but I counted over a dozen in all. I watched as the other boats scrambled away but knew it was unlikely they'd make it far. I focused the lens across the lake to where we donned our dive gear and waded into the water. Just up the hill from there, a few cartel were running on a dirt road and jumping into their vehicles as the Mexican military closed in on them.

"Shit," I said. "Looks like they're making a run for it."

"They won't get far."

"You can't underestimate these guys. I've been fighting them for years, and they're powerful, smart as hell, and reckless."

Our conversation was interrupted by the sound of automatic gunfire echoing over the lake.

"Time to go," I said. "Sorry about your Jeep, but I'd rather not get caught up in all of this any more than we already have. If we stay, there will be a lot of questions and a lot of dealing with crap, and that's all before the media gets ahold of it."

"Don't worry. Based on our past experiences, I knew to pay extra for the good rental insurance. Got any idea how to get out of here? We're too close to the action to call in for a chopper."

"I saw a river coming into the lake just a short ways from here. We should motor to it while sticking close to the shore, then go upstream as far as we can. We'll beach the boat and call in for a pickup once we're far enough away from this mess."

"Sounds good. Just keep a steady eye out for any cartel. We're far from the cave, but you never know . . . A few may have staggered from the pack."

I surveyed the area around us one more time, then hammered the throttles. Within a few minutes, we reached the river I'd spotted earlier. It was much smaller than I'd expected, and the mouth was narrow, but the water was deep enough for me to navigate without the propeller grinding against the riverbed. The flowing crystal-clear water weaved through cuts in the rock faces and eventually right through the side of a mountain, giving us views of sheer cliffs on both sides. Waterfalls splashed down around us from a hundred feet above, and brilliant green vegetation blanketed the cliffs.

"The water's getting pretty shallow up here," I said as we neared a part of the river where the shore became flatter. I gave the engine everything she had and forced the boat up a shallow patch of white-capped water. Rocks scratched the hull of the boat, and I turned sharply to port and forced the boat up onto the shore. Even with having to overcome the river, we hit a sandbar at fifteen knots. The boat slid up onto the sand, and I killed the engine just as our momentum brought us completely out of the water. Scott and I grabbed our things and jumped out of the boat.

"Let's see if we can find a good extract point up the hill," Scott said, leading the way.

A moment later, we disappeared into the jungle, still putting distance between ourselves and the conflict on the other side of the lake. After an hour of trekking, we reached the top of a large hill that flattened out to form a plateau.

"Time to call in the bird," Scott said, reaching for his satellite phone.

Within thirty minutes, a dark blue and white Bell 206 helicopter appeared on the horizon. After grabbing a signal flare from my pocket, I removed the cap, held it downwind, and pulled the tab. A burst of orange smoke filled the air, and within minutes the pilot landed. He loaded us up and took off, speedily taking us away from Sierra Gorda.

"This place will be swarming with air support soon," the pilot said into the mic. "Just got the call to clear the airspace as soon as possible. You two going back to International?"

He was referring to the airport in Mexico City, but I knew we'd have to go somewhere else. Landing at as big of an airport as that and coming from Sierra Gorda would look suspicious.

"Take us northeast to Tampico," Scott said. "Logan, I have the jet waiting for us there."

I nodded and gazed back out the window at the ground below. This part of Mexico was rural, filled with farmers and cattle drivers. The landscape was far less green here than back in Sierra Gorda. There were few rivers and no lakes in sight for miles.

Scott shifted over beside me and changed the

channel on his headset so we could talk privately. I did the same.

"They took it, Scott. Somehow, the conquistadors found it and made off with the entire haul on one of their ships."

"They were mad with it," he said. "Possessed. Willing to annihilate an entire civilization for it."

"And yet the ship never reached its destination, or any destination for that matter." I turned away from the window and shot my old friend a confident gaze. "You and I both know damned well where that treasure is. There can be no doubt about it now."

Scott shook his head. "We've searched that ledge over and over again and never found a thing."

I sighed and paused for a moment. "It has to be there somewhere, and I'm going to find it."

Scott smiled and patted me on the back. "I think I can extend my trip for a few more days, especially since it involves a trip to the Keys."

I turned and gave my old division officer a "you've got to be kidding me" look.

"To hell with that," I said sternly. "I don't want you involved in this any more than you have to be. Those were some close calls back there. Far too close. You're too important to be getting into stupid shit like this, Scott. You're a damned senator, for goodness' sake."

"What the hell is that supposed to mean?"

"It means that I'm going to the Keys," I said. "I'm going, and I'm going to find the gold, and you're going back to Washington where you belong. For the sake of your family and everyone you represent, don't come with me."

He turned away from me, shaking his head in frustration. Scott was smart, much smarter than me, but he had a wild side to him. It was the side that had kept him, as well as the entire platoon, alive countless times in countless skirmishes. But it was also a part of him that, now that he was a senator, he'd have to let go of every now and then.

"What about Black Venom?" Scott said. "What are you going to do if and when they come after the treasure?"

I leaned back and relaxed my body. "It's a big ocean. All they know is that it left Central America on a Spanish ship and never arrived at its destination. It could be anywhere for all they know. They have no reason to assume it's in the Keys."

"Just be careful, and watch your back."

Telling a SEAL, former or active duty, to watch his back is a useless statement, but I knew what he meant. What he was really saying was don't do anything stupid, and don't try to take on too much for one guy to handle—SEAL or not.

"And promise me that if you get in over your head, you'll give me a call."

SEVEN

Miami, Florida

Scott's jet dropped me off at the private terminal at Miami International Airport. I told him once more to keep his distance and to be expecting a phone call with an update as soon as I learned anything, and he told me that if I did something stupid like get myself killed, he'd never forgive me.

"Still alive," I said. "You know how much I hate to disappoint."

His jet fueled up then took off for D.C. while I made my way to the rental car center and got myself a red Mustang convertible. Before leaving Miami, I made a quick stop at Dante's Armory and purchased two new Sig Sauer P226 pistols, along with a holster, three magazines, and a hundred 9mm rounds. I ordered a few more specialty weapons and arranged to have them delivered to Jack's house in Key West.

Half an hour out of the city, and I was on US-1, heading south to one of my favorite places in the world—a little piece of paradise where anything involving a boat, a scuba tank, or a fishing pole is possible.

I decided to get a hotel in Key Largo in order to get an early start in the morning and avoid the tourist traffic. It was March in the Keys, meaning it was that perfect time of the year where it wasn't too hot for Northerners or too cold for Southerners, and I had just barely caught the end of the lobster season.

I stayed at the Largo Inn, a quaint place littered with beautiful palm trees and rooms just steps from the sandy beaches. My room had a balcony with two chairs and a little charcoal barbeque grill. I was on the ground floor, which made it easy for me to haul in the fish I caught using a speargun and a net I'd purchased at a dive shop just down the street from the inn.

Since spearfishing isn't allowed in the parks, I went after the one fish no one would ever bat an eye at you for spearfishing in Southern Florida: the lionfish. Lionfish are a colorful, alien-looking, invasive species in Florida. They have thirteen long, needle-sharp dorsal fins, along with a few pelvic and anal fins that are coated with venom. Though not deadly to humans, their venom is incredibly painful once it enters the bloodstream and can lead to immense swelling. Due to their overpopulation and lack of predators, the killing of lionfish is allowed and highly encouraged at all times.

I cleaned each of the eight fish, careful not to poke myself with their spines as I cut two filets, one off each side, and disposed of the rest properly. I seasoned the fresh white meat with No. 1 and a dash of Swamp Sauce, a local seasoning made just a few miles north near the Everglades. I sat in the chair and watched the sun drop down below the horizon, the smell of grilled fish tantalizing my taste buds. Eating fresh fish was the perfect ending to a perfect day of snorkeling and spearfishing near John Pennekamp Coral Reef State Park.

"Sure smells good over here," a voice said, coming from the direction of the beach.

I'd been so relaxed with my eyes closed, enjoying the salty air, that I hadn't noticed someone approach. I opened my eyes, tilted my head skyward, and saw a woman standing with her bare feet in the sand, wearing a thin sundress and smiling at me invitingly. She was beautiful, with short blonde hair and smooth, tanned skin.

"I promise it tastes even better," I said, smiling back at her. I sat up and lifted the lid from the barbeque, and smoke filled the air as I grabbed and plated one of the cooked filets. After blowing a little to cool it off, I handed it to her.

The woman peered down the beach, then back at me. She looked to be in her mid-twenties and had a sexy, athletic build.

"I really wouldn't want to impose," she said, taking a step down the beach. "I'll let you enjoy it."

I held it out in her direction. "I have more than enough for two," I said. "Besides, it would be a shame if I were the only one to enjoy it."

She hesitated a moment, then grabbed the plate from my hand and took a bite of the lionfish. Her eyes grew wide. "This is incredible." She chewed quickly and then took another bite. "Where did you learn to cook like this?"

"I'm glad you like it. My dad taught me. There's nothing like fresh fish, and these were swimming right out on that reef just a few hours ago."

She joined me on the patio, and we ate all of the fish, along with a few grilled mushrooms I'd picked up at a market. We talked about what had brought us to Key Largo and how we were enjoying it so far, and of course, I left out everything about the Aztec treasure. Her name was Catherine, and she was a paralegal from Atlanta who'd come down to the Keys for a wedding and decided to spend a few extra days with some of the other bridesmaids. When the food was done, I wanted to offer her a drink but realized I hadn't purchased anything but the seasoning, a speargun, and other snorkel gear since I'd arrived.

Catherine stood up. "Don't worry," she said. "I've got it handled. Just give me a minute." She moved quickly down the beach, shooting me a grin before disappearing out of sight.

A few minutes later, she returned with a bottle of rum and a case of glass-bottled Cokes. She told me they were her favorite drink, and after putting down three quick glasses, I believed her.

~ ~ ~

The next morning, I woke up to find Catherine already awake. The smell of coffee lured me from the bedroom and into the kitchen. She was wearing one of my shirts, and it reached only to the top of her thighs.

"You sure know how to show a girl a good time for her last day on vacation," she said as she grabbed a nearby mug, filled it with coffee, and handed it to me.

We migrated to a nearby restaurant, had breakfast, and then exchanged numbers.

We strolled to the surf, then she fixed her hair and beamed as we made eye contact. "If you're ever in Atlanta, I'd love to show you the town."

I told her that sounded good, kissed her on the cheek, and watched as she walked down the beach, back toward her resort.

Keys Disease, the laid-back island vibe mentality, was kicking in much faster than even *I* thought it would.

After getting back to my room, I took a quick shower, packed up the Mustang, and headed south. At 0930, it was already over seventy degrees, and the breeze with the top down made the drive all the better as I headed down US-1 out of Key Largo and toward the Middle Keys.

The drive through the Florida Keys is probably my favorite drive on Earth. I love looking out at the endless blue in all directions as I hop from one island to another over the bridges. I tuned my radio to Pirate Radio, a local station that plays classic island jams, and turned it up to pay homage to Jimmy Buffet's "Margaritaville."

I texted Jack, letting him know I would arrive in Key West in about two hours. I'd called him the day before, letting him know I was in Florida and that I was going to be heading to his neck of the palm trees.

A few minutes later, he replied, telling me to meet him for lunch at the Greasy Pelican, a local restaurant we'd both enjoyed as kids.

I drove on through Marathon and remembered why I'd loved that part of the Keys so much as a kid. It's much quieter there than down south, and there are some great campgrounds and beaches that few people ever go to. It's also where my dad and I lived and spent most of our time together.

While driving through the town, I spotted a used car dealership that was almost completely hidden behind a Mobil gas station. It only had about six vehicles in the lot, but one, a black pickup truck, caught my attention. I pulled my rental into the lot beside it and gave it a quick inspection before the salesman came over. I smiled as I saw the word *Tacoma* etched on the backside of the tailgate. It was the same make and model as the truck my dad bought me back when I first started driving, though it was about fifteen years newer.

"Just got her in on Tuesday," said a bald, round-bellied man wearing sunglasses and a black visor. He was also wearing a name tag, which I thought was funny considering how small of a business it was.

"Give me the rundown on her, Jerry," I said.

He gave me a quick overview of the truck. It was a 2001 four-door with an extended cab. It had a little over a hundred thousand miles on it, with four-wheel drive and new off-road tires.

Liking what I heard, I parked the Mustang beside the office and walked over to do an inspection of the engine and the interior. Everything looked good, and the seats looked like they'd never been sat in before.

The engine started up perfectly, and I took a quick drive around the block, testing the brakes and acceleration, and making sure the engine didn't make any strange noises.

"She's a great truck," Jerry said. "One of the best I've had here in a long while."

"How much do you want for it?"

Jerry stared off into the distance, rubbing his chin. "Well, given its condition, I'd say it's worth no less than twelve thousand."

I knew he was trying to pull a fast one on me. The truck was probably worth close to ten, maybe a little more for the island markup.

"How about eleven?" I replied. "Cash."

Jerry sighed. "Eleven five. Can't do any better than that, my friend."

"That's too bad," I said, grabbing my keys and heading toward my rental. "Thanks for your time."

"Are you really willing to walk away for five hundred bucks?"

I grinned and turned around. "Are you really willing to let me walk away for five hundred bucks?"

When he didn't answer, I took it as a yes and opened the door to my rental.

"Wait," he said. "All right. Eleven thousand even, it is."

I turned around and shut the door to the Mustang.

He sighed. "I'll get all the paperwork started."

My dad had taught me always to be willing to walk away when negotiating, and that cash talks. I'd negotiated for the truck the same way my dad showed me when we bought my first truck years before, and his advice still held true.

Less than an hour later, after a quick trip to the bank, we shook hands and signed the title, and I drove out of there in my new truck. I called the rental company, and they agreed to pick up my rental and bring it to Key West International Airport for a small fee.

It was just after noon when I merged back onto US-1, and soon, I was entering one of the most popular and craziest tourist destinations on Earth: Key West, Florida.

EIGHT

As much as I'd always liked the quiet and relative seclusion of the Middle Keys, Key West was an exciting place to be. The nightlife, restaurants, and tourist attractions made it a truly unique place to visit. It was also where Jack and his dad had lived, and where we'd met each other when I was young. Our dads introduced us to each other, but it was our shared love for the ocean that forged a friendship between us.

I drove to the Conch Harbor Marina and pulled into the lot. A young man with curly blond hair and a backward snapback greeted me as I stopped just beside his wooden booth.

"Good morning, dude," the kid said. "It's eight bucks to park for the day."

"Eight?" I asked. "Why not just charge ten?"

"I'll take ten if you want," he replied with a grin.

I laughed. "Who's your boss?"

"Mr. Henderson."

I recognized the name but couldn't quite place it. A second later, it came to me. "Gus?" I asked.

The kid looked at me, confused. "Yeah. Look, I can give you his information if you need to contact him for something, but I gotta charge you eight bucks to park. We take Visa, dude."

I told him that I'd be coming and going frequently over the next few weeks, and he offered me a monthly pass for fifty dollars. I bought it, then the barrier rose, and I drove through to the parking lot.

"Welcome to Conch Harbor," the kid said as I drove away.

I waved back at him and soon found a spot right in front of the Greasy Pelican. It was just after one in the middle of the week, but the place was already filling up quickly. I killed the engine, and as soon as I hopped out of the truck, my mouth started to water. The smell of fresh seafood mixed with the tropical air made me wonder how anyone could ever leave such a place.

I walked up the steps and through the double doors, which had old helms chopped in half for handles. The Greasy Pelican was exactly how I'd remembered it. Just as I walked in, I saw the walls covered with stuffed fish, knickknacks, and pictures of famous people who'd eaten there. Right by the front door was an impressive saltwater fish tank filled with various colorful hard and soft corals and everything from clownfish to gobies.

"Just one today?" a waitress standing behind the host stand asked.

"No," I replied. "I'm actually supposed to be

86

meeting someone for lunch. Jack Rubio."

The restaurant seemed pretty busy, even given the season. Looking past the waitress, I noticed that the patio was almost empty, seeing as how it was now well over eighty degrees. Still, I decided I'd rather sit out there and watch the boats come in and out of the marina.

"Haven't seen Jack at all today," the waitress replied. "My guess is, he's on his boat. It's moored just down the dock."

"Which one's his? Is it still the *Calypso*?"

She nodded. "Yes, sir. You can see it from the patio. Slip forty-seven, I think."

"Thanks," I said.

I turned around and left the restaurant through the same doors I'd entered. I expected Jack to be late. He'd always been bad with time and had always told me it was because he was an islander. "Blame it on the heritage, bro," he used to say. "Conchs are too laid-back to arrive at an appointed time. Hell, I've never even owned a watch."

I walked past my new Tacoma and down a few wooden steps to the dock. It was a beautiful marina, filled with boats of all shapes and sizes. Some were small Catalinas and Tahoes, and others were million-dollar yachts that sparkled in the Florida sun and cast shadows over the dock.

It wasn't far to Jack's boat. Slip forty-seven was at the tip of the dock closest to the Pelican. The *Calypso* was the name of Jack's dad's boat we used all the time as kids. His dad had been a fishing charter captain, along with his father before him. Jack was a fourth-generation conch and had grown his father's business to include scuba diving charters, as well. He'd done well for himself, and the last time I was down there, he had more than one boat and a scuba shop downtown.

Nearing the end of the dock, I saw a black pirate flag flapping in the wind alongside a dive flag. Below it was the white hull of a forty-five-foot Sea Ray with *Calypso* stenciled on the side. It was a beautiful boat with plenty of deck space and a pilothouse above. As I walked closer, I saw someone hunched over, under the cockpit. It was Jack. His tanned skin from years of being on the water and curly blond hair were unmistakable. He was shirtless, wearing only board shorts, and when I reached the boat, I saw that he was cleaning up beer cans.

"Nice boat," I said. "What's the rate for a dive out on the reef?"

Jack looked up, then smiled as he realized who I was. He grabbed his cellphone from the chair beside him and glanced at the time.

"Dammit. I'm sorry, Logan." He jumped over the transom, landed on the dock, and wrapped his arms around me. "I was hoping to be done with this by now."

"Don't worry about it. It's great to see you, Jack."

"You too, my brother. It's been too long since the last time you came down. How've you been?"

He welcomed me onto the boat and offered me a seat on the padded bench.

"Can't complain," I said. The entire deck was littered with beer cans, and there was fish blood and guts against one of the rails. "What the hell happened here?"

Jack shook his head. "Just got back from a morning charter. Bunch of loud-mouthed guys from the Midwest who'd never fished the ocean before."

"I don't get how you put up with it."

Jack shrugged. "It pays the bills."

A young man appeared from the cabin, walking up the steps and carrying two full black garbage bags that were tied off at the top. He was scrawny, pale, and looked like he was around fourteen.

He dropped the bags on the deck beside us. "That's the last of it for in there," he said. Using the top of his forearm, he wiped the sweat from his forehead.

"Isaac, this is Logan," Jack said. "You met him once before, but you were really little."

The young man scanned me over, then tilted his head. "Yeah, I think I remember. You pulled me out of the water one time. I was fishing off the dock, and I leaned a little too far over."

"It's good to see you again, Isaac," I said, extending my hand. "You've sure grown up a lot since then."

Isaac was Jack's nephew. Jack's older brother had gone to college up north and then gotten a job in Chicago. For some reason, he always preferred colder weather to the tropical climate of the Keys. He got married, and they had one child, Isaac. But when Isaac was only seven, Jack's brother died in a tragic car accident, leaving behind his wife and son. When his wife decided she couldn't take care of him, she left him with Jack, who'd raised Isaac ever since.

We shook hands, and Isaac said, "You want me to spray down the deck?"

Jack patted his nephew on the back. "Nah, I've got it."

"I'm gonna head home, then," Isaac said, stepping over the transom and grabbing a bike that was leaning up against a piling. "It was good seeing you, Logan. Thanks again for saving my life."

I laughed. "I'm sure you would've been fine. Rubios are born able to swim."

He waved and pedaled his bike down the dock and out of sight.

"It's a good thing you saved him," Jack said, smiling at me. "He may bear the name, but that boy's a mainlander at heart." He opened the lid of a nearby cooler. "You want a drink? I'm afraid all I got left are a few Cokes."

I accepted the offer, and we sat in the shade, enjoying the cold beverages.

"How long are you here for anyway?" Jack asked, leaning against the railing across from me.

"Well, that depends."

"Depends on what?"

I started to open my mouth, then felt my stomach grumble. "Why don't you let me help you finish cleaning up here, and then we can talk over some lunch at the Pelican. I'm starving."

NINE

After we cleared the deck of cans and sprayed down the blood and fish guts, Jack threw on a cutoff shirt and locked up the *Calypso*. We drifted over to the Pelican and got a table on the patio overlooking the marina and the rest of the bay beyond.

"Lucy," Jack called to the waitress before she even stepped out of the door. "Could you get us a couple of hogfish sandwiches and two beers?"

The pretty waitress with long brown hair, tanned skin, and freckles, smiled and continued walking toward our table. She was the same waitress I spoke to earlier when I was looking for Jack. I pegged her to be in her mid-thirties and was surprised to see she didn't have a wedding ring on her finger.

"Will that be all?"

"For now," Jack said.

"Lucy," I said. "Could we get an order of coconut shrimp, as well?"

"Sure thing. I'll be right out with your beers."

"She's cute," I said when the door shut behind her. "I think she likes you."

"Who, Lucy? Nah, man. I've given up dating the locals here, even though she just moved here less than a year ago. It's a small island, you know? It's hard to avoid your ex when there are only a few grocery stores in town. It can get awkward."

Lucy came back out and set two beers on the table in front of us, then strode back inside.

"Besides, it's nice having a few women that are just friends, you know? You start dating, and that all goes to hell."

I grabbed the beer and took a long pull. Leaning back in my chair and looking out at all of the boats and the blue water behind them, I let out a long sigh.

Jack laughed. "You look like a fish that's just been thrown back into the water."

"Sure is good to be back. It feels like it's been forever."

"You know, you still haven't told me why you're here. What, did you finally get sick of going on dangerous adventures around the world?"

I took another sip of beer. "Funny thing is, it was one of those dangerous adventures that led me here."

"Uh-oh. Is everything okay?"

"Yeah," I assured him. "It was just an unexpected encounter, that's all. Scott and I were in Mexico, and we ran into some trouble. But we both made it out fine."

Jack grinned. "I should've guessed Scott would be involved. You two could find danger in the Vatican, for goodness' sake. What does any of that have to do with you coming to the Keys, though?"

I waited until after Lucy brought us our food, ensuring she wouldn't walk out and overhear part of our conversation.

The hogfish sandwiches were smothered in melted Swiss cheese, onions, and mushrooms, and they smelled delicious. I took a bite, savoring the flavor, and was amazed by the freshness of the fish and the Cuban bread.

"You remember that coin I found years ago? Well, we found another one, and let's just say there's a hell of a lot more."

I told Jack the story of our going to Sierra Gorda and exploring the cave—how we'd found Spanish writing along with a conquistador's helmet and sword. I also told him about how Scott had found the coin we'd found all those years ago and how he'd learned that it was actually an Aztec medallion.

"The treasure was taken, Jack. It was taken from the cave by the Spanish, and it hasn't shown up anywhere since."

"So, what are you saying? You think Montezuma's treasure, the gold of the Aztec empire, is somewhere here in the Keys?"

I grabbed a shrimp, dipped it in cocktail sauce, and scarfed it down in one bite. "All I'm saying is that there's a damn good chance. How else could that medallion have gotten here?"

"That ledge isn't a popular dive site down here. Only a few locals know about Neptune's Table. Hell, it's been nearly a year since I made it out that way myself, and that was just because the lobster are still plentiful there. But we've searched it over countless times before, bro. Heck, we probably know every inch of that area for four hundred feet in all directions, and yet we've never found any more gold or anything to hint at a treasure being there."

I took a bite of my sandwich and washed it down with beer. "But it's possible we could've missed it. Even a massive treasure like that is tiny compared to the ocean, and it's been hundreds of years." I shot my friend a confident grin. "What's your schedule look like the next couple of days? Any chance we could head there soon and explore it some more?"

Jack chuckled then shrugged. "Sure, bro. I would take the *Calypso* out today, but this weather's about to turn on us. Tomorrow's gonna be blue skies all day, so we can head out early in the morning and have a look around."

I gazed out over the water, then up at the nearly cloudless sky. "*This* weather's gonna turn? What makes you think that?"

Jack grinned. "Thinking's got nothing to do with it. I've been living here all my life, same as my father before me. It's called islander instinct. Mark my words, by no later than three this afternoon, there will be rain."

I looked at the sky again and just laughed. "The funny thing is, you're probably right."

"Of course I am. Why don't you come by the dock in the morning and we'll take her out for the day?"

He asked where I planned to stay, but the truth was, I hadn't really thought about it or even had a chance to look for a hotel yet.

"It'll be tough luck finding a vacancy this time of the year," Jack said. "Why don't you stop by the house, and I'll put you up in the guest room?"

I thanked him and told him it would just be for a day or two until I found a more permanent place to stay.

After lunch at the Pelican, I spent the rest of the afternoon strolling around downtown Key West, revisiting the historic tourist town I used to call home. A lot of it was exactly how I'd remembered it: the same local eateries, the same gift shops—though there seemed to be a lot more of them—the same oddballs doing tricks or singing in the streets, and of course, the same laid-back vibe in the air. I roamed the length of historic Duval Street, then past the southernmost point and on to Fort Zachary Taylor State Park, which was always one of my favorite places in Key West.

Sure enough, just after 1300, clouds rolled in over the island, and by 1430, there were tropical showers along with the occasional lightning strike. I made it back to my parked Tacoma just in time, and rain pelted the vehicle as I cruised over to Jack's place. Pulling into the drive, I felt like a kid again. His house looked exactly as it had when we were little when I used to pedal my bike there almost every day. It had the same white seashell driveway surrounded by large palm trees and palmetto plants.

I stepped out of the car, grabbed my duffle bag, and headed for the large wraparound porch. It had been his parents' house before they'd passed away, and though it was old, it was well taken care of and had been remodeled a few times. I passed a few paddleboards and wetsuits hanging out to dry and then knocked on the door. Jack answered and welcomed me inside.

It wasn't a large house, maybe twelve hundred square feet, and it seemed even smaller since the top floor was just the master bedroom, but it felt homey. Out the back of the house was a sliding glass door that led to the other side of the porch and a grassy area, along with a narrow channel where Jack kept his smaller center-console. I dropped my bags in the spare bedroom, passing by Isaac, who sat glued to his computer screen in his bedroom.

"Video games?" I asked, pointing at Isaac.

Jack shook his head. "Kid's crazy about computers. Can't understand how he spends so much time on it when he lives in a place like this." Jack motioned to the kitchen. "Here, I'll put some potatoes in the oven, and we can have a drink on the porch. This rain's about to die off, so in a few minutes, let's take out the twenty and pull up my crab pots. How does fresh stone crab, clams, and garlic potatoes sound?"

Fifteen minutes later, we were climbing aboard his twenty-foot Key West and untying the lines. He started the outboard, and we cruised leisurely out of the channel, keeping the speed down to keep from making a wake. After a few minutes, we reached a larger bay, and Jack hit the throttles, shooting us out toward the open ocean.

It wasn't far to his buoys, and when I pulled the first one up, I saw that it was nearly full of Florida stone crab. I removed one claw from each of the biggest ones, making sure they were of legal size first, then threw the crabs back into the ocean, along with a few freeloading spider crab, blue crab, lobster, and even a hogfish. Stone crab can lose their claws as a defense mechanism to escape predators. In less than eighteen months, these crabs would regrow their claws just as big as before.

"Damn, this trap reeks," I said, covering my nose with the top of my hand. After clearing the trap, I eagerly threw it back into the water. "What the hell do you use for bait?"

Jack laughed. "Pig's feet, bro. It's the most potent stuff out there. But keep it between us . . . it's a local secret. Crabs come running for miles when that nastiness hits the water."

Jack piloted us back from the open ocean and into the narrow channel, and we were soon tied off against the little private dock in front of his house. After carrying the crab claws toward a large pot of boiling water on his porch, I grabbed the lid, let the steam rise out, and dropped each claw into the water.

Jack went inside to check on the potatoes and then brought out a container of seasoning. "Swamp Sauce," he said, grinning at me.

"Just like old times," I replied.

Swamp Sauce had been a favorite of ours since we were kids. Jack introduced me to the stuff, and though I was skeptical at first, after trying it, I soon found myself putting the miracle seasoning from the Everglades on just about everything.

Jack opened the lid and dropped some into the boiling pot, along with a dozen or so clams from a nearby bucket of seawater resting on the porch.

"Should be just a few minutes," he said, walking to a cooler resting by the sliding glass door. He pulled out two Paradise Sunset beers, which were from a local brewing company in Key West called Keys Disease Brewery.

It was a classic brew they no longer sold, but it had always been a favorite of our dads. I recognized them instantly by the palm tree and orange sunset on the label.

"I was saving these for a special occasion," Jack said. "Welcome home."

I smiled and opened the top. It had been years since I'd had one of my favorite brews. It wasn't a popular drink, especially among locals, but upon completion of dive school, it used to be a tradition for Navy divers to come down to Key West and get wasted off the brew. And though Jack had never served in the military, he was as good of a diver as ever dropped below the waves.

TEN

The next morning we woke up early and grabbed a quick breakfast and coffee before heading out before the sun. I moved for the front door of the house, but Jack stopped me.

"Let's take the twenty, bro," he said. "It's less than a mile to the marina."

We packed up what we needed from the house, loaded it all into his boat, and motored to the marina. Jack had quite the lifestyle, I thought. He commuted via boat to his job, where he worked on a boat.

As we neared the marina, the sun began to rise up out of the ocean, and streaks of pink and gold lit up the horizon. We pulled up to the *Calypso*, unloaded our gear, then untied the lines and headed out toward the ledge.

The boat was much roomier and fancier on the inside than I expected it to be. Stepping down into the lounge, I saw it had a well-appointed galley with a beautiful table, a wraparound bench covered in blue cushions, and clean wooden cabinets. Jack showed me the main cabin, which was all the way forward and had an oversized V-berth. The other cabin was on the starboard side and had a full-sized bed. He'd removed the third cabin to accommodate more guests in the saloon on his afternoon charters.

I climbed the ladder and joined Jack in the pilothouse as we reached the edge of the marina.

"It's a little under an hour to the ledge," Jack said. "You wanna take her out?"

He stepped away from the helm, and I grabbed hold of it, along with the throttles to the right.

"Due southwest," I said, pointing forward and verifying with the compass attached to the panel. "Just around Sunset Key, through the West Channel between Crawfish Key and the Sand Key Lighthouse. Then onward to Neptune's Table six miles south of Marquesas Keys."

Jack smiled. "Very good. Nice to see you're still an islander at heart."

Holding on to the helm, I gunned the throttles, testing the twin four-hundred-and-thirty-horsepower engines. The *Calypso* shot through the calm morning water with ease. The view from up in the pilothouse was amazing, and since it was a clear day, we could see far across Key West National Wildlife Refuge. Within ten minutes, we cruised past Sand Key Light in the distance off our port side, and I thought of all the times I'd spent diving there before.

I felt eager and excited as we made our way closer to the ledge, but before I knew it, Jack was patting me on the shoulder and encouraging me to slow down to a stop.

I eased the throttles, and when we were just barely moving, I looked at him, confused. "This isn't right. The ledge is farther still. What are we doing here?"

Jack grabbed a pair of binoculars. "Look," he said, pointing at a boat on the horizon.

I grabbed the binos and peered through them. It was one of those fancy go-fast boats, and it was coming toward us at full speed.

"That orange Thundercat has been following us since we left the marina this morning. I first noticed it just as we were hitting open ocean."

"Ever seen it before?" I asked, lowering the binos.

Jack shook his head. "Never."

I handed him the binos, and as I did, I noticed that he'd grabbed a compact Desert Eagle, his handgun of choice, and had it lodged in the back of his shorts, just beneath his button-up shirt.

"What are you thinking? Pirates?" I grabbed my bag from the deck and pulled out my Sig.

He shrugged. "Sure as hell aren't the coasty patrollers." He pointed toward the boat. "They're slowing down."

We watched as the boat with the massive bow and sleek side panels pulled up closer. It turned slightly, displaying three enormous outboards mounted to the stern. At least two guys were in the cockpit, one shirtless and wearing large sunglasses, and the other, a huge black man wearing a cutoff shirt and a black do-rag. Another guy appeared from the cabin, skinny and sunburned, making it three in all. They stared at us as their boat idled up right beside ours. I felt for my Sig lodged into the back of my shorts. I had fifteen rounds and was ready to use them at a moment's notice if I had to.

The shirtless guy stepped against the port gunwale and glared at us. The large black man stood behind him and grabbed a coil of rope with a metal grappling hook tied to the end. These guys weren't asking for directions.

"Stand down," Shirtless said. He had a thick Spanish accent. "We're boarding your vessel. Neither of you will be hurt as long as you don't resist."

Jack stepped right up to the transom. "The only way you scumbags are getting on this boat is over our dead bodies. And if you don't tell your friend the Hulk to drop that hook, I'm going to force him to drop it by putting a bullet right into his arm."

Do-Rag was furious, along with Shirtless, who stood frozen, staring at Jack and me. Suddenly, Shirtless bent over and reached for something out of view.

"Freeze!" I yelled, sliding my Sig out of my shorts and taking aim at Shirtless in one quick motion. "Drop whatever you're grabbing, shithead." I eyed the other two guys. "All three of you, get your hands up!"

Jack grabbed his Desert Eagle and was now aiming it at them, as well. The three guys stared at us and said a few words in Spanish to each other that I couldn't hear.

"You've got three seconds until I start firing!" I yelled, and when they kept talking to each other, I fired a 9mm round straight through the port side of their boat.

The guys jolted down, then looked back up at us

with eyes wider than the horizon.

"I'm not fucking around here!" I yelled. "Get your damn hands up, now."

Reluctantly, Shirtless slowly raised his hands over his head, followed soon after by the two guys behind him. Their boat had drifted close to ours, leaving only about a six-foot gap between our hulls. Keeping my Sig raised, I stepped up onto the transom and vaulted over to their boat. Shirtless stepped back but kept his hands raised.

"Either of you moves a muscle, and you're getting a bullet in your chest," I said, looking at the two guys behind Shirtless.

Glancing down at the deck, I saw an Uzi, which Shirtless had been reaching for only seconds prior. I picked it up and flung it over the side, hearing it splash into the water. Forcing Shirtless to the deck, I used the coiled rope with the grappling hook to tie his hands behind his back.

As he struggled against the restraints, Shirtless said, "You have no clue who you're messing with, asshole."

I tied the knot tighter, making him wince in pain.

"Neither do you."

When I finished tying him up, I raised my weapon to the other two and yelled at Do-Rag to get down on his knees. He grunted, then sluggishly dropped to the deck.

"You," I said, pointing at Skinny. "Tie him up."

Do-Rag glared at Skinny, but seeing the barrel of my Sig zeroed in on him and Jack providing cover from the *Calypso*, Skinny moved toward his friend and started tying the rope around his wrists. For a moment, I thought he was actually doing a good job, but it was soon obvious that the knots weren't secure enough.

"Tighter," I said, but Skinny didn't tighten the rope. I stepped closer to them both, my finger on the trigger. "Tighter, dammit!"

In an instant, Skinny lunged at me and tried to grab my Sig from my hands. I fired off a quick round into his shoulder, and he fell back, slamming against the deck. Do-Rag slid his hands effortlessly from the knots, grabbed a buck knife from under his cargo shorts, and swung its blade straight for my left leg.

I turned away from Skinny and stepped back to avoid having my leg sliced in half, then took aim at Do-Rag. But before I could fire, he swooped his other hand beneath me, knocking me to the ground.

He dove toward me, and using his hulking momentum against him, I forced my legs into his chest and kicked him over the top of me. He crashed into one of the seats, breaking it into pieces. I grabbed his buck knife, which had fallen to the deck, and threw it overboard as I approached him. Dazed, he stumbled to his feet to continue the fight he didn't realize was already over. He took one strong swing at me, which I avoided by stepping back. Digging my left heel into the deck, I finished him off with a strong roundhouse kick, smashing my right foot into the side of his face and knocking him to the ground. He lay sideways against the broken seat, unconscious.

Shirtless was still tied up in the corner, watching helplessly. Skinny was cursing and rolling on his back in pain, his hands pressed against his shoulder, where blood was pouring out onto the clean white

104

deck.

"You all right, bro?" Jack asked, watching from the *Calypso*. "I was about to take out that guy when he came at you with the knife, but I couldn't get a clear shot over here."

"No problem," I replied with a grin. "These amateurs never stood a chance."

Confident that all three were incapacitated, I stepped toward the stern. Leaning over the three engines, I loosened the clamps holding them in place, then gave each one a strong kick. One by one, the engines flipped over the stern of the boat, their weight snapping their respective control and fuel lines before sinking toward the bottom of the ocean below.

"These guys aren't going anywhere now," I said.

I searched the boat but found that it was almost completely empty. Aside from a few backpacks with personal belongings and a case of Modelo beer, the boat was spotless. Stolen, no doubt. I stepped up from the cabin and saw Jack up in the pilothouse of the *Calypso*, talking into the radio. When he finished, he leaned over the railing.

"Patrol's on their way," he said. "They're asking for a call sign. What do you think?"

I stepped over the guys, opened a hatch on the bow, and grabbed the anchor. Making sure the chain was locked in first, I threw it over the side. "It would be a shame to spend a day like today talking to the police," I said, looking out over the clear water. "If we stay, it'll take hours, probably even days to clear up our story." I jumped back over to the *Calypso*. "Let's let the police take it from here."

Jack threw a thumbs-up, then changed the station

on the radio.

"Besides," I said, climbing up beside him, "that boat's clearly stolen. This isn't the first time they've boarded a boat."

I eyed the orange Thundercat and the three guys one more time. Skinny was still thrashing in pain. The damn fool would've been fine if he knew anything at all about first aid.

"Keep pressure on it!" I yelled over the *Calypso*'s engines after starting them up.

I watched as Skinny forced his hand against the wound, slowing the bleeding from his shoulder.

"Damn, Logan," Jack said. "In the Keys less than a day and already causing mayhem."

ELEVEN

I eased the throttles forward, wanting to put distance between us and the disabled boat. As I brought the *Calypso* up on plane and got us back on course for the ledge, my mind began to fully grasp the gravity of the incident we'd just had. "You ever had to deal with pirates before?' I asked my beach bum friend, who was still staring back at our unwanted visitors.

"Not like that. I've seen them around, and I've heard about things like this happening before, but I've never had it happen to me. I'm lucky that you were here, bro. I'm just as hard-headed as you are, but I'm a little rusty in the combat-experience department."

"I wouldn't say that," I said, thinking it over. "Maybe I'm the reason they tried to board us."

"What are you talking about? Why would anyone be after you here?"

I popped open a can of coconut water and took a long swig. Peering out over the endless blue, my mind took me back to Sierra Gorda. "They could be cartel. They didn't have the typical Black Venom tattoos etched into their wrists, but that doesn't scratch them out."

"What are you saying? You think those guys somehow figured out who you were and followed you all the way from Mexico?"

"It's possible. All I'm saying is that it's quite the coincidence that the day after I show up to Key West, your boat is attacked." I reached for the binos and handed them to Jack. "Here, make sure there aren't any more boats following us. We need to be cautious whenever we go to the ledge. If they are cartel, then they're after one thing . . . the Aztec treasure. We can't give them any more hints as to its whereabouts."

We throttled the *Calypso* up to her max speed just until we were out of sight of the disabled boat. Jack only saw a few other boats as we headed out toward the ledge. Most were fishing boats, and one was a Coast Guard patrol cruising full speed through the water toward the coordinates we'd given them.

"Gonna check the *Keynoter*," Jack said. "Should be a story about that boat over the next few days."

"Harper Ridley still writing for it?"

"Yeah," Jack replied. "In fact, she just did a story on the marina last week. Truth is, it was a rather uneventful summer. I bet she'll be happy to see a little excitement around here."

If we were lucky, that would be all the excitement we'd see, but I had a gut feeling that wouldn't be the case. Those guys on the boat worked for somebody, whether they were drug cartel from Mexico or not. And when word got back to whoever was running the show that three of their men had been incapacitated and their boat sabotaged, they would want some answers. Another good reason for not getting involved with the authorities.

Less than half an hour later, we reached the ledge referred to by locals as Neptune's Table, easing the throttles to a stop and dropping anchor just fifty feet from where I'd found the medallion years before. Jack and I both took another look around, making sure there weren't any suspicious-looking boats on the horizon. When we were both satisfied, we carried out a few tanks from the deck locker, and Jack grabbed the BCDs and gave them to me. He removed a pair of first- and second-stage regulators and inspected them as I dipped both BCDs into the water before strapping a tank behind each.

We slid into full wetsuits, then Jack cracked open a hard case and handed me a Suunto dive computer. "Already got your info plugged into it, bro," he said as he tightened his computer around his left wrist.

I thanked him and did the same, then we donned the rest of our gear.

"I'll be leaving the cabin locked," Jack said. "And the starter switch and ignition key are both with me, so even though we shouldn't ever be too far from the *Calypso*, we won't have to worry about someone coming aboard and taking her." Jack sat down beside me and put on his fins. "We should stick together. If one of us sees a boat approach, we'll notify the other and head for the surface."

I nodded, then slid my mask and snorkel over my head.

"Let's go find us a treasure," I said before

splashing back into the waves.

The warm water felt good as we bobbed for a moment, making sure we were weighted properly, then we vented the air from our BCDs and descended toward the ledge. It was only twenty feet down, so we would have about an hour and a half of bottom time before having to head back to the surface.

The ledge was teeming with sea life and surrounded by large masses of coral in all directions. Surveying the area, I noticed a few antennas sticking out from crevices, and I suppressed my desire to grab and bag a few bugs. Neptune's Table had gotten its name due, in part, to its large rectangular shape, and also because it's always loaded with seafood fit for the Roman god of the sea.

Kicking softly and keeping myself neutrally buoyant just over the ledge, I kept my eye out for anything unusual, anything foreign to the landscape, and of course, anything shiny. When I reached the spot where I'd found the Aztec medallion years before, I stopped. It was easy to tell that it was the right place. The ledge met the reef at a right angle, and the narrow crevice where the golden artifact had been lodged was still clearly visible. I followed the crevice in both directions, sliding my fingers through the cracks.

I glanced at Jack, who was pointing at the seafloor. The ledge rose up from the bottom about five feet or so, shadowing patches of coral and white sand below. I followed him down to the sand, and we searched the base of the ledge. Circling around it, I met back up with Jack, who shook his head, letting me know he hadn't found anything, either. I checked my dive computer and saw that we'd only been down about thirty minutes. We kept looking over the ledge, in the cracks between the coral, and in the sand below, but didn't find anything. It was clear that if the rest of the treasure was there, it must have been hidden extremely well.

After forty-five minutes passed, Jack and I met up at the base of the ledge. He grabbed a foldout bag I didn't notice had been attached to his BCD. Holding it out in front of him, along with a metal tickle stick, he gave a thumbs-up. I grinned, and less than ten minutes later, we broke the surface with a bag full of lobster that were well beyond regulation size.

"At least we won't go hungry," Jack said after we climbed aboard the *Calypso* and removed our dive gear. One by one, he pulled each lobster out of the bag and dropped them into a holding tank he had installed at the aft end of the boat. "There's no better place in the Keys to find a nice bug."

After we set our BCDs aside and strapped our tanks to the starboard gunwale, I climbed to the bridge and grabbed hold of the binoculars.

"See anything?" Jack said, not bothering to look up from the catch.

I scanned the horizon and was surprised by how empty it was. Aside from a few fishing boats and a sailboat, there was nothing but ocean and the occasional patch of land.

"Nothing."

Unable to dive for an hour while we waited for the nitrogen buildup in our lungs to dissipate, we cracked open a few coconut waters and cooked the lobster on Jack's outdoor gas grill. We sat, watching the ocean and relaxing on the cushioned seats. Jack set up his hammock, and I swayed in the breeze while listening to Jimmy Buffett stream through the boat's sound system. He cooked the lobster to perfection and dabbed lemon over it before handing me two decadent tails stuck to a kabob.

We spent the rest of the afternoon taking intermittent dives down to the ledge and the surrounding corals and seafloor. Using Jack's computer and his underwater camera, we were able to do a basic survey of the floor over the ledge and a hundred feet radius around it. This would allow us to study the intricate details and look for any unusual formations while out of the water. We spent hours filming and uploading to Jack's laptop, filling our bellies with succulent lobster and enjoying the tropical sunshine.

Despite the great conditions and animated conversations, we never let our guards down. We took intermittent scans of the horizon and routinely checked the *Calypso*'s radar. Needless to say, the incident with the three guys on the go-fast boat wore heavily on our minds.

Over the years, I'd learned that coincidences rarely occur. Whoever those men were and whoever they worked for, I was confident we hadn't seen the last of them.

TWELVE

At four in the afternoon, we weighed anchor and motored our way back to Conch Harbor Marina. We decided to head back the way we came and check for remaining patrol boats in the area, but we didn't see a single one.

"I'm sure they took care of it," Jack said. "Drug runners are pretty prevalent down here—compared to most places stateside, that is. These guys are usually pretty good at what they do."

As we pulled the *Calypso* into the marina, a sparkling yacht caught our attention. It was moored in a neighboring marina—one of the fancy yacht clubs—and it was hands down the largest and most extravagant-looking vessel there, with sleek silver trim bordering a creamy white hull.

I was the first to speak. "Damn. Who owns the floating palace?"

Jack stared at the yacht, which must have cost

113

more than a small country's annual budget. "Never seen it before. It must've just pulled in today."

"Another coincidence?" I asked, thinking about the guys who'd tried to take the *Calypso* earlier.

"I've never heard of a drug runner running around in something like that," Jack replied. "Must just be some billionaire from up north. We get a lot of big yachts around here from time to time. Everyone loves the Keys, after all."

"Any *that* big?"

Jack shook his head. He tried to convince me there was no way that I was the reason the yacht was there, but I still couldn't get it out of my mind. I'd dealt with drug cartels many times before in South America, Europe, and all over Africa. I knew the kind of money and power that was possible and knew that even a yacht like that could be well within the scope of a drug lord who ran a large enough operation.

We docked the *Calypso* and tied her off. I helped Jack wash down our diving gear and tidied up the main deck and cabin a bit before we took the center-console back to his house.

"Where are you planning to stay, anyway?" Jack said as he piloted the boat. "I mean, you're more than welcome to keep staying at my place, bro, don't get me wrong. I'm just sure you'll want your own pad, especially if you're gonna be here for a while."

I thought it over for a moment. "I'm thinking about a liveaboard. Preferably something fast and with a lot of space."

Jack laughed. "Hope your pockets are deep, because that's a tall order. But if you're looking to buy a boat down here, you should check some of the nearby marinas. All sorts of boats are always for sale down here."

On the way back to his house, we passed by a few yachts with for sale signs. Most were old yachts or sailboats, but we drove by one that caught my attention from the moment I saw it.

"Pull up close to that one." I pointed at a long, sleek boat attached to the end of one of the docks in a passing marina.

Jack brought us right up to it, and it looked even better up close. It had plenty of deck space with a huge swim platform, a sunbed, and a cozy topside dinette. It was at least forty feet long, and I knew it couldn't be much more than just a few years old.

"That's a Baia Flash," Jack said. "Probably forty-eight feet. A badass boat, for sure. Must have at least two cabins to go along with a gorgeous lounge, and it'll probably push you through the water over forty knots. But it's gonna set you back a fortune."

I leaned over the transom of Jack's twenty to get a better look at the for sale sign. The price was listed at four hundred thousand dollars or best offer. I grabbed a pen from a shelf next to the wheel and wrote down the phone number.

"You're seriously considering it? I didn't know mercenaries got paid so much."

"If it's still available, yeah, I am. I mean, I'm planning to be here for a while, so I might as well get a nice place. And it depends on how good you are at it."

He threw his hands up in the air. "Well, from what I saw today, I'm sure you're the best there is."

~ ~ ~

I called the number that evening, and a man, who I later learned was a retired surgeon, answered the phone and told me the Baia was still available. I asked him if he was able to meet the next day, and we agreed on ten in the morning.

That evening, we grilled the rest of the lobster and a few steaks and drank beer as the sun dropped down over the water.

"You know," Jack said, lounging beside me, "if you're serious about finding this treasure, we're gonna need some specialty gear. I know a guy who lives just on the other side of the island. His name's Pete, and he's really into treasure hunting. He even owns a restaurant with a museum on the second story. I could give him a call and let him know we're looking for some advice on treasure-hunting equipment."

Jack went on to say that Pete had been a friend of his father's and that he knew more than anyone about the Keys and treasure hunting.

"See if he can meet me tomorrow afternoon."

Jack brought out his laptop, and we spent a few hours looking over the surveys of the ocean floor. Despite repeatedly scanning every square foot, we couldn't find anything unusual. It was just the same ledge surrounded by corals.

"If the Aztec treasure did sink, the bulk of the treasure could be anywhere," Jack said. "I don't know a lot about sunken treasure, man, but I know that after nearly five hundred years, for all we know, the ocean could've brought that medallion you found from miles away. You remember that treasure they found off Florida's eastern coast? The remnants of the seventeen fifteen Spanish fleet? Well, those guys found coins from Jupiter, all the way up north to Sebastian. That gold's scattered all over the place, bro."

"Which is why your idea of getting better equipment will help us track it down."

After the sun fell and the bugs came out, we decided we'd had enough work and shut the laptop. Jack, who drank five bottles of beer, decided it was time to call it a night and entered the house through the sliding glass door, leaving only the screen open so the ocean air could flow into the house at night. I only had a few beers and decided to stay up a little longer.

"That reminds me," Jack said through the screen door. "Isaac told me a few packages arrived for you today. He put them in the spare bedroom."

I was filled with a sudden rush of excitement. I'd almost forgotten about the orders I'd made while back in Miami, and as I examined my new arsenal, I felt like a kid on Christmas morning.

After opening all of my new weapons, including a .338 Lapua sniper rifle, I stowed and locked them in the toolbox in the bed of my Tacoma. Then I went around the house, across the grass, and stood on the wood pilings that formed the edge of the channel. I looked up at the moon through the clear night sky, then surveyed the area around me. The truth is, I didn't feel right. I felt like something was off, and I'd felt that way since we'd arrived back at the marina. After years of taking part in special operations in the Navy and years of fighting as a mercenary, I'd developed a sort of sixth sense that alerted me whenever trouble was nearby. Right then, that sense was going off like an alarm clock. I couldn't stop thinking about the guys who'd attacked us earlier . . . and then the mysterious yacht.

After scanning the nearby bushes and trees, I headed back toward the house. I decided, even though I hadn't even stepped aboard it yet, that I would buy the Baia the following day. I didn't like the idea of putting Jack, and especially his nephew, at risk. If I was right and Black Venom had somehow managed to track me down to the Keys, I'd want them to come for me, not the two of them.

When I was satisfied with my survey around the outside of the house, I came in through the sliding screen door, shutting it softly behind me before heading to the guest room to crash for the night.

The next morning, Jack and I drove the Tacoma to the marina and met with the owner of the 48 Baia Flash. Stepping aboard the boat was easy, as it had one of the largest swim platforms I'd ever seen on a boat. As I stepped up to the wheelhouse, I realized that the yacht was even more immaculate than I'd anticipated. The attention to detail was incredible, from the leather cushioned seats and freshly waxed cabinets, to the shiny steel wheel and handrails. It had a dark blue hull and a brilliant white deck. Dropping down a few steps to the saloon, I admired the galley and dining area that could comfortably seat eight people. It had two cabins, a master suite, and a guest room. A king-sized bed was in the middle of the master suite, along with a closet, which had a built-in safe and plenty of storage space.

The owner of the boat, George Shepherd, was a retired surgeon who loved the island lifestyle as much as any man. He gave me a tour of the boat, and I could tell by his voice that he loved it dearly. When I asked him why he was parting with it, he told me it was because he and his wife were going to buy a sailboat and cruise around the world for a few years.

"I hate to see it go," George said, admiring the yacht, "especially considering she's only two years old, but if we put off this trip any longer, we won't be able to take it."

George walked me through every inch of the yacht and answered all of our questions.

"What's she got for power?" Jack inquired, motioning below to the engine room.

George smiled as he bent over and pried open the entire aft deck sunbed, revealing two huge engines that looked brand-new.

"She's got twin six hundreds," he said, grinning from ear to ear. "This baby can hit fifty knots. I've taken day trips from here all the way up to Key Largo in under two and a half hours."

After explaining more about the engines and telling us how top-of-the-line they were, he shut the hatch and pointed at two cameras mounted sleekly to the boat.

"It's got a state-of-the-art security system," George said. "Anybody comes near the boat when the system's up, you can have it alert you anywhere on board."

After seeing all that the yacht had to offer, I felt more and more like it was clearly the boat for me. It was big enough for me to live on, had plenty of speed, and was easy on the eyes. Whether I ended up staying in the Keys for a few months or a few years, it would be a hell of a nice place to call home.

We agreed on three hundred and seventy-five thousand, and later that day, I wrote out the check and exchanged it for the title and registration.

"It was a pleasure doing business with you, Captain," George said. "Take good care of her. I'll be around for a few more months, so if you have any problems or questions at all, just give me a call." There was something about being called *captain* that caught me off guard, but boy did I like it. Wrapping an arm around my shoulder, he added, "There's a bottle of champagne in the fridge for you to celebrate."

When he left the dock, Jack and I sat on the padded seats on the deck and broke open two bottles of beer to christen my new home, thinking it a little odd for a couple of dudes to enjoy a bottle of fine champagne together.

"I can't believe you bought this thing," Jack said, laughing. "You must be an even better mercenary than I thought."

The truth is that even though I'd done well for myself as a gun for hire, most of my money came in the form of an inheritance from my dad. He had owned a house in California to go along with his condos in Mexico and Curacao. After he died, I'd sold everything but the condo in Curacao, not having the heart to see it go.

Jack and I sat for a bit and polished off our beers before he got up to leave.

"I got another charter this afternoon, man," he

said. "But look, if you need any help finding a place to keep this baby, give Gus a call over at the Conch. I know he's got a few slips available that are big enough. Just don't let him charge you anything over fifteen a foot." He jumped onto the dock, then turned back to me. "Oh yeah, I almost forgot. Pete said he'd be at his place all day today if you want to stop by to ask about treasure-hunting gear. I'll text you the address."

I raised my beer high over my head. "To the Aztec treasure."

"Just try and stay out of trouble, bro. At least for the afternoon, try not to beat anybody up."

"I can't make any promises," I said, and chugged the rest of my beer.

THIRTEEN

It was only twelve thirty, so I decided to take my new boat out for a test drive. I would take the long way to Conch Harbor Marina, circling around Mule Key. Having already checked out with the office, I unloaded my weapons from the bed of my truck and locked them in the safe inside the master stateroom. Then I untied the lines and threw them aboard before hopping into the cockpit and grabbing hold of the wheel. Using the engines to guide the boat away from the dock, I brought her out of the marina where she was moored and into the open ocean.

It was a calm day, so I'd find out for myself just how fast she could go. After getting up on plane, I slid the throttles all the way forward. The boat flew through the water, the ocean streaming by in a blur as I got the engines up to fifty knots. The feeling of taking my own boat out on the water and letting it loose was incredible.

After spending an hour cruising around Mule and Crawfish Keys and up toward Barracouta Key, and getting a handle on my new boat by testing different high-speed maneuvers, I headed toward Conch Harbor Marina. I called Gus on my way back to get an idea on price, and he told me that since I couldn't commit to a year, it would be fourteen dollars a foot, and that included electric, water, internet, and access to all of the marina facilities. I agreed, and less than fifteen minutes later, I was pulling my boat into slip twenty-four, which was just a short walk down the dock from the *Calypso*.

While meeting with Gus and handling all of the paperwork, I got a text from Jack informing me of the location where I could find Pete. After finishing up at the marina office, I locked everything away on my boat, then headed down the sidewalk to the parking lot a few marinas down, where my truck was still parked. I typed the address into my GPS, and four minutes later, I was pulling into the parking lot of what looked like someone's house, aside from the sign out front that read "Salty Pete's Museum and Grill." When I stepped out, I realized I was the only car in the gravel lot. I looked around, then walked up to the large wooden porch. A bell rang as I entered, and a woman appeared from the kitchen.

The restaurant made good use of its space, with booths lining the walls and a few tables and chairs in the middle. In the back was an old wooden stairway, and beside it was the door to the kitchen. The walls were covered with old pictures of boats and various locations around the Keys. There were a few old boat helms and other marine memorabilia, giving the run-down place a nostalgic feel to it. In the distance, I heard the Eagles' "Take It Easy" playing over the radio.

"Welcome to Salty Pete's," the woman said. She had light brown hair that she pulled back in a ponytail. She appeared to be in her early twenties and wore a green shirt tied behind her back that had the words "Salty Pete's" emblazoned in bold letters, along with a picture of a guy fishing. Holding a notebook and pen in her hands, she said, "It's your lucky day, Mister . . . ?"

"Dodge," I said with a friendly smile. "Logan Dodge."

"Well, it's your lucky day, Mr. Dodge. We just got a fresh haul of grouper, and Osmond's got them marinating and ready to grill." She motioned to the tables. "Go ahead and have a seat anywhere. What would you like to drink? The Key limeade is my favorite."

I slid into one of the middle booths and eyed her name tag.

"That sounds great, Mia. Thanks."

As much as I'd wanted to find this Pete guy and find out what kind of stuff I would need, I was starving after buying my new toy and cruising around the islands. I realized that I hadn't eaten since dinner the night before.

Mia smiled and walked back to the kitchen. It was just after two o'clock, and it made me wonder why the place was so empty. I chalked it up to the poor location since it wasn't near the main rows of stores and restaurants in downtown Key West. It was also in desperate need of a renovation, from the old

124

scratched-up wooden floors to the faded paint on the walls.

Mia appeared with my drink and set it on a napkin in front of me. "What will it be, Mr. Dodge?" she asked, her hands resting on her hips.

"Just Logan," I replied. "And I'll take the grilled grouper." I hadn't even bothered to look at the menu on the table in front of me. "But to be honest, I'm not really here for the food."

The young woman wrote on her pad, then smiled. "It's the location, right? We get that a lot here." She slid the menu from the table and walked back to the kitchen.

I glanced again at the run-down establishment that bordered a tourist gift shop on one side and an empty alley on the other. Both could be seen from open windows with weathered curtains hanging down their sides.

A few minutes later, Mia returned with my plate. The grouper appeared to be cooked perfectly, its surface lightly blackened. It was served with wild rice and a kabob of mixed vegetables. I took a bite of the fish and was taken aback by how delicious it was. Mia wasn't kidding about it being my lucky day. I'd wager this fish had been swimming carefree less than a few hours ago.

"So what brings you here?" Mia asked. "I mean, since you're not here for the food."

I swallowed a bite of fish and rice, then washed it down with a gulp of the Key limeade.

"The truth is, I'm looking for somebody."

She shrugged. "It's just me and Osmond in the back."

I grabbed my phone and brought up Jack's message from earlier that day and held it up to her.

"I was told I could meet with Pete this morning."

"Salty Pete's out diving," a man said, appearing from the kitchen. He had a scruffy face and long blond hair braided in the back. He was wearing a dirty apron and wiped his hands on a rag. "That's the guy that owns this shack."

Mia nodded, then turned to me. "Oz works for him sometimes on his boat. Pete's a collector. He has a museum upstairs."

I shook Osmond's hand and introduced myself. I hadn't been prepared for the smell of marijuana that radiated from the large Scandinavian-looking man.

"It's quite the collection, really," Osmond said. "He spends most of his time out on the water, though. I go out with him occasionally." He placed his fingers on a gold earring dangling from his left earlobe. "He helped me find this."

"Where can I find him?"

"He has a boat just down the street a few blocks," Mia said. "It's in the harbor, moored to a buoy. Poor guy can't afford to keep it on a dock."

A few tourists who'd stumbled off the main streets entered through the front door, and Mia ushered them to a table.

I took a few more swigs of the cool limeade and finished off more of the grouper. When I glanced up at Osmond, I saw that he was watching me awkwardly.

"It's good, isn't it?" he said.

The guy looked stoned out of his mind, but he sure cooked up some mean fish. I nodded and told him it

126

was delicious.

"Well, if you need anything else, just let either of us know," he said before turning back toward the kitchen.

"Where did you find it?" I said.

Osmond paused, then turned on his heels and eyed me with a crooked brow.

"The earring," I said, turning on a lightbulb in his head.

"Oh, uh . . . Voodoo Reef." He placed his fingers on the golden earring once more. "It was from a shipwreck first discovered years ago. It's just north of Cottrell Key, about forty feet down. Near the sunshine rim of the reef."

"You find a lot of gold around here?"

He shook his head. "The Keys are scarce these days. Better luck fifty years ago," he said as Mia motioned for him to walk with her into the kitchen. "But you can get lucky sometimes."

Before they reached the kitchen door, it swung open in front of them. A man stormed through the door, carrying a large net filled with lobsters over his shoulder and holding a line of fish in his left hand.

"Get the grills hot, Oz!" the man shouted enthusiastically. "We're gonna cook up some fresh bugs tonight!"

"Well, speak of the sea devil," Osmond said. He looked over at me and pointed at the man. "This is Salty Pete, Logan. Pete, this is Logan Dodge, and he wants to talk with you about something. He's friends with Rubio."

"Dammit, Pete," Mia said, walking angrily toward the older man. "How many times have I told you not

127

to bring your catch into the dining area? You're dripping water everywhere."

Pete smiled and patted the young woman on the back as she grabbed a rag and started to dry the floor. "It used to be a tradition here in the Keys," Pete said. "It's the conch thing to do."

"Well, your tradition is scaring away customers." Mia pointed to the door just as it was closing behind the group that had sat down a few minutes earlier.

Pete handed the net to Osmond, who took it into the kitchen. He walked toward me, unable to remove the smile from his face, despite the fact that he'd just driven away probably the only other customers he'd see for a while.

I guessed him to be in his early sixties. He had a few gray hairs, but his head was mostly tanned bare skin. He was short and had a decent belly but still moved with ease across the restaurant. He was wearing the same shirt Mia was but in gray instead of green. The first thing I'd noticed about Pete, however, was that his right arm was missing just above the elbow.

"Welcome to my restaurant, Logan," Pete said, offering me his left hand. "Don't worry about my arm. People stare at it all the time. Care to know how I lost it?"

Mia walked away from the table, rolling her eyes as Pete continued.

"Well, I was deep-sea diving off the Goblin Gull, and I ran across the largest great white any sailor ever saw. She was over six fathoms from tail to snout, no lie."

Osmond shook his head. "You're telling me a

shark the size of a school bus came after you, and all he took was your arm?"

"Aye, and I took a hell of a lot more from him."

"You're a lucky man," I said. "Where is this Goblin Gull? I've never heard of it."

Pete smiled, liking the fact that I'd humored him. "It's a secret blue hole roughly twenty to a hundred miles southeast of here."

I chuckled. "That's very specific."

Pete leaned in close, revealing two gold teeth as he practically whispered, "If I wasn't vague, it wouldn't be a secret, would it?" He peeked down at my plate. "How do you like the eats? Oz is the best chef in the Keys, if you ask me."

"It's great."

"But he didn't come here for the food," Mia said, appearing behind him.

Pete eyed me suspiciously, then gave a soft smirk.

"Yeah. Look, do you think we could talk in private?" I asked. "Jack told me you'd be a good person to ask for advice on a particular venture we're undertaking."

Pete's eyes lit up. "He called and said you'd stop by sometime today." He motioned toward the stairs at the back of the room. "My collection is just upstairs, along with my office."

When I finished eating, I walked with Pete up the old, creaking stairs, hoping with each step that I wouldn't break through the floorboards. The second floor was a wide-open space with rows of glass cases and shelves, each filled with an assortment of artifacts. On the walls were paintings, pictures of big fish, and other relics from the Keys. I stood in awe of

129

the enormous collection, admiring the pieces that were closest to me. One was an antique pistol, like the ones you see in the old pirate movies.

Pete motioned toward the back of the room. "My office is just back here, mate."

I followed him to a room that was taken up mostly by a huge wooden desk covered in old charts, maps, and various equipment. The room was lined with bookshelves filled top to bottom with everything from Cussler to the encyclopedia.

"Have a seat," he said, removing a bunch of papers from an old leather seat. He sat across from me on a squeaky office chair, then leaned back and regarded me curiously. "Well, what can I do for you, Logan?"

"I'm looking to get ahold of some salvage equipment."

He tilted his head toward me. "Oh? What are you trying to salvage?"

I looked him over, wondering how much I should say, then decided to be as vague as possible. "I'm looking for a shipwreck."

Pete then shot a barrage of questions my way, from the year the ship went down to the approximate expected location of the wreck.

"That's nearly five hundred years ago," he said. "Years of shifting sands, changing tides, storms, erosion, and corrosion can make a wreck almost impossible to find with the naked eye. I'd recommend you pick up some heavy side-scan sonar equipment and a magnetometer so you can pick up cannonballs, anchor chains, stoves, and other large metal objects. Then you could get yourself a computer guru to hook you up with good GPS software to help pinpoint unique formations under the water, at least in the shallower areas. You'll also need a mailbox if you want to find a treasure that's been down that long."

"A mailbox?"

"Yeah. It's a metal shroud that directs prop wash to the seafloor to clear away sand and other loose debris. It would work well on Jack's Sea Ray."

He went on to explain a few other necessities for treasure hunting and gave me the address and phone number of a place up by Marathon that could hook me up with most of the stuff I needed.

After we'd talked a while and he'd written down the gear I would need, I thanked him, and we walked out of the office. While heading for the stairs, I caught a glimpse of a dirty sliding glass door that led out to a porch. I changed direction and looked out the glass, staring at the ocean that peeked over a patch of palm trees.

"The view's amazing from up here," I said.

"Oh, it's of the best in the Keys. You can watch the sunrise and sunset from right out there." He gazed out over the water, then at me. "Anything else I can help you with?"

"Yeah, actually." I decided to trust this guy a little more based on both Jack's recommendation and my own gut instinct. "Does the name Francisco de Cavallos mean anything to you?"

Pete stood frozen for a moment. He looked at me quizzically, then gave a grin. "I haven't heard that name in over thirty years." He turned away from me and focused on one of the nearby glass cases. "You know, my grandfather opened this place almost a hundred years ago. He was a brilliant treasure hunter

131

by the name of Theodore Jameson, and he used to tell me all sorts of stories."

I was surprised to learn of the relation. I'd heard of Theodore Jameson, as had many people in Florida. In fact, he ranked right up beside Walt Grissam as one of the most famous treasure hunters ever to explore the Caribbean.

"My favorite was always the story of Francisco de Cavallos," Pete continued. "He was a Spanish rogue who lived in Cuba and stole a ship from Cortés himself, sailing with a crew of ragtag outcasts in search of gold in the Americas. However, after leaving Havana in fifteen twenty-eight, the *Intrepid* and her crew were never seen nor heard of again. There is no doubt that she sank. When and where is the only question. And there's also no doubt that most of the crew died."

"Most of the crew?" I asked, intrigued by his story.

"Well, there's more to the story—at least, whenever my grandfather told it there was. The history books will claim otherwise, but he was confident there was one man who survived."

"One man?"

Pete nodded. "This is where the story gets interesting. A few years after they set sail from Cuba, a man washed ashore on a beach not too far from here. For three days he lived here on his own before traveling north in search of a settlement. He was found by a Calusa hunting party, and after a few years, he assimilated into the group and became a part of the tribe, the only white man ever recorded as doing so with the Calusa Indians. To the astonishment of the natives, the man remembered very little about where he came from. It wasn't until much later in his life that he started having dreams about gold and nightmares of a catastrophic shipwreck. Until the day he died, he told stories about a massive treasure that he claimed was under the waves just a few miles off the coast of what is now Key West. His story was passed down, and it's still well known among the handful of remaining Calusa, but very few others have heard it before."

"What do you think happened? Do you believe the story about the gold?"

"I hope so. I like a good treasure yarn." He reached into a nearby glass case, grabbed a model ship, and set it on a table beside me. "All that's certain is that this ship sailed out of Cuba and never returned. And she hasn't been found to this day."

I was happy with the way it went with Pete. Jack had been right—he was clearly the right person to talk to about a treasure anywhere in the Keys. Now, in addition to the captain's name, I had the name of his ship and a list of all the equipment I would need to find her. I was anxious to get out on the water and find the rest of the gold.

I thanked Pete for everything, but before I left, he stopped me.

"I gotta tell you, I sure like you more than the last guy," he said.

"What are you talking about?" I asked, unable to hide my confusion.

"You're not the first person to walk in here and ask me about a shipwreck. A guy came in here just yesterday. I got a bad vibe from him, though. Didn't give him much information."

"What did he look like? Did he threaten you in any way?"

Pete laughed. "He was temperamental. But at my age, I don't take easily to threats, so if he had, I'd have flipped him off. He was tall and well built, with dark skin and hair cut close to his head. He spoke with a Spanish accent, sounded like. I already called Sheriff Wilkes, and he said he'd keep an eye out. Either way, I'd say you've got yourself a little competition."

FOURTEEN

I thanked Pete again, then rushed down the stairs and out the door. I started the engine of the Tacoma, then called Jack on my cellphone. He picked up on the third ring.

"What's up, bro?" he asked. "How was your meeting with Pete? You get some good info?"

"Yeah," I replied. "More than I bargained for. We need to get this gear pronto and find the rest of that damn treasure before someone else does. Can you meet me at the marina?"

"Already here, man."

I backed out, then hit the gas pedal, shooting down Whitehead Street toward the waterfront.

I pulled into the marina parking lot, and before stepping out, took a quick look around. Between the guys trying to hijack Jack's boat the other day, the mysterious mega yacht, and the stranger asking questions of Pete, I knew something was up.

Someone else was trying to find the treasure, and whoever they were, they knew I had information regarding its whereabouts. By force of habit, after many years of fighting off bad guys, I assumed the worst, which was that Black Venom was here in the Keys. I grabbed the Sig from my center console, checked to make sure the mag was loaded up—even though I knew it was—and strapped it to my chest.

Seeing nothing suspicious in the parking lot or visible portion of the marina, I slid on a pair of aviator sunglasses and stepped out.

Jack was lounging on the topside seats when I strode up to the *Calypso*. He was leaning over a newspaper and glanced up when he saw me approach. "What's up, man?" he asked. Jack, per usual, was shirtless, wearing only board shorts and flip-flops.

"Does he always introduce himself by telling the story of how he lost his arm?"

Jack chuckled. "That old sea dog has a different story every week explaining how he parted ways with that limb. Gets more exaggerated each time, too. What did he tell you, that he lost it while fighting off a gang of alligators in the Everglades with his bare hands?"

"This time, it was a shark," I said, grinning.

"Well, crazy or not, he's got a lot of info if you pick his brain. What'd he say?"

"He said there's someone else interested in our shipwreck. And whoever it is isn't friendly."

"Who do you think it is? Those drug lords from Mexico?"

"Could be. You know how I like to plan for the worst." I scanned the marina, making sure there was no one approaching. "Come on. Let's head up to Marathon. Pete's got a guy there who can hook us up with the gear we need."

Jack grabbed a shirt from below deck and removed his keys from his pocket to lock up the *Calypso*.

"Oh, and don't forget your Desert Eagle," I said.

Before we reached the Baia, I called the number Pete had given me, and I agreed to meet the owner of the shop in forty-five minutes. I jumped onto the Baia, and Jack followed right on my heels.

"It's a buck fifteen to Marathon, bro," Jack said, untying the lines and throwing them aboard.

I started the massive engines and eased on the throttles. A few minutes later, we reached the end of the no-wake zone.

"Not today it isn't," I said right before letting loose on the throttles. The engines roared and shot us through the tropical water like a rocket.

Within no time, we were circling around Key West and heading northeast along the Lower Keys toward Marathon. The sun was shining, and the seas were calm as glass, allowing me to really test out what she had for power. When we reached fifty knots on the speedometer, I yelled at Jack, pointing at the gauge. The ocean flew past us in a haze, and I had to keep a sharp eye out for other boats to avoid having a collision at such high speeds.

We cruised past the Saddlebunch Keys, then wrapped around Big Pine Key and under the Seven Mile Bridge. Reaching the opening to Boot Key Harbor, I slowed on the throttles, easing the Baia through the narrow channel between Boot Key and US-1.

137

Marathon had always been one of my favorite places in the Keys. It had a much quieter and more natural vibe to it than the rip-roaring wild ride that was Key West. I'd spent many days swimming the reefs just offshore and camping with my dad on her pristine and isolated beaches. Looe Key particularly had always been a special place for me, my dad, and Jack when I was young.

We pulled into Westside Marina, and I eased the Baia into one of the day moorage spaces right beside the office. We tied off, and a moment later, we hopped on the dock, paid the office manager the daily mooring fee of forty dollars, and marched down the dock toward a large commercial building surrounded by boats stored on racks. We entered and quickly found the guy Pete had recommended.

I took all of Pete's recommendations to heart, and after a few hours of going over their equipment, Jack and I were cruising the Baia away loaded with everything we would need to find a treasure. I got top-of-the-line sonar, including a side-scan sonar device that, when dragged behind your boat, sweeps the bottom with twin sonar beams. The reflected sound waves are recorded to create, in essence, an "aerial map" of the seabed. I also got a magnetometer to locate large metals and a laptop preloaded with high-tech GPS programs. I held off only on the mailbox, deciding with Jack's approval to install it on his boat when we had the chance.

We spent most of the next few days at the ledge, testing out the new toys I'd bought and seeing if they could help us pinpoint the location of the treasure. Regardless of the excitement we felt and the fun we were having, we kept our heads on a swivel at all times, maintaining an ever-watchful eye for anyone or anything suspicious. A few times while piloting the Baia out, we thought we were being followed, so we hit the throttles hard and weaved in and out of a few small islands and shallow reefs. Both times we ended up losing whoever it was, whether they were following us or not. Buying a boat that could really fly on the water seemed to be paying off.

After two days, we'd done enough scanning with the sonar to have a complete digital replication of the seafloor around the ledge, and it was much more accurate and helpful than the one we'd made with my action camera on the first days out. This one provided intricate details that really gave us a chance to study for any abnormalities at the bottom of the ocean. The magnetometer appeared to work almost too well. Each and every time we dragged it anywhere near the ledge, it rang out like an angry seagull, indicating that there was more heavy metal under us than at a Metallica concert. We questioned whether or not it was broken because we never found any metal on or around the ledge. Jack explained how it could have been a natural iron deposit of some kind, and that was explanation enough for me to trust the device over the rest of the seafloor.

Regardless of the strides we felt like we were making, we still had yet to find another piece of jewelry or any artifact from the *Intrepid*. I was growing impatient, knowing that our luck in avoiding the other guys after the treasure could run out in the blink of an eye.

FIFTEEN

One morning, while Jack and I were sitting on the bridge looking over the sonar scans on the laptop, a woman approached the *Calypso*. The sun had risen over the water just a few hours prior, and despite it being only nine in the morning, it was already seventy-five degrees.

"Are you Jack Rubio?" a voice called out from the dock below.

We peered down and saw a woman standing with her hands on her hips, staring at us behind dark sunglasses. Behind her was a young blonde woman and a short Asian guy who wore a large beach-style hat that I'm confident he'd bought at a gift shop down the street.

The woman with her hands on her hips began impatiently tapping her foot against the dock. "Well?" she said. "Are you or aren't you? We're burning daylight."

Jack and I looked at each other, surprised. Neither of us had heard anyone approach, our eyes having been glued to the laptop screen.

"I thought I was free today," Jack muttered, hoping only I would hear him.

"I have my confirmation," she proclaimed, "as well as my receipt from my partial payment."

Jack climbed down the ladder to the cockpit, then stepped over the transom and onto the dock. "Jack," he said, holding out his hand, which she took reluctantly. "And you must be . . ." She handed him the confirmation letter, and he read the name that it had been sent to. "Miss Samantha Flores."

"Sam is fine," she said. "And this is Tony and Claire." She gestured to the two behind her.

I couldn't help but notice how attractive the woman with the attitude was. She looked about five and a half feet tall with a great, lean figure, and jet-black hair that she kept in a ponytail beneath a faded Florida Seminole ball cap. She had bronze skin, spoke with a subtle Spanish accent, and looked to be in her early thirties. All three had backpacks on, and Sam had a rolling hard case balanced in front of her, her hand resting on the handle.

"Well, Sam, I apologize that I'm not more prepared," Jack said. "I don't usually handle reservations, and I was told no one was going out today." He inspected the *Calypso*'s main deck, which was freshly cleaned but lacked any of the gear needed to take a group out on the water. When Sam didn't reply, he continued. "It'll take me some time to get everything ready." He pointed to the Greasy Pelican. "They serve a good breakfast over there if you three

141

want to stand by for a bit. I can call you when everything's good to go."

I stretched and climbed down the ladder as Jack spoke. Leaning against the port railing, I got a front-row seat to witness the woman's dissatisfied reaction.

"We're not hungry," Sam said, then slid the handle of her rolling bag down into itself, picked it up, and handed it to Jack. Without a word, she plopped down onto the transom, slid her long, tanned legs over the horizontal beam, then stood up beside us. "I can help." She slid her backpack from her shoulders and held it out in front of me. I stared at her for a moment, then smiled and grabbed it. "Better pick up the pace if you want a tip at the end of the day."

I laughed and gave her my best smile, but she just glanced away. Apparently, Keys Disease hadn't kicked in for her yet.

"Logan's not a deckhand," Jack said, cutting in between us. He grabbed his phone and sent a quick text. "My mate lives just down the street. He'll be here in a few minutes."

Irritated, Sam ripped the bag from my hands and called for Tony and Claire to get the rest of the gear from the car.

"I can get the tanks," I said, striding into the lounge. "Miss Flores, you can stow your stuff in here for now. Would you care for some coffee?"

Reluctantly, she followed me down through the door, and I showed her the closet where she could put their gear.

"I said it's just Sam, and I'll get some once we're out on the water."

"Logan Dodge," I said, holding out my hand.

She shook her head and strutted back toward the steps. "If you're not part of Jack's crew, I don't have time. Not today."

I couldn't help but grin. She was the sexiest angry woman I'd ever seen.

She disappeared topside and said something to Jack. I filled my mug with another cup of coffee, then Jack came down.

"Sorry I can't help out more," I said.

"Don't worry about it. I think you have a friend here to see you, though. A woman is leaning up against a red Camaro in the marina parking lot. She just pulled up, and she's been eyeing the boat."

I squinted at him, confused. "What makes you think she's here to see me?"

He shrugged. "Just a hunch."

I helped Jack carry the tanks up to the deck, where they could be filled as necessary.

"You should just cancel it, man," I said when the other three were out of earshot. "It's gonna be hell dealing with that woman all day."

Jack laughed. "That's the charter business, bro. You gotta learn to deal with difficult people and not cancel on them because that can kill you on the reviews."

I jumped over the transom and onto the dock. Eyeing the shore, I saw the Camaro and a woman leaning against it, staring straight at me. I smiled and strolled toward her.

Halfway down the dock, I ran into the young blonde woman who was part of the charter group. She lumbered past me, carrying a stuffed, oversized duffle bag over her shoulder and rolling another hard case.

143

"Here, I can help you with that," I said, taking the load off her back.

"Thanks," she replied.

She was strikingly pretty at around five foot ten and with hair that flowed freely in the wind. I pegged her to be around nineteen, maybe twenty.

"Claire, right?"

She nodded.

"What's the deal with all this gear? Are you three underwater photographers of some kind?"

"No, it was Professor Flores's idea. She wanted to play it safe, so she brought every piece of survey equipment in the *entire* world."

"What's her deal anyway?"

"She's just mad about how the trip's gone so far. She's usually not like this. If you ask me, I think we should hit the beach, relax, and enjoy the nightlife for a few days. That's what I was hoping for when I signed up for this. I never thought it would be so much work."

We reached the boat, and I helped Claire carry her bags onto the deck.

"Thanks again."

"Anytime," I said as I turned back toward the shore.

Having time to think it over, I realized Sam did sort of give off the professor vibe. She was intelligent and articulate and seemed used to getting her way. I was curious as to what type of work they were doing here, but not curious enough to turn back around and ask.

Isaac appeared, riding his bike around the corner and pedaling toward me.

"I thought we were off today," he said, shaking his head. "Sure could've used a heads-up."

"Here's a heads-up," I said, holding up my hand as he stopped beside me. "There's a cute girl over there who looks even less thrilled than you do to be here." I nudged his shoulder. "You should go introduce yourself. Who knows? You two might hit it off."

"Yeah, right. I'm sure she'll be impressed by my skinny, pale physique, and my computer-coding skills. Just call me Casanova."

"Aren't you in the chess club, too? You can't forget about that."

"Gee, thanks, Logan, but I think I'll pass. Last time I tried flirting with a pretty girl didn't go so well. The last couple of times, actually."

"It's worth a shot. A lot of girls appreciate intelligence, and at least you'll have a nice view for the day, if nothing else."

He shook his head and pedaled toward the boat.

"Just don't let her drown when she falls head over flip-flops for you!"

I advanced to the end of the dock and grinned as I approached Angelina, who was leaning gracefully against the side of the 1968 Z28 Camaro with black stripes down the hood. Her eyes were covered by big dark sunglasses, and her hair was tied back.

"Nice wheels," I said, wrapping my arm around her and kissing her soft cheek. "I didn't think I'd be seeing you again so soon."

"Hop in," she said, showing no emotion. I'd heard that tone from Angelina many times before. It was her "There's no time for pleasantries, and we need to get out of here" tone.

145

I gave a quick scan of the parking lot, then opened the passenger door and plopped down onto the leather seat. Before I shut the door, Angelina had the engine roaring, and she drove out of the marina parking lot and down Margaret Street.

"Sorry about being short," she said, glancing at the side mirrors to make sure no one was following us. "I just don't trust some of the other guys I'm working with." Angelina turned down a quiet, almost empty street, and pulled behind a large dumpster and a few palm trees. She kept her eyes forward.

"You wouldn't happen to be in the Keys for the reason I think you are, would you?"

She didn't answer, but she didn't have to.

"How did your employer learn about the treasure?" I asked.

She raised her eyebrows, then looked away from me, out the window. "I don't know."

"Tell me it wasn't some of his boys that tried to commandeer our boat the other day."

Agitated, she said, "I heard about that and did a little research on them. Those boneheads usually pull that kind of shit all on their own. They're Caribbean thugs. Small-time criminals. But I know one of them, and he's worked as a gun for hire before."

"Are you saying someone hired those guys to come after us the other day?"

"I'm saying you need to watch your back, Logan. If Black Venom figured out who you are from your hijinks with Scott in Mexico, then they're gonna come after you. I wouldn't be surprised if they were already here in the Keys."

I sighed. "I was thinking the same thing, Ange.

146

What about your boss? How does he play into all of this?"

"He's rich, powerful, and wants to find the treasure badly, but he wouldn't come after you like Black Venom. He's a good man, Logan. He's not a criminal."

We sat in silence for a moment, and as Angelina pulled the Camaro back onto the road, I said, "So, what, your boss is gonna have you guys follow me now?"

"No, that's why I'm here. He wanted me to tell you that we'll leave you alone so long as you do the same."

"Who is he? Anyone I know?"

"I'm sure you've heard of him," she said, "but I doubt you've ever seen him in person. His name's Arian Nazari."

My mind instantly shot back to my conversation with Scott as we were driving to Sierra Gorda. Scott told me he'd gotten the medallion back through a wager of some kind. I guessed Nazari must have learned of its importance, and being the avid collector he was, wanted the rest of the treasure for himself.

"That explains the mega yacht," I said as Angelina drove back onto Margaret Street, heading toward the marina.

A few minutes later, she pulled up alongside the curb, and I stepped onto the sidewalk.

"Good seeing you, Ange."

"You, too," she said. "And I'm serious about watching your back."

"I'll message you if I learn anything."

"I'll do the same," she said.

147

I shut the door, and she cruised down the street, disappearing around the corner.

SIXTEEN

I made my way back to the marina, and after seeing Gus in the office, I stopped in to see how he was doing.

"Just living the island dream," he said as I walked in.

He sat on an old bean bag chair behind the counter with his feet propped up on a nearby stool and his face glued to a flat-screen TV mounted on the wall. A reporter on the local news was walking downtown, admiring the different shops and talking to the tourists as they passed by. Gus's parents had owned the marina, and their parents before them. For three generations, the Hendersons lived in Key West and were as much a part of the town as Key lime pie.

"Everything all right with your slip?" he asked, leaning up from his chair. "Sure is a beauty you got there."

"Yeah, I love the place. Gus, do you think you

149

could do me a favor and let me know if you see anything suspicious going on here at the marina?"

He muted the television and gave me his full attention. "What kind of suspicious activity are you expecting?"

He seemed worried, so I did my best to ease him down.

"I've been followed a few times lately, and I got word that there may be some guys who've recently arrived in the Keys looking for trouble."

"Have you talked to Sheriff Wilkes? I'm sure he'd be much more informative than me."

I nodded, though I had no desire to go to the authorities. I always liked to handle things on my own and in my own way. I knew that if I went to the police, things would only get more difficult.

"Thanks, Gus. I'll do that."

I turned to the door, and before I left, Gus said, "But I'll let you know if I see anything."

On my way to my boat, I was surprised to catch a glimpse of the *Calypso* still moored to its slip near the end of the dock. It was nine forty-five, over thirty minutes since I'd left. Hoping that nothing serious had happened, I rushed over to the *Calypso*, but upon seeing Claire lounging in the shade with Tony sitting beside her, I relaxed.

Claire was staring at her phone, and Tony was tinkering with a piece of equipment they'd brought for the dive. When I reached the boat, he pointed at the deck. I peeked over the transom and saw Jack wedged between one of the engines and the hull. Sam was hovering over him with one foot on the deck and the other bent against one of the steps leading down to the engines.

"Everything all right?" I asked, peering down at Jack.

He looked up when he heard my voice and then shook his head before wiping the sweat from his brow with a dirty rag. "She was working fine yesterday," he said, then glanced over at Sam. "I'm sorry, Miss Flores."

"It's Sam," she said.

"My apologies, Sam. But it looks like we're gonna have to reschedule."

"You filled the fuel tanks, right?" she asked, a hint of snark in her voice.

"It's not that. Must be something internal. It would take me a few hours to take her apart and figure out what's wrong."

Jack climbed up to the deck and reached for his phone. "Is there another day that would work for you this week?"

"We're on a tight schedule," Sam replied, agitated. "We've had this planned for months, and you aren't even ready for us. Do you have any idea what we're trying to do? Any idea how important this research trip is?"

Claire, who was playing a game on her phone, almost laughed.

I wondered again what it was they were researching and why her crew didn't share her enthusiasm for it. "You can take them out on the Baia," I said.

Sam acknowledged my presence for the first time since I'd returned. Her hazelnut eyes locked onto mine, then she glanced back at Jack.

"I can't ask you to do that, Logan," Jack said.

"You don't have to."

"What kind of boat do you have?" Sam asked. Her attitude had simmered down a little bit.

"It's a forty-eight-foot Baia Flash," I said. "Plenty of deck space to accommodate, along with a comfortable saloon. It's just down the dock a short ways if you want to take a look at it. Using the carts Gus has at the office, we could have all of this gear moved over and be out on the water in no time."

Sam thought it over for a moment, then grabbed one of her bags from the deck. Motioning to Claire and Tony, she said, "All right, let's move all the gear. Looks like Captain Dodge will be taking us out today."

I grinned. "Just Logan," I said. But I had to admit, I liked the way Captain Dodge sounded, especially coming from her.

Isaac ran over to the marina office and came back with a big metal cart on rubber tires. We loaded it up with the tanks, BCDs, regulators, and all the other necessary gear, including the research equipment the three had brought with them.

When Sam first stepped aboard the Baia, she was taken aback. "This boat is beautiful, Logan."

We stowed all of the gear, utilizing the outside lockers and hatches, as well as the saloon, and strapping the tanks onto the port and starboard bulkheads.

When all the gear was aboard and Jack was carrying the cooler over the transom, he spoke quietly to me. "You know, you're supposed to have a license to charter, bro. You're looking at a pretty hefty fine if

152

someone checks us."

"Well, *you* have a license," I said. "And if they give us any kind of trouble, we could bring up the fact that we handed them three criminals on a silver plate."

Sam poked her head up from below deck. "You did what?"

"It's a long story," I said. I loosened up the lines holding the boat to the dock. "Not sure about the rest of you, but the Conch Republic's clear tropical waters are calling my name."

I leapt onto the swim platform, manned the cockpit, and started up the engines. Isaac finished handling the lines on the dock and pushed us out as I eased the throttles, bringing us away from my slip. As I took us out of the marina through the no-wake zone, Jack and Sam stood on either side of me. Sam unfolded a sheet of paper and held it for me to see.

"There are three sites," she said. "I have the coordinates for each, along with a map showing their locations. The three sites form a triangle, so I figured we could start at this one"—she pointed at the map—"then work our way around."

"You're the boss," I said with a grin, "though I won't be needing the map."

I typed the coordinates she'd printed out on the paper into my top-of-the-line Garmin GPS, and a few seconds later, the screen displayed the destination on a digital map, also showing various potential routes, along with depths along the way.

"That's one sweet gadget you got there," Jack said. "I might have to get one myself one of these days. That's just northwest of Little Mullet Key." He pointed to the screen. "The reef's beautiful over that way. There are some unique rock formations, as well. We're looking at about thirty minutes, depending on how much Logan wants to show off."

"You know me," I said.

"Make it twenty-five."

I looked back and saw Claire sprawled out on the sunbed. Tony was on the bench, leaning over the table, while Isaac sat beside him with his feet propped up on the cooler.

"Isaac, toss me a drink, would you?"

He flipped open the Yeti, pulled out a can of coconut water, and lobbed it to me. I caught it and told the others to help themselves.

When I cleared the no-wake zone, I slowly brought us up on plane, then up to thirty knots, which I'd found out was a good cruising speed for her. I scouted the horizon with a pair of binos, and seeing no boats that would interfere with our path, pushed the throttles forward as far as they would go. I yelled for everyone to hold on as the Baia smoothly accelerated up to forty knots, then forty-five, and soon maxing out at just over fifty.

Claire, no longer looking at her phone, stared forward in apparent disbelief at how fast we were going. Tony was no longer working on his equipment. He was holding on to the table with Isaac beside him. Sam stood next to me, her hands bracing against the supports overhead. Jack began to howl, I joined in, and soon all six of us were bellowing at the top of our lungs as we rocketed through the water toward the first site.

Within twenty minutes, I'd maneuvered the Baia

around a few shallow reefs before easing my way to the location of the coordinates. I was pleased to see that we were the only boat nearby, so we would have that part of the reef all to ourselves.

I stopped the Baia directly over the coordinates, then dropped anchor. It was just over forty feet deep, meaning we would each be able to stay down for about an hour on a normal tank of air before having to resurface. The three of them quickly got to work, opening their bags and setting up all of their gear, with Sam taking charge. When Jack and I had all six tanks strapped to their respective BCDs, we checked over the first- and second-stage regulators, verifying that they were functioning properly.

When we finished staging the dive gear, I stepped closer to Sam and the others. "Anything I can help you with?"

Sam nodded. "Do me a favor and throw a dive flag in the water." She grabbed her wetsuit from the storage space, then strode toward the saloon. After taking a few steps, she turned back to me. "Is it okay if I use your head to change?"

I told her it was fine with me, then reached for another wetsuit and handed it to Claire. She grabbed it and followed Sam down into the saloon, and minutes later, they appeared, ready for the dive. Somehow Sam managed to look good even in a wetsuit, which I hadn't thought was possible. Her athletic, lean figure probably looked good in anything. She removed her Seminoles cap and her sunglasses and set them on the dash above the wheel.

Jack, Isaac, and Tony slid their wetsuits over their swim trunks, then Jack helped the others into their

BCDs.

"You're not coming, Logan?" Sam asked.

I grabbed Jack's dive flag, which was connected to a white buoy, and tossed it over the side. "I'm gonna stay up here and keep an eye on the boat. Maybe I'll go down for the next dive."

Jack, Isaac, and I helped the three get ready and checked to make sure their gear was donned properly. Sam and Tony had been diving hundreds of times and looked like they could have put on their gear blindfolded. Claire, though not as experienced, had her open water diver certification and knew the basics well. I helped them carry their gear into the water, which included an expensive-looking digital camera in a waterproof housing, an underwater metal detector of sorts, and a large, handheld sonar scanner.

"What's in that one?" I asked, pointing at another large plastic case in the corner.

As Sam donned her mask, she said, "That's our top-of-the-line underwater ROV."

"An underwater drone?" I asked.

"Yeah." She stepped down the ladder attached to the swim platform. "I'll show it to you later. We use it to explore caves too small for us to enter."

The three members of the team went over the dive, including roles and key things Sam wanted them to document and study. Within a few minutes, they were all in the water, getting properly weighted and making final adjustments.

"Sixty minutes," Jack said as he gave the okay for the others to submerge. After the other four were underwater, he added, "If you see anyone approach, pull up the buoy, and I'll ascend."

I nodded and gave Jack a thumbs-up before he submerged below the tropical water.

After watching them for a few minutes to make sure they were making it down without any hiccups, I grabbed another coconut water from the cooler, climbed around the cockpit, and strode up to the bow.

With my Sig strapped to my side, I scanned the horizon with my binos. It was a calm, clear Tuesday morning, and though there were a few boats on the water, none looked suspicious—just a passing shrimping boat, a sailboat, and two jet skis far off in the distance. Opening the can, I took a long pull, then looked around one more time before dropping back down to the shade of the cockpit. I turned on Pirate Radio, sat on the semicircular cushioned seat, and slid my laptop out from the storage space beneath it. The sounds of the Beach Boys' "Kokomo" streamed through the boat's speakers as I studied the sonar projections of the seafloor where we had been looking for the treasure. Every five minutes or so, I'd stand up, grab my binos, and perform a quick sweep to make sure there weren't any boats zeroing in on our position.

I couldn't shake the feeling that there was trouble nearby, and it kept me slightly on edge as I sat in the cockpit, surrounded by an endless blue horizon.

SEVENTEEN

After a little under an hour, a cluster of bubbles rose out of the water near the dive buoy, just behind the stern. A few minutes later, all five broke the surface. I stepped onto the swim platform in my bare feet, grabbed their equipment, and hauled it onto the boat.

Jack slid his mask down to rest around his neck, revealing a big smile. "The reef looks beautiful today, bro."

I helped them one by one as they handed me their fins and climbed the ladder.

"Did you get what you needed?" I asked Sam as she sat on the transom. I supported her BCD as she unclipped it, then slid it from her back and set it beside the others.

"Won't know the answer to that until later when we bring everything up on the computer and analyze it. But it looked promising."

They all unzipped their wetsuits and pulled them

off. Sam was wearing a bikini under her wetsuit, and though it wasn't one of those flashy, dental-floss types, I couldn't help checking her out. After drying off and setting all of the gear aside, we sat in the topside dinette for drinks and snacks Jack had packed in the cooler.

After a few animated discussions about the dive, I finally asked the question that had been on my mind since back at the marina.

"So, what exactly are you guys studying down here in the Keys anyway?"

"We're investigating seismic abnormalities on the seafloor," Sam said enthusiastically. She was in a much better mood than she'd been in when she arrived at the marina. I guessed diving into paradise and enjoying the reefs and sea life was a good way to turn her mood around.

"You mean, like earthquakes?" I asked. "I didn't know there were any down here."

Sam nodded. "Earthquakes occur everywhere on Earth. Some are just much more noticeable than others." She motioned to Tony, who was hunched over his laptop. "Can you bring up the GPS plots?"

He punched in a few keys, then turned the screen of the laptop so Jack and I could see it. Sam pointed to various points on the screen that appeared to display a map of the Lower Keys.

She pointed a finger at a portion of the map filled with light-green dots of various sizes. "This cluster here. This is where we are now. Each of these green marks represents seismic activity of various magnitudes. As you can see, there are many incidents in the Keys, especially at our current location and at the other two locations we've chosen to study. When they group together like this in other places in the world, unique geological formations are usually the direct result."

I listened to her with interest as she explained in more detail how the GPS software worked and how they managed to use satellite imagery in connection with highly sensitive buoys that were able to detect even the slightest deviations in the water.

"Using this technology"—Tony nodded toward the laptop and pushed his glasses up to rest at the top of his nose—"we're able not only to predict when larger seismic activities might occur, but also pinpoint these bustling seismic regions we call 'hot spots.'"

Jack sliced a chunk of apple with his dive knife and brought it to his mouth. "You guys work for the government or something?"

"FSU," Sam replied.

"Dr. Flores is a professor of marine geology," Claire added. She'd been looking at her phone while lounging on the boat and posting pictures she'd taken during the dive. "Tony's an assistant professor, and I'm an undergraduate research intern."

"What about you guys?" Sam asked, motioning to Jack and me. "Have you both always worked in the charter business?"

"I have," Jack said. "Spent my whole life on these waters taking people out fishing and diving. And my father before me." Jack motioned to me. "But Logan here isn't in the charter business. It's much too safe for him."

"Too safe?" Sam asked, raising her eyebrows.

I grinned at Jack. "I think what Jack means to say

is that while he possesses customer service skills, I possess, well, a different set of skills."

Everyone was now looking up at me, intrigued.

"Don't let him beat around the bush with you," Jack said. "Logan here was Naval Special Forces. He's one of the best-trained warriors on the planet."

"You were a SEAL?" Sam asked.

I bowed my head slightly.

"But you're not a SEAL anymore?" Claire said.

"That's right," I said. "I guess you could say I'm in the business of trying to make the world a better place, one bad guy at a time."

That piqued their interest even more, and they hurled a barrage of questions my way, but I managed to deflect them all. I'd gotten pretty good at keeping what I do a secret. I usually never even mentioned to anyone that I was a SEAL, preferring to let people figure it out on their own after I whooped their butt or beat down some bad guys in front of them. I'd always had a distaste for the guys who went around bragging to everyone and their mother that they were a SEAL. But that's just me.

After finishing the snacks and downing a few cans of coconut water to stay hydrated, we decided to head to the second site. It was now eleven in the morning, and we were nearing the peak heat of the day. I climbed onto the bow with my binos and had another look around. When I was confident that there were no boats following us or heading in our direction, I raised the anchor and climbed back down to the cockpit. Jack had already grabbed the dive flag, along with the line, which he coiled and set on the swim platform. I turned the key, started the engines, and punched in the coordinates. It would only take fifteen minutes at cruising speed to reach the second dive site, which would allow the five divers to get rid of the remaining nitrogen buildup in their lungs prior to the next dive.

The next site was just north of the Marquesas Keys. Sam and Tony spent the majority of the ride hunched over their laptop and tinkering with their equipment in preparation for the dive. Isaac, interested in the technology behind their equipment, peered over their shoulders and asked the occasional question. Claire helped out but seemed more interested in working on her tan and staring at her phone. And Jack stood by me and kept a lookout while I cruised through Boca Grande Channel and then piloted us straight to the dive site.

In just over twenty minutes, I slowed to a stop then dropped anchor. The depth finder showed that we were floating on a little over sixty feet of water, meaning the divers would have less bottom time than at the previous site. They donned their gear and dropped below the surface with their survey equipment in hand. Jack told me they'd be down about forty minutes, and again I stepped up to the bow, had a quick look around, then plopped down into the half-moon seat with a cold drink in my hand.

Soon they were rising back to the surface and climbing onto the swim platform.

"That was even better than the last site," Sam said as I grabbed the sonar scanner from her hand and then helped her climb the ladder.

After I helped everyone aboard, they removed their gear, and we lounged for a quick lunch before heading to the third and final site of the day. Anxious to get started on analyzing the data they'd gotten, Sam and Claire went fast to work uploading to their laptop while Isaac helped Tony take apart and dry off their underwater camera.

Sam stepped over to her BCD to retrieve a sample she'd left in the front pocket and slipped on the wet deck. She reached out her hands and grabbed onto the transom to stabilize herself but accidentally knocked off her mask. It tumbled over the swim platform and into the water, quickly disappearing beneath the surface.

"Shit," she said as she regained her balance and watched as her mask sank to the bottom.

"Are you all right?" Jack said, rushing over to help her.

When it was clear that she wasn't injured, she shook her head and reached for her BCD.

"Mind if I borrow your mask?" she asked, looking at Jack.

"You can't go down yet," he said. "You need to off-gas the nitrogen from your body."

Before Sam could reply, I was on my feet. I quickly slid my shirt over the top of my head, handed Jack my Sig, and grabbed my mask from the nearby storage space in the outboard. "I'll be right back," I said.

"That's over sixty, bro," Jack said.

Moving aft, I leapt over the transom, flying high into the air and splashing headfirst into the water. The water felt good against my previously sweat-covered body as I dove down toward the seafloor. I kept calm and swam with slow, deliberate strokes, using as little oxygen as possible. Holding my nose and trying to force air out of my ears, I equalized the pressure a few times before reaching the bottom. Sam's mask was resting on a piece of elkhorn coral beside an anemone and a patch of seagrass. As I grabbed it, I realized how familiar the ocean floor looked. Right below me, under the coral, was a large ledge eerily familiar to the one where we'd been looking for the treasure. Holding Sam's mask in my hand, I swam over the top of the ledge, examining the cracks and the intricacies of its edges. After inspecting it for a minute, I peered up toward the bright surface and started my relaxed ascent.

Freediving always reminded me of my time at Basic Underwater Demolition School. It's six months of physically rigorous training that every SEAL undergoes prior to receiving their gold trident, which is the symbol for the SEALs. In BUDS, we'd spent weeks in the water, swimming with our hands tied behind our backs and our masks flooded with water for hours on end while instructors yelled at us and called us every name in the book. After going through BUDS, everything suddenly becomes incredibly easy, especially everything to do with the water.

I broke the surface while letting out the rest of the air from my lungs, then took a slow breath to recover while I treaded water aft of the boat.

Claire, Sam, Tony, and Isaac were leaning over the transom when I came up.

"He got it!" Claire said.

I slid my mask down, then grinned as I handed Sam her mask.

"How did you do that?" she asked. "That's over

164

sixty feet down. You were under for at least three minutes."

"'Bout time you came up," Jack said.

I climbed onto the swim platform and saw that he was lounging casually in the shade with a beer in his hand, grinning from ear to ear. "And what did I tell you about Logan? He probably did that dive without even trying. The man's a fish."

Sam handed me a towel, and I began drying off. "I was intrigued by the formations down there," I said.

Tony plopped back down beside the laptop. "That's what we're studying. Remarkable, isn't it?"

I nodded and opened the cooler. "Who's ready for lunch?"

We ate sandwiches Jack had ordered from the Pelican before we left the marina and talked more about what they were studying and how each had realized their desire to study geology. I was intrigued to learn that Sam was a first-generation American and had moved to San Antonio, Texas, from Mexico with her family when she was twelve.

After eating, I grabbed a beer, spread a towel on the bow, and relaxed in the sun before taking them to their third and final dive site for the day.

I was surprised when I heard footsteps and saw Sam approach. She spread out her own towel and sat down beside me. "Mind if I join you?"

"Not at all." I put my arm under my head. My aviator sunglasses allowed me to look at her without having to squint too much under the tropical sun.

We sat in silence for a moment, then she said, "I'm sorry I was rude earlier." She took in a deep breath, then sighed. "It's just . . . it had been a rough trip up

165

to this morning, and I was worried we'd end up wasting all of our time here." Her tanned, smooth skin sparkled in the sun, and her long dark hair swayed gently in the breeze.

"Don't worry about it. I hope today has made your trip a little better."

"Infinitely so. We've gotten a lot of great research in, and I know the third site will yield even more than the others."

"What makes you think that?"

"It's by far the most active site in all of the Keys. The seismic activity there is unlike any place I've seen in the world."

That piqued my interest. "When are you gonna use that drone?" I asked, trying to subdue my desire to take her toy out for a test drive. I'd seen ROVs—Remotely Operated Vehicles—while I was in the Navy, but I'd never been given the opportunity to operate one.

She laughed. "Planning to at the next site."

We spent a few more minutes relaxing on the bow and enjoying each other's company before I stood and folded my towel.

"Well, now you've got me interested," I said. "I guess your passion's contagious."

We climbed down to the cockpit, and after Sam gave me the coordinates for the third site, I punched them into the GPS. A moment later, the location appeared on the digital map, and after scanning it, I motioned to Jack. As I pointed to the screen, he looked at me with a confused expression and then froze.

"What do you think?" he said quietly.

I shrugged. "Maybe they can help our search."

The coordinates Sam gave me were for the exact location of the ledge Jack and I had been searching for the Aztec treasure for the past week. I handed Jack the binos and told him to keep a lookout for anything suspicious.

It was just after thirteen hundred when we weighed anchor and cruised toward the third site. The sun was now right overhead, warming the air around us into the upper eighties. The sky was still clear, and the sea was as calm as I'd ever seen it. I brought the Baia up on plane, then kept her steady at thirty knots.

When we cruised past the Marquesas Keys and were only a few minutes away from Neptune's Table, Jack tapped me on the shoulder. "Ease off a bit," he said while staring into the binos.

"What's wrong?"

"Not sure, but bring her to a stop."

I slowed the Baia to a halt, then kept her idling.

Jack handed me the binos. "There's a boat anchored right where we're heading."

I saw a center-console probably thirty feet long, with two guys walking about the deck. There were no fishing rods, so they weren't a fishing charter, though it could've been a dive charter or just a few locals out catching lobster. Jack had told me that although it wasn't a well-known site, the few who did know about it liked to take advantage of the abundance of bugs.

Suddenly, a diver appeared on the surface. He climbed the ladder and onto the boat wearing full scuba gear.

I handed the binos back to Jack. "What do you

think?"

"I don't recognize the boat or anyone aboard."

"What's going on?" Sam asked. She stepped beside Jack and me, her gaze drawn forward.

I didn't know how to respond, and Jack also appeared tongue-tied.

"Just another boat at the site we're heading to," I said. "Couple guys diving."

"What's wrong with that? Lots of people dive all over the Keys. I'm sure you both know that as well as anybody."

"Yeah, but Jack doesn't recognize the boat or anyone aboard. We're trying to figure out if they're friendly or not, but it's hard to tell."

Sam shook her head in frustration. "I don't understand." She snatched the binos from Jack's hand and took a quick look at the distant boat. "What is it you two are so worried about? It's just a couple of guys out enjoying the water. We could pull up fifty yards from them, anchor down, and share the site."

"What are we worried about?" I said. "First of all, Jack's been living down here his whole life. He's seen all sorts of things and knows just how dangerous this part of the country can be if you're not cautious. There are drug-running pirates in the Caribbean, Gulf of Mexico, and the Straits of Florida that would love a boat like this. And I'm sure they'd try to take you and Claire, as well." The mention of her name caused Claire to look up from her phone and stare at us with a worried gaze. "Second, you hired Jack to take you out on the water today, which means you're in his care. If Jack decides it's too dangerous to approach this unknown boat, then we don't do it. End of story."

"We're in the Florida Keys!" Sam exclaimed. "US soil. There's nothing dangerous about this place."

Just as she said those words, I heard the unmistakable roar of a loud diesel engine far off in the distance. I grabbed the binos, stepped to the edge of the bow, and searched in the direction the sound was coming from. Out to the west, to the right of the anchored boat, I saw another boat flying across the water. This one was larger, and it was fast, probably going at least forty knots and heading straight for the boat anchored above the site.

"I'm guessing you don't recognize that boat, either?" I said.

Jack shot me a worried gaze, then shook his head. "I don't like the look of this, bro. We shou—"

His words were cut off by the booming reports of automatic gunfire echoing across the water.

EIGHTEEN

I hit the deck, yelling for everyone to get down and Sam to get back into the cockpit for cover.

Jack was kneeling beside me and pointing at the boat cruising full speed over the water. "It came from that one."

I stared at the boat and saw three men standing in the cockpit. One was piloting the craft, and the other two were holding rifles against their shoulders, their barrels leveled at the anchored boat they had almost reached. More shots filled the air, and we watched the men on the anchored boat take cover as bullets rattled against their hull. They tried to fight back by firing off a few rounds, but were quickly overtaken by the speeding boat.

The attacking boat pulled up alongside the smaller one, and the guys holding rifles sent their victims to the deck, shooting them in the chest multiple times. A few men aboard the larger boat jumped over to the other one. I tried to get a good look at the attackers. One of the men was in a white tank top and had a bald, shiny head. Another guy was big and muscular and wearing camo cargo shorts.

After taking a split second to burn their images into my mind, I climbed into the cockpit and patted my old friend on the back. "We need to leave. Now!"

After telling Isaac to take our guests below deck and hold on to something, I eased forward on the throttle while turning sharply to port. A moment later, the men climbed back over to their boat, and a loud explosion filled the air as the anchored craft blew up from the inside. Flames shot out from all openings. Glass shattered, and pieces of fiberglass burst in all directions. Black smoke billowed from the wreckage, rising in a thick cloud through the clear sky.

Just as I was completing my turn and about to put the explosion behind us, I peeked over my shoulder and saw that the guys aboard the attacking boat were staring in our direction. They pointed and yelled out, though they were much too far away to hear what they were saying. One of the men jumped in front of the wheel, and a moment later, the boat was turning in our direction.

I pushed the throttles forward as far as they could go. The Baia accelerated like a rocket, shooting us over the waves and spraying water over the bow. The boat was now following us and quickly coming up on plane. I watched as the speedometer inched higher and higher until we were cruising at fifty knots. Our pursuers were still far off, but they were gaining on us. There was no doubt in my mind that whoever these guys were, they'd do the same thing to my boat as they had done to the other one. I opened the small locker beside the wheel and handed Jack his Desert Eagle, which he shoved behind the waist of his shorts.

"Take the wheel and keep us straight as you can," I said, stepping aside. Jack grabbed the helm with a firm grip.

I climbed down into the saloon and found Sam standing by the steps, holding on to a support brace beside Isaac, while the two others were sitting nervously around the table, holding on to anything they could get their hands on.

"What's going on?" Sam asked. "Who are those guys?"

I walked right past her, heading for the main cabin. "Drug-running pirates," I said as I headed straight for the closet adjacent to my bed, pushed aside the hanging clothes, and made quick work of the combination lock. It clicked open, and I pulled the door, revealing my stash of rifles, handguns, and other assorted weapons I'd purchased since arriving in the Keys. I grabbed my 338 Lapua, which had a Nightforce NXS scope attached to it and two magazines, then shut the door to the safe and spun the combination lock.

Carrying the rifle and ammo, I moved back into the saloon.

Sam pressed a hand to her lips when I appeared. "What are you gonna do?"

I loaded one of the magazines into the bottom of the rifle in one clean, smooth motion. "I'm gonna get them off our backs," I said as I made my way topside.

The boat was even closer now, and soon we would be within range of their rifles. Jack glanced back at me as I climbed over the seats and sprawled on my stomach over the sunbed. I unclipped the bipod legs and extended them to support the barrel of my rifle as it aimed toward our attackers.

Focusing through the scope, I put the boat right in my crosshairs, then chambered a round and clicked up the safety. I calmed my breathing and took aim at one of the guys whose upper body peeked over the cockpit through the windscreen. The wind had picked up a little, and both of our boats were bouncing slightly over the waves, making it difficult to get a clear shot. I held my breath and steadied. Predicting when their boat would rise up, I pulled the trigger just as the guy appeared in the crosshairs. The rifle boomed to life, and I watched as the round crashed through the windscreen and struck the guy center mass, sending a spray of blood behind him. He instantly disappeared from view, along with the pilot, who, having seen his buddy get sent to Davy Jones's locker, decided it was best to stay low in the cockpit.

I fired off a few more rounds into the windscreen, shattering the glass. Unable to hit the engines at that angle, I took aim at the hull, piercing a few holes in the fiberglass, hoping to slow the boat down. It didn't. I didn't know if the boat was armor-plated, but they kept gaining on us regardless. I rose from my position, switched on the safety on the rifle, and set it on the half-moon bench. I'd been in many boat chases before, and there's only two ways to come out of the situation on top. You either outgun your opponent, or you outmaneuver them. Fortunately, in the Navy, I'd been sent to small boat school and was frequently appointed to the helm when we needed to get our

173

team out of a jam in a hurry.

I glimpsed at the digital chart beside Jack. "Where are we?"

"Approaching the Southern Reef." He pointed ahead of us, then motioned to the screen. "You can see it on the chart. The reef stretches across a few miles here."

I examined the reef on the chart, which was indicated by shallower water. I noticed an abnormality in the reef, and studying the image closer, realized that I recognized it.

"Is that Sierra Reef?"

Jack didn't have to look at the chart. He'd spent his whole life on that water and knew every reef, island, and sandbar like the back of his hand. "That's her all right."

Sierra Reef was named after its shape since it featured a cut through the coral and rock that clearly formed the letter S from overhead.

"Let me take over." As soon as I had control, I immediately turned us slightly starboard, positioning us on a straight-shot course for the uniquely shaped reef.

"What are you doing?" Jack stared at me, and then the digital chart, and then shook his head violently. "Are you crazy?"

"That reefs gotta be only a foot or so beneath the surface," I said, then pointed forward. "Look, you can even see a few whitecaps."

"It's probably even less. We gotta turn this thing before our hull gets torn to shreds!"

"Oh, I'll turn," I said with a confident grin. "But not yet."

Jack kept eyeballing me like I was insane, then, catching onto my plan, said, "You can't hit Sierra at this speed and expect to make it through, Logan. It's not possible."

"We used to do it all the time in my dad's boat," I said, remembering the days Jack and I would spend out on the water together, maneuvering in and out of shallow reefs for the thrill of it.

"That was years ago, and that was a twenty-four-foot navigator, not a damn yacht. Also, I'm pretty sure we never hit it at fifty knots!"

Jack was right both about the speed and size difference, but we had no other choice. We were too far to make a break for Key West, and I didn't like the idea of facing those guys head-on, given the fact they had high-powered automatic rifles, and all we had were semiautomatics. Even amateurs can hit a target with a spray of bullets, and I doubted the guys after us were amateurs.

"I'm serious, Logan. There's gotta be another way out of this."

"There's no other way! Look, I'll slow down right before we reach the reef. Just enough to hit the turns."

Jack went silent.

The boat behind us was still moving closer and closer with every passing second, and we were inching closer to the reef. My eyes darting between the water ahead and the Baia's speedometer, I eased off the throttles as we were almost over the reef, bringing our speed down to just over forty knots.

"That's still too fast, bro!"

There was no time to debate with him.

"Hold on!" I yelled over the roar of the engines so

175

the others below deck could hear.

As the boat behind us maintained its speed, cruising to within two hundred yards of us, I entered the opening between the reef, then rolled the helm sharply to the right. The boat jerked hard, and the starboard side lifted out of the water. I gripped an edge of the roof with my left hand and kept the wheel turned with my right. Keeping my eyes glued to the screen, I let off the turn slightly, and the Baia leveled as I kept it in the narrow gap between the reefs. The side-scan sonar and depth finder allowed me to see exactly where the reefs were. It was close. So close that even the slightest mistake would ruin part of the hull. I turned hard to port, then eased back to starboard, maintaining thirty-five knots throughout the turns until I reached open ocean, then pushed the throttles forward. Gunshots echoed across the water at our backs, and I watched water splash around us as bullets pelted the surface.

Our pursuers were less than a hundred yards behind us and about to reach the reef at full speed. They tried to turn sharply at the last second, but it was too late. Their boat smashed into the shallow reef, splintering their hull into pieces before the weight and velocity of the boat caused it to flip over and tumble wildly. The propellers roared as the engines flew out of the water, muffling a chorus of faint screams as the craft tumbled over and over again before finally coming to a stop.

When the chaos settled, all that remained of the boat was a scattered mass of debris. Jack and I knew there was no way anyone on board could have survived. There was no doubt in our minds that the fuel tanks were punctured, meaning that if by some miracle one of them had survived, they would be gone in a matter of minutes when the wreck blew sky-high.

NINETEEN

Jack patted me on the back as I kept the throttles full, putting distance between us and the two wrecked boats.

"Hell of a maneuver, man." He scanned over the horizon to make sure there weren't any other boats following us, then stepped down to the saloon to let the others know the coast was clear.

Sam rose up from below deck first. I could tell she was about to ask what had happened, but she paused as she stared at the crashed boat behind us. Claire and Tony appeared, followed closely by Isaac. The three stood in awe as they gazed back at the wreckage.

A few moments later, Sam turned to me. "Who were they?"

"Don't know. All we know is they killed everyone on that other boat and tried to kill us, too."

I stepped aft and grabbed my rifle, which was still resting on the half-moon bench. Removing the magazine and ensuring the chamber was clear, I carried it back into my stateroom, locked it up, then returned to the cockpit.

"Aren't you gonna call the police?" Sam asked.

"We'll wait until we're closer to the marina, then we'll give an anonymous tip. I personally try to deal with law enforcement as little as possible." I looked at Claire and Tony, who were still in shock after what happened. "Look, but that's just me," I continued. "You are Jack's and my guests. If you want to speak to the police about this, I'll respect that decision."

Sam thought it over for a moment. "You're the locals, and we'll trust your judgment. I don't have a lot of time to spend down here in the Keys, so every hour counts for our research."

Jack nodded. "Sheriff Wilkes is a good man, but trust me, if we tell him exactly what happened, we'll be wrapped up in this mess for a week. Best to leave it all to them."

Jack was interrupted by the sound of a loud explosion coming from a quarter of a mile behind us. We all turned back in unison and watched as a black cloud fumed up over the crashed boat, now engulfed in flames.

"That's something you don't see every day," Claire said.

Cruising through the water at forty knots, it didn't take long for the Baia to reach Key West. We arrived just before fifteen hundred, and I eased on the throttles and pulled us into the harbor. We called the local authorities via channel sixteen on the radio and gave a detailed emergency report, then hung up before giving away any information about ourselves.

"You weren't kidding about not liking to deal with authorities," Sam said with a grin. "You spat those words out so fast I could barely understand them."

"I worked for the government for eight years while in the Navy. There's little that's simple or logical about how they go about their business when it comes to dealing with people."

We cruised through the no-wake zone and into the marina. After refueling, I brought the Baia right into slip twenty-four, then killed the engine and tied her off. We spent the next half hour rinsing off the scuba gear and cleaning up the boat. We loaded everything onto one of the marina's carts and rolled it back over to the *Calypso*. Once all the scuba gear was in its rightful place and the tanks were refilled, we helped carry their gear to the parking lot and loaded all of it into the back of a silver Pathfinder.

"Is there any chance either of you would be willing to take us out to that third site tomorrow morning?" Sam asked as we finished loading her SUV and shut the back door. She had changed into a pair of short shorts and a flannel shirt with her sleeves rolled up and the top buttons undone, revealing part of her bikini top underneath.

"Are you serious?" Tony asked.

I was surprised to hear him talk. He hadn't said much since we'd been chased across the Straits. The whole thing had shocked him pretty badly, a common response when people unaccustomed to grave danger experience it first-hand. "You want to stay here and keep going out after what happened today?"

"Of course. It's our job, isn't it?"

"Getting chased by a bunch of bad guys with guns

isn't my job. I'm a geologist, not a warrior."

"All great intellectuals took risks for their discoveries," Sam said enthusiastically. "Besides, thanks to Logan, there are fewer bad guys out on the water than there were before."

"I have to agree with Tony," I said. "I think it's too much of a risk to take you all anywhere on a boat right now, especially where we ran into those guys today."

Agitated, Sam opened the driver's door and hopped inside. Claire got in the passenger side, and Tony sat in the back.

Before Sam pulled away, she rolled down her window and handed me a ripped piece of paper. "Let me know if you change your mind."

I grabbed it and saw that it had a phone number written on it.

She smiled. "Or if you just want to have drinks sometime."

I told her to be expecting my call, then waved as she started the engine and pulled out of the lot.

I kept my head on a swivel as Jack and I walked back toward the Baia. After giving her one final wipe-down, I grabbed the laptop bag and duffle, then activated the security system and locked her up. We headed over to the *Calypso* and did the same, deciding it best that we both stay at Jack's house tonight. We couldn't be certain no one was following us, and we wanted to stick together. Jack started up his twenty and piloted us out of the marina and over to his house. Isaac was spending the night at a friend's house, having ridden his bike there after we'd arrived back at the marina, so we spent the evening cooking up food and trying to figure out what our next course of action would be.

I called Sam the following evening, and we listened to live music at the Pelican while enjoying some of the best cocktails in the Keys. But she ended up cutting the evening short in order to get back to her work.

"Are you always such a workaholic?" I asked as I walked her out of the restaurant.

"Mixing work and play doesn't usually go well for me," she said.

I drove her home, then made my way back to Jack's place.

A modest storm blew up from the south for the next couple of days, turning the sky black, and blowing winds in excess of sixty miles per hour. It made the seas too rough to do much of anything, so Jack and I spent most of our time looking at what footage and sonar scans we had of the ocean floor over and around the ledge.

One night, the day after the storm passed, I had dinner with Jack and Gus at Pete's place. Afterward, we were pulling into the parking lot at the marina when I received an alert on my phone. It was my boat's security system informing me that someone was on my boat. I gazed through the windshield, trying to catch a glimpse of the Baia, but I couldn't see it beyond the other boats in the dim dock lighting.

"What's wrong?" Jack said.

I grabbed the Sig from my hip and checked to make sure the magazine was full, even though I already knew it was.

"There's somebody on my boat."

I stepped out of the truck and shut the door quietly. Jack and Gus got out just behind me.

Gus held his hands in the air. "Look, I don't want any trouble here."

"Me, neither. That's why I'm packing."

I kept my eyes and ears on full alert as the three of us headed toward the docks. Jack had also grabbed the Desert Eagle from his hip, and we moved in slower as we hit the stairs and reached the dock where the Baia was moored.

"I'm gonna call the sheriff," Gus said as he turned and ran for the marina office.

The marina was usually quiet at night, a contrast to the loud nightlife of downtown Key West. This night, it was silent aside from the shifting docks, occasional conversations of night owls, and the distant sound of a radio playing. A few people sat on their boats, lounging and enjoying each other's company as we crept by. The few who noticed the pistols in our hands sat with wide eyes and open jaws. As we closed in on slip twenty-four, I realized my boat was gone.

"What the hell?" I picked up my pace, nearly sprinting as I raced toward the empty slip where my boat had been moored just a few hours earlier. I stopped and took a quick scan of the marina.

Jack pointed toward the end of the dock. "There, bro."

I saw movement in the water illuminated only by the distant glow of the marina. It was my boat, and it was rounding the narrow opening at the end of the dock, heading out toward the open ocean.

I took off down the planks, sprang onto a small

Catalina moored at the tip of the marina, and jumped as far as I could, launching my body toward my moving Baia. I landed softly on the sunbed, rolled into a somersault, and rose into a crouching position with my Sig aimed straight at the guy manning the helm.

"Cut the engines and put your hands up!" I gritted my teeth and kept a close eye on the stranger in a hooded black sweatshirt, watchful for any of his sudden movements.

He eased the throttles back and turned the key in the ignition, killing the engines.

"I'm not gonna say it again. Get your hands in the air!" I clicked up the safety, revealing the red dot and indicating that it was ready to fire.

The man lifted his hands into the air and turned around. My jaw dropped when the light from the dock touched their face.

"Holy shit. Sam?" I stared at her blankly as she slid the hood of her sweatshirt off her head. "What the hell are you doing?"

She was staring straight at the Sig in my hands, and I noticed her relax a little as I lowered it. I was angry but impressed.

How did she manage to get past my security system? And where did she get a key to start up the engines?

"I have to go to that site," she said. "I told you my research is important to me. I figured I could take it out and return it before sunrise without anyone noticing."

"You mean steal it?" I said.

"Borrow it." She sighed. "Look, I'm sorry. I

184

shouldn't have tried to take it, but you didn't want to go out, and I didn't know what else to do. Every charter in town is fully booked."

I paused for a moment, then heard the sounds of footsteps coming from the nearby dock.

Jack was running to the end, and when he saw us standing in the cockpit, he gave a confused look, followed by a grin. "I guess you don't need backup." He slid his Desert Eagle back into his waistband at his lower back.

I stepped over to the wheel, started the engine, and brought the Baia in a slow circle back toward my slip. When I reached the dock, I threw the lines for Jack to tie her off.

"So, Sam, let me get this straight. You planned to steal my boat, cruise over an hour from here, and scuba alone and in the dark at a site you've never been to before? And you're a professor?"

"I'm an experienced diver," she replied. "And boater. I've gone out many times before, and I'm successful at what I do because of my drive and willingness to take risks in order to find answers."

Jack said, "Why do I get the feeling this isn't the first time Miss Flores here has borrowed someone's boat without asking?"

"This is the only time, I swear," she said. "Hell, I can't swear to that, but it's the only time in the Keys, and I promise I won't come near your boat again."

I tried not to smile, but damn, it was hard. Truth is, I would've been mad as hell if she hadn't been so damn sexy. She was wearing a sweater big enough to cover the end of her shorts, but small enough for her long, toned legs to be visible in the moonlight. Her

185

hair was a mess over her face from the evening breeze, and she occasionally brushed it back, revealing her soft brown eyes.

A moment later, Gus appeared, running wildly down the dock. He stopped right in front of the Baia and bent over, resting his hands on his knees. "They're on their way!" he said before looking up and seeing the three of us standing there.

"Gus, can you get the sheriff on the line?" I said.

He nodded, reached his hand into his pocket, and pulled out a cellphone.

"That really isn't necessary," Sam said. "Look, I'm sorry about the boat, but there's no reason we can't handle this ourselves. Here, I can even pay you." She grabbed her bag from the deck and reached inside. "What's the rate for a day's rental for a boat like this? Five hundred?"

"More like seven," Jack said.

"Fine."

I shook my head. "That's not necessary."

Gus, after standing for a few moments with his phone held up to his ear, informed me that he had the sheriff on the line.

"Tell him not to come out," I said. "It was a misunderstanding, that's all."

Gus shot me an incredulous stare, but before he could voice his confusion, I added, "Apologize for me, will you?"

He paused a moment, rubbing his chin as his eyes bounced back and forth between Sam and me. Still catching his breath, he cleared his throat and relayed my message to the sheriff. A moment later, he hung up, then walked to the edge of the dock beside the

Baia. He stood with his hands on his hips, looking straight at Sam. "You caused quite the ruckus here tonight, Miss Flores. You're lucky Logan here isn't getting the authorities involved. If he did, you'd be spending the night at the station tonight and calling your lawyer."

Sam apologized again, and looking defeated, grabbed her things. She'd brought a few major pieces of gear with her, including the black hard case containing the underwater drone.

When she reached for the sonar device, I grabbed the other end of it and looked her in the eyes. "Why don't you leave it here for now?" She gave me a blank stare, and I turned to Gus. "Thanks for your help tonight, Gus. And I'm sorry for the commotion."

"No problem," he said, then turned on his heels and headed back down the dock.

Sam, who was still holding the other end of the sonar device, said, "I'd rather take it all now, thank you."

"No." I stepped over the transom, grabbed the hard case containing the ROV, and brought it back onto the Baia. "How about you wait a few hours? There's a site out there waiting to be explored."

Her face brightened, and she beamed as if she'd just won the lottery.

I glanced over at Jack.

"Isaac's home tonight," he said. "I'd love to help, but I gotta look after him." Jack jumped over the transom, then turned to us both. "Be careful out there. Maybe Miss Flores here can keep you out of trouble for one night."

"You're talking about the woman who just tried to

steal my boat," I said.

Sam hit me with a playful punch.

"Just don't get killed," he said before flip-flopping out of sight.

TWENTY

Sam helped me untie the mooring lines, and I started up the engines.

"Professor, I've gotta ask ..." I said as I accelerated us away from the dock. "How did you manage to get past my boat's security system and take it out by yourself?"

She winked. "Impressed?"

"Yeah," I said. "And slightly embarrassed. I installed the system myself."

"Well, you can sleep soundly. I had to cheat to pull it off."

I raised my eyebrows. "Oh yeah?"

"I peeked over your shoulder when you punched in the key code."

"And the spare key? I had it locked in my nightstand drawer. Let me guess ... you're a part-time MacGyver?"

She chuckled. "I swiped it when you left the drawer open after the shootout."

189

So, she'd been planning her little grand theft vessel for some time.

As we motored toward the opening out of the harbor, I changed the subject. "Before we get there, there's something I have to tell you about this site . . . Something you're probably not gonna believe."

The trip to the site went quickly as I relayed to Sam the story about the Aztec treasure and how I'd found the gold medallion. She was engaged the entire time and found it hard to believe that the site where I'd found the valuable artifact was the same place where a large amount of seismic activity occurred. It was a crazy coincidence, and one that could explain why the treasure had remained hidden from view for so many years. During the hour it took for us to cruise through the darkness from the marina in Key West to Neptune's Table, I kept my eyes peeled, making sure no one was following us.

"So, those guys chasing us yesterday weren't ordinary drug runners," Sam said. "They were after the treasure."

"As far as I can tell, yes. But the truth is, we're not certain who those guys were or where they came from. We've tried to keep the treasure on the down-low, but something this big is sure to find its way out."

The water above the site was clear of boats when we approached, along with the rest of the ocean's surface as far as we could see. There were no lights over the water except our own and the glowing reflection of the moon breaking through the partly clouded sky. We anchored, set up and donned our scuba gear, then dropped below the waves. We agreed that we'd spend about twenty minutes just doing a brief visual inspection of the ledge before deciding which piece of Sam's equipment to utilize.

Using high-powered dive flashlights, we descended to the ledge. I kept close to Sam, watching as her mannerisms changed when she examined certain portions of the seafloor. She seemed particularly interested in the narrow openings that lined the base and sides of the ledge, where hundreds of lobster antennas were sticking out. Those unique formations are what make Neptune's Table one of the best places to find bugs in all of the Keys. She pointed upwards, and we ascended, breaking the surface a few minutes later.

Sam slid her mask down to her neck. "That ledge was formed by abnormalities in the Earth's crust. And it looks to me like the majority of it isn't more than a few hundred years old. I've never seen such an astounding underwater site before."

I climbed the ladder onto the swim platform and helped Sam up behind me.

She motioned toward the large plastic case. "I think it's time for the drone. Hopefully, it's small enough to fit through those crevices."

Excited to use the toy, I picked up the case and set it on the outdoor table. Unclasping the hinges and opening the case revealed a white rectangular device with a long yellow tether attached to it. When I picked up the ROV, I saw that it had a built-in camera in front, along with adjacent lights. It also had two forward/reverse thrusters and top and bottom thrusters.

Sam hooked the other end of the tether to a control

unit with a built-in flat screen. We set up the controller on the sunbed, then turned on the drone and launched it into the water. I was amazed how clear the image was on the screen. The lighting on the little vehicle worked great, allowing us to see clearly in the dark water.

"I'm going to try to take her into one of those openings," she said, piloting the machine like she'd done it a hundred times.

The drone flew through the water, reaching the ledge in just a few seconds, then Sam eased it toward the openings. Shining the light into the largest gap, she hit the forward thrusters softly, easing the device into the cave. When she'd barely entered, we realized the way was blocked by the local inhabitants.

"I'll be right back," I said, grabbing my mask, a flashlight, and a tickle stick. Wearing only my swim trunks, I leapt over the side of the boat, splashing into the water, then dove down to the ROV, following its yellow tether the thirty-five feet to the base of the ledge. The vehicle had backed out of the opening when I reached it, so I shined my light on the hole and peeked inside at the five lobsters hiding with their long antennas sticking out.

Using my tickle stick, I prodded the closest bug, causing the lobster to shift its body and tuck its tail under its abdomen, rapidly propelling the crustacean out of its hiding place. I moved the end of the stick from one to the next until they were all gone. Some had been well over regulation size, and as I watched them swim out, all I could think about was how I'd be back for them another day.

When the opening was clear of all of the lobsters, I

stabilized myself on the ledge and faced the drone. Holding my hands palms up, I pointed toward the opening, letting Sam know that the way had been cleared. A moment later, I heard the forward thrusters spin, propelling the craft into the cleared opening. Shining my flashlight into the cave, I watched as the device eased inside, quickly disappearing from view.

I switched off my flashlight and kicked my feet, reveling in the view of the water around me as I ascended through it. The dark ocean turned light, with hints of a silver glow as I broke the surface. The clouds had completely abated, allowing the three-quarter moon to illuminate the scene.

I swam to the Baia, grabbed hold of the swim platform, and heaved myself up out of the water. We had no lights on the Baia, trying to remain as unnoticeable as possible, but I could see Sam huddled over the drone controller and screen on the sunbed.

"What a gentleman," she said as I grabbed a towel and patted myself down. "The cave's opening up a little."

Intrigued, I quickly dried off, flattened out a fresh towel on the sunbed, and sat down beside her to look at the screen. The underwater vehicle had entered a cave that appeared to be getting larger the deeper it went.

"You see these wavy grooves on the sides of the wall?" She pointed to distinct features of the cave, and I nodded. "Those are the result of portions of a tectonic plate breaking apart, then being forced back together by the crust's extreme pressures."

We kept our eyes glued to the screen as Sam piloted the drone deeper and deeper into the cave. She reached a turn and carefully maneuvered around it. On the other side, the lights of the ROV shined upon a set of bright eyes bobbing back and forth. She stopped the vehicle a moment, and we saw that it was a jewfish swimming against the back wall of a narrow portion of the cave, staring at the camera, and clearly unhappy to have visitors in its home. As Sam eased the drone forward, it got spooked and swam out of the frame in a hurry.

I pointed at the bottom of the screen, where just a tiny portion of the cave's bedrock was visible. "What's that?"

She accelerated the upper thrusters, then angled downward slightly. A few ladyfish swam into view, and a huge stone crab crawled over the rock, but that wasn't what caught my attention.

"Right over there." I pointed to a portion of the cave's floor ten feet in front of the device.

Sam piloted it slowly to prevent the thrusters from churning up too much silt and sand, but regardless, the clear water had a fine cloud, making it difficult to see farther distances. There was a crack in the rock, but there was something strange about it—something abnormal about its shape. As the drone moved closer, it began to take form.

Sam tilted her head as the vehicle hovered just in front of the object. "What is it?"

It wasn't natural, we were both certain of that, but it was covered in barnacles and silt, which gave it the same color and texture as the rock surrounding it. After studying it for a few moments, I realized what we were staring at.

"It's the barrel of a Falconet," I said, then wrapped

194

my arms around Sam and smiled, completely mesmerized by what we were seeing.

She kept her eyes on the screen, trying to discern what she was looking at, but I was certain what it was. The narrow barrel gave away that it was most likely that particular type of light cannon utilized by the conquistadors during their wars in the Americas. As the drone angled across to its side, Sam's eyes grew wide.

She looked at me, astonished, then smiled as she also saw that it was the barrel of a cannon. "Unbelievable," she gasped, unable to look away.

Manipulating the controls, she ascended, then shined the lights forward and headed deeper into the cave. Just ahead of the vehicle, the cave appeared to dead-end, stopping at a large rock face. But after looking around the cave, we saw that the same crack below where the cannon had been lodged was now much larger. In fact, it was large enough for Sam to angle the ROV down and pilot it in.

She navigated through the crack, and a few moments later, the cave opened up, revealing a large open space. As the drone entered the large cavity, Sam noticed something shiny against the wall, and she eased the camera closer, stopping right in front of a shiny gold object resting on a ledge. It took only a second for me to realize that it looked exactly like the medallion I'd found on the ledge nearly ten years earlier. Its large size and the image stamped on its surface were unmistakable.

As she piloted the ROV around the outer walls of the cave, we saw more pieces of gold jewelry scattered about. There were bracelets, necklaces, rings, and a few more medallions that bore striking resemblances to the one I'd discovered. The underwater cavity was at least fifty feet in diameter and over a hundred feet deep, the lights from the device unable to illuminate the bottom. After circling to the other side of the cave, we counted almost thirty gold artifacts in all, then Sam angled the drone downward and hit the top thrusters.

I gazed over the stern of the Baia, watching as more yellow cable unraveled and slid into the water. "How long is the tether?"

Sam continued the vehicle's descent. "Four hundred feet."

We were glued to the screen. Excitement took over, and my heart pounded in my chest as the lower portions of the cave were revealed by the light of the drone. As it descended, we noticed more sparkling objects resting on ledges and lodged into crevices around the walls. When the light touched the bottom of the cave, we both sat in silence for a moment, and Sam kept the vehicle hovering in place, the camera aiming straight at the cave's floor.

The ground was covered with scattered remnants of the *Intrepid*, including more Falconets and hundreds of chests piled together, some with their tops cracked open, revealing piles of gold bars and jewelry that littered the bottom of the cave. We couldn't remove our eyes from the Aztec treasure that had been hidden from mankind for nearly five hundred years.

"It's unbelievable, Logan. I . . . I can't believe what I'm seeing."

I could barely believe it myself. Thousands of gold

bars and countless pieces of gold and silver jewelry were in chests and spread out over the bedrock. The great Aztec treasure had finally been found, and as I'd hoped would be the case, I was the one who'd found it.

"I'd say this is cause for celebration," I said. I stepped down into the galley, opened up the refrigerator, and pulled out the unopened bottle of champagne that had come with the boat. Stepping back up to the cockpit, I propped one leg up on the transom, then blew the top off the bottle. Raising it high in the air, I said, "To Professor Samantha Flores."

Once the bubbles settled, I took a few gulps, then handed the bottle to Sam.

She grabbed it from my hand and held the bottle in the air. Before taking a long pull, she said, "To Logan Dodge . . . and to the Aztec treasure."

We spent another half hour piloting the drone around the bottom of the cave, exploring and getting as much footage as possible before navigating out of the caves and back up to the boat.

I grabbed the ROV and set it on the deck in front of Sam. As I wound up the tether, she dried off the device and removed part of its waterproof shell, then slid out the storage cartridge. She inserted the micro SD into her computer and quickly transferred all of the files.

Once everything was stowed, we sat beside each other on the sunbed and stared out over the water. I grabbed a few flutes, and we drank champagne while watching the waves glow in the moonlight.

"And you said you don't like mixing work and

play," I said.

She laughed. "I guess it's okay every now and then. What are you going to do with the treasure, Logan?"

The night had cooled off a bit, so she sat up against me with a blanket. It felt good to have her smooth legs pressed against mine.

"First, we've gotta get it all up somehow. These waters are still gonna be infested with bad guys looking to take the whole haul for themselves. And we sure as hell can't bring up all of that gold using this boat, so we're gonna need a bigger one with cranes."

Sam took a drink, then inched closer to me. "I'd like to help more if I can. I'm supposed to leave in a few days, but I'm going to call the university and get an extension."

"You don't have to do that," I said, polishing off the rest of my champagne. "Not that I don't want you to, but it's dangerous here."

"I know that. I was here the other day when we were being chased, remember? This isn't my first time in a dangerous situation. I know the risks, and I accept them."

Instinctively, I wrapped my arm around her and brought her in closer. She leaned back into me and sighed.

"It's amazing how it all wound up down there under that ledge," I said.

"My initial theory is that the ledge used to be a lot shallower. The *Intrepid* must have run aground, then years later, the seafloor rose up and over the wreck somehow."

It made sense but seemed so unlikely that it bordered on impossible. What were the chances that, out of all the shallow reefs and ledges in the archipelago, the *Intrepid* would run aground on that ledge, where seismic anomalies would surround it with rock for hundreds of years? I was too tired and buzzed to think it over anymore. Instead, I just enjoyed the moment and the company of a beautiful and intelligent woman.

It was just after two in the morning, and we decided it was time to head back to the marina. I gave a quick scan of the horizon, and after seeing that we were the only visible boat on the water, pulled up the anchor and started up the engines. Putting it in gear, I eased the throttles forward and brought the Baia up on plane, heading back toward Key West.

The marina was as calm as glass as we cruised up to slip twenty-four and I maneuvered the boat steadily up against the dock. Sam stepped over the transom, tied off the mooring lines, and connected the shore power cable and water lines. I put the Baia in neutral and killed the engines. The only sounds in the marina were the soft shifting of the boats in their slips.

Sam stepped back onto the deck, then after grabbing one of her smaller bags, wrapped her arms around me. "Thank you for a most memorable evening."

She started to let go, and I clasped her hand in mine. "It doesn't have to end so soon."

She smiled at me, and then keeping my hand in hers, stepped down toward the saloon.

I turned on the security system, locked the cabin door, and led her into the main stateroom.

TWENTY-ONE

The next morning, I woke up just after seven. Sam was curled up in the white comforter beside me, so I tiptoed out of the main cabin and into the saloon. I started up the coffeemaker, then walked barefoot up the steps and out the door into the cockpit. After taking a quick look around to make sure nothing had been disturbed on the Baia while we were sleeping, I stepped back into the galley, where I cut open a few mangoes and placed them in a bowl beside freshly sliced banana.

Grabbing my cellphone from a nearby drawer, I saw that I had a message from Jack letting me know he'd be at the Pelican for lunch around noon. I replied that I'd be there, then texted Scott using a code similar to the one he used when contacting me in Curacao a few weeks earlier. The gist of it was that I'd found something, and I needed him to come down to Key West as soon as he could get away. He replied a few minutes later saying he'd let me know when he was coming.

The saloon quickly filled with the smell of fresh coffee. I checked on Sam and saw that my movements hadn't disturbed her. She was curled up on her side, her raven-black hair brushed back and revealing her smooth, tanned skin. Somehow she managed to look even better in the morning.

A few minutes later, the smell of the coffee drifting into the main cabin caused her to stir. She appeared at the door wearing one of my T-shirts and nothing else. She stood for a moment, resting her head against the frame as I filled a mug and handed it to her. I grabbed my own mug and the bowl of fruit, and we headed up to the sunbed to watch the goings-on in the marina.

As we were about to finish our breakfast, Gus appeared down the dock. He was stopping to talk to people out on their decks, and as he got closer to the Baia, I saw that he was holding a newspaper and pushing a cart with a large package on it.

"Ahoy, Captain Dodge," he said, waving at us. "Have you read the *Keynoter* this morning?"

"Good morning, Gus," I said, sitting up on the sunbed. "Come aboard and have a seat. You remember Sam, right?" I grinned as I looked back and forth between the two. "From last night. . . ."

"Right," Gus said, stepping over the transom. "Did you two end up going out of the harbor?"

"Yeah," Sam said. "Logan showed me Joe's Tug. I'd been wanting to see it at night for quite some time now."

It was just a little white lie, and though I was fairly

certain Gus would keep his mouth shut, I liked where Sam's head was at. After all, Joe's Tug, which is actually a sunken, 75-foot steel-hulled shrimp boat, is nowhere near Neptune's Table.

"Did you see anything suspicious? Any signs of danger?"

I shook my head. "The water was calm, the night sky clear, and we were the only ones out there."

"Good," Gus said, giving a sigh of relief. "You two were lucky, then. Check out what's on page one of the *Keynoter*." He handed me the folded newspaper.

I held it flat to the first page on the table in front of us. There were mugshots of three men, each staring angrily into the camera. They were the same three guys I'd beaten the crap out of when they tried to board Jack's boat a week earlier. The bold-lettered caption said they were being charged with over twenty counts of theft, drug trafficking, smuggling, and assault.

"There was an explosion yesterday, as well," Gus said. "Two boats went into the drink, or so I heard. Now obviously, I can't stop any of the boats here from going out late at night. You can all come and go as you please, of course. But I highly discourage it. At least until the waters get clear of all the other scum like these guys."

I leaned back into the cushioned seat and polished off the rest of my coffee. "Thanks for the heads-up, Gus. We'll be careful when we go out." Not having read the whole article, I asked, "How many more do the authorities suspect are in the Keys?"

Gus shrugged. "Been crazy around here, especially

lately. Could be none, or could be a lot more. The article just says to be cautious when unknown boats approach or when cruising at night."

I slid the bowl of fruit across the table. It still had a few slices of mango and half of a banana. "There's coffee in the pot if you want to fill a mug."

He waved me off. "No, thanks. I gotta inform the rest of my tenants." He stepped over the transom, lifted the large package off the cart, and handed it to me.

I set the package on the deck beside me and handed him back his newspaper.

He continued on his way. "You two enjoy your morning."

Sam turned her body to face me. "You've seen those guys from the paper before, haven't you?"

I didn't reply, but I couldn't help but grin.

"I thought so. You looked at them like you knew them."

"I may have been involved in their capture in some way, yeah."

Sam took a quick shower as I stowed my newly arrived toys. She stepped out of the main cabin barefoot, wearing denim cutoff shorts and one of my flannel shirts with its sleeves rolled up. She left most of her gear on the Baia after I told her we'd be heading back to the ledge as soon as I was able to get a bigger boat.

Grabbing her bag, she kissed me, then hopped onto the dock. "I'm gonna meet up with Claire and Tony. Let me know when you learn anything. And you better not get that gold without me, Dodge."

"Be careful! If you run into any trouble at all, I'm

only a phone call away. It's a small island. I can make it almost anywhere within a few minutes."

Just as she disappeared, I received a message from Scott saying, in our encrypted style, that he would fly into Key West International the following day. I took a quick shower, then spent the rest of the morning researching nearby salvage vessels and contacting the owners to find out how much it would cost to rent one for a week.

Pete wasn't in his office when I drove to his restaurant looking for him, and the old-timer didn't use a cellphone, so there was no way of contacting him.

"I think he might be out on his boat," Mia said as I walked back out toward the seashell lot. "Could be gone all day. You never know with Pete."

After finding a few potential salvage ships north of the Keys, I spent an hour polishing up the engines and performing routine maintenance to make sure the Baia was in tip-top shape. I met Jack for lunch at Salty Pete's, and we sat at a table upstairs on the balcony. It was right against the railing and overlooked the marina and the ocean far off in the distance.

When I told Jack what had happened the night before at Neptune's Table, his jaw fell so hard it nearly broke through the mahogany decking under our feet. I showed him footage of the site and explained how the treasure was located deep beneath the ledge and that we were only able to reach it using Sam's underwater drone.

"That's a lot of rock between us and that gold," Jack said. "How do you plan on hauling it all up?"

I thought it over for a moment. "Well, first things first. We'll need to identify the wreck. Salvage laws in the US are pretty strict, and I'm sure both Spain and Mexico will claim ownership of the wreck and all of its contents. We'll be lucky if we get a few scraps of leftovers from the haul."

"Well, I'm sure Pete has a few ideas on how to identify it." Jack drew his gaze through the sliding glass door toward Pete's office.

Just as he did, Mia approached with our drinks.

"Still no sign of him, Mia?" I asked.

"The ocean is his therapy, and it hasn't been a good year for him. In reality, it hasn't been a good couple of years."

"It's all these cookie-cutter tourist shops, bro. People just aren't interested in real artifacts anymore. They'd rather buy a dead shark in a jar. Pete's used to be a landmark around here. Now it's gone off the deep end. It's a damn shame."

Mia walked back into the restaurant.

I took a drink of the Key limeade. "In the meantime, we're gonna have to head back to the ledge and explore more around the treasure," I said. "Maybe find a cave big enough for us to squeeze through."

"Those drug runners we saw out there the other day don't give a damn about salvage laws. How do you plan to deal with them?"

I took another sip and looked out over the water, still amazed by how great of a view the place had. It was now almost one in the afternoon, and a few patches of gray clouds covered the blue sky above. A strong breeze was blowing in from the west, shifting the palm fronds and forming scattered whitecaps on the water.

"I plan to avoid them as best as we can. But I'm going to bring that gold up, Jack. If I have to fight them off again, so be it. Besides, Scott's flying in tomorrow. There's nothing in the Caribbean more dangerous than the three of us fully armed." I grinned, but Jack still seemed unconvinced. "Look, I'll understand if you don't want any more part in this."

"It's not me. I'm worried about Isaac."

Mia came through the door holding two plates of food. After setting them in front of us with a smile, she turned on her heels and headed back inside.

"I'm sending him to his grandparents' for a few days. They live in Chicago, and I know he'll be safe there. I just don't want him here with everything that's been happening lately."

"When does he leave?"

"Got him on a flight first thing in the morning."

I thought it was a pretty good idea.

We ate the delicious grouper sandwiches along with their specialty sweet potato fries. When we were finished, we headed back to the marina and boarded the Baia, where I showed Jack more footage of the treasure on the laptop.

We spent a few hours studying the space beneath the ledge and trying to formulate a way to reach the treasure. The weather turned even worse as darker clouds rolled in and the wind picked up, and we decided that we'd wait for the following day to return to the ledge with Scott and Sam.

Around five in the afternoon, Jack headed to his

house to be with his nephew on his last night in the Keys and to make sure he was packed. I texted Sam, telling her the plan, and she invited me to have dinner with her, saying she'd already made reservations at the Paradou Chateau, one of the higher-end restaurants in Key West.

I got a long workout in, running the Old Town loop course, which is about four kilometers and circles around town to White Street Pier, then back to the marina. Then I did a combination circuit involving pull-ups, planks, and various push-up variations. Being in the SEALs had taught me how to get in a good workout anywhere and at any time, so I'd never had much use for a gym membership.

After the workout, I grabbed a quick shower on the boat, then dressed in the nicest clothes I had—gray slacks, a dress shirt, and black Converse All Star high-tops. After locking up my laptop in the safe, I killed all of the lights on the Baia except the ones in the cockpit, then locked the door and turned on the security system.

TWENTY-TWO

The main streets of Key West were bustling with people, and when I reached the Paradou Chateau, I hopped out and handed the valet my keys. The place was full, and a few groups were sitting in the lounge waiting to be seated. I told the host I was reserved under a party of two for Samantha Flores. She smiled and led me along a row of elegant tables and chairs in the fancy French restaurant. She ushered me to a booth right next to one of the restaurant's front windows, overlooking a long sandy beach and distant crashing waves that white-capped in the moonlight.

I ordered a few drinks and an appetizer, and a few moments later, Sam arrived wearing a sexy black dress and high heels. The dress was just tight enough to show her lean figure and short enough to show her long, tanned legs. Her hair looked different. It was straighter and seemed to fall slightly past her shoulders.

I slid out from my seat and held out my hand as

she sat down across from me. "You look incredible."

"Thank you. I never imagined I'd be wearing a dress on this trip. Luckily, Claire and I are about the same size."

"Well, you wear it well. I think you might need to do the world a favor and take it off her hands."

She blushed as the waitress arrived and set a mojito and a mai tai on the table in front of us, along with a plate of escargots with melted butter and garlic that looked amazing.

"I took the liberty of ordering you a drink," I said. "I hope you don't mind."

She took a sip of the mojito, then the mai tai. "One of the best I've ever had," she said, setting the mai tai back on the table. "I'd heard this place was good."

"It's one of the finest restaurants in the Keys."

I grabbed the mojito and took a few sips, savoring the delicious flavor and smelling the fresh mint. It was a perfect blend of white rum, club soda, sugar, and fresh mint leaves between clear cubes of ice. Shaken to perfection. The escargots were equally good, and we both decided on the chef's special, which was bouillabaisse with cream of watercress soup. The main course tantalized our taste buds as we savored the seafood stew, which was loaded with fresh clams, lobster, and fish.

When we finished the meal, we walked out onto the patio, then down to the beach. The wind was strong, and the sun had fallen hours earlier, but it was still over seventy degrees with a cool breeze. We walked barefoot in the surf by the light of the moon and talked about where we were from and how we'd ended up where we were in life. Turned out, her mom had immigrated from Mexico when she was only twelve years old, taking her and her older brother to live in the States, and eventually settling in San Antonio.

"She raised us both on her own," Sam said. "You'd like her, Logan. And you'd also like my brother. He's a Marine."

I raised my eyebrows. "No kidding. I believe I would like him, then."

I'd always liked Marines, regardless of how much our branches always trash-talked each other. If I hadn't been so hell-bent on being a SEAL, I would've joined the Marines, no question.

"They still live in Texas?"

She shook her head. "Mom lives with me in Wakulla Beach, just outside of Tallahassee, and my brother lives in San Diego."

"Really? There's great cave diving in Wakulla Springs."

"Yeah, I've been down there a few times."

"I didn't think it was legal anymore."

"One of the benefits of having the backing of a university. I found mastodon bones there while exploring some of the unknown portions of the cave system. You know, there's over twelve miles of mapped caves there, and much more that isn't discovered."

"You found mastodon bones?"

She grinned. "Yeah. A friend and I did a piece on the cave, and we stumbled into them accidentally, believe it or not."

A large wave broke on the beach, splashing past our ankles, and as it slid away, I noticed something in the sand five feet in front of us. I grabbed ahold of what looked like a shell, but after bringing it up and examining it in the moonlight, I realized it was a shark's tooth. After rinsing it off in the next crashing wave, I handed it to Sam.

She inspected it as we continued to walk.

The conversation turned to the treasure and how we would spend the next few days trying to haul up as much as we could.

At just after eleven, her phone rang.

"Hello?" She listened for a moment, then froze in place. A wave receded, sucking the sand from beneath her feet, but she didn't move a muscle. Her face turned from pleasantly happy to shocked in an instant. "Where are you?" she asked frantically.

I listened and watched Sam intently, trying to figure out what was happening.

"Okay, we'll be right there." She hung up the phone, then looked at me with wide eyes. "We have to go, Logan. I need your help." She grabbed my hand and started running up the beach, back toward the parking lot.

"What's going on?"

"It's Claire." Sam was racing as fast as she could, and when she reached the wooden steps of the restaurant, she kept up her pace, not bothering with her heels. "She's in trouble."

We ran to the valet, and I handed him my ticket, urging him to fetch my truck as quickly as possible. A moment later, my Tacoma pulled around the corner. The valet hopped out, and Sam and I jumped in.

"Where?"

"Club Indigo."

I peeled out of the driveway, burning rubber as I floored it onto the main road.

"I need you to calm down, okay?" I said, looking deep into Sam's eyes.

She was breathing frantically and urging me to drive faster.

"I need you to tell me who that was on the phone and what they said. We'll be at the club in a few minutes, and I need to know as much as I can before we get there."

She took in a deep breath, then let it out. "Tony said Claire's dancing at the club, and there are a few guys who won't leave her alone. He says she's drunk and they keep touching her and trying to take her home. One of the men has a gun lodged in the back of his pants."

I thought it over for a moment as I weaved in and out of pedestrians crossing the busy road. Key West during the busy tourist months is incredibly chaotic, but in the evening on weekends, it's more like a zoo if the walls all disappeared.

"That's all he said?"

Sam nodded. "Please, Logan. We have to help her. She's in my care. I . . . I told her parents that I'd . . ."

"She's gonna be fine," I said sternly.

A moment later, we arrived at a large building with a blue neon sign that said "Club Indigo." All the parking spots out front were taken, so I turned down a small street that went around to the back of the building. I pulled up alongside the back entrance, shut off the engine, and we hopped out.

A large group of people stared at us as we rushed to the back door. Sam, being well dressed, beautiful, and a woman, had no trouble getting past the big black guy standing with his arms crossed at the front door. When I tried to walk in behind her, he held up his enormous hand and pressed it against my chest.

"The club's full," he said in a strong Jamaican accent.

He tried to say something else, but before he could, I'd already grabbed his wrist and twisted his right arm behind his back. He cursed as I pushed him hard against the wall and told him I was going inside.

"I'm calling five-oh!" the man said angrily.

"Good."

Before a few of his buddies reached me, I pushed him to the ground and disappeared into the club. Sam was nowhere in sight as I navigated through the thick crowd of people. The club was dark, and lines of tables and a few bars surrounded a large dance floor that resembled a mosh pit at a concert. Strobe lights flickered through the darkness, and fog machines made it even more difficult to see anything. A DJ in the corner played music that shook the entire building.

Unable to see anything, I ran up a set of stairs and looked down at the dance floor. After scanning the crowd for a moment, I saw Sam just below me and watched as she forced her way through the dancing people toward the center of the floor. Tony was just behind her, and I realized they were moving toward a group of five rough-looking dudes. A blonde-haired woman was dancing in the middle of the guys, and I recognized that it was Claire. She was clearly wasted, and I imagined the only reason she was still on her feet was because the guys she was dancing with were holding her up.

When they reached the men, Sam and Tony each said something to the guys, who looked back at them angrily. In an instant, one of the guys pushed Tony in the chest, and when he regained his balance and moved back toward them, a guy wearing big sunglasses and a glittery cutoff shirt punched Tony in the side of his face, sending him to the floor. At the same time, a large Hispanic guy grabbed Sam forcefully by her arm, pulled her into the middle of the group, and started grinding on her as she tried to break free of his grasp.

Before I consciously knew what my body was doing, I was already rushing for the stairs and toward the dance floor. I forced my way through the dancing people to the group of guys.

The first man I approached was the Hispanic who'd grabbed Sam. Engaging five guys at once is never easy, especially if they know how to fight, so the first thing I had to do was even the odds a little. I grabbed him by the arm, and when he swung around to see what was happening, I slammed my right elbow into his head. He collapsed unconscious to the floor like a sack of potatoes. Two of the other guys saw what was happening and came at me. The first swung his fist at my head, and I easily dodged the blow and landed a roundhouse kick to his side. I heard a bone crack as he fell to the floor in pain. The second guy in the glittery cutoff shirt grabbed me from behind and wrapped his arm around my neck. I stood tall, then curled forward, hurling him over me and slamming him to the floor.

The center of the dance floor opened up a little as

the intoxicated tourists realized in a daze what was happening around them. A shirtless ripped guy in slacks came at me with a switchblade. I quickly avoided his attempt to slash me with the shiny edge, and when he stabbed it toward my chest, I slid to the side, grabbed his arm holding the blade, and jammed his elbow down into my knee. His hyperextended elbow cracked, and he yelled out in pain as his knife fell and rattled to the floor.

A big bald guy covered in tattoos was moving Claire toward the back of the club. As soon as I approached him, he pushed Claire aside and reached for something in his pants—the *something* I soon identified as a handgun. Before he could level the barrel at me, I kicked it out of his hands, and it tumbled across the room, stopping against a far wall. He grabbed a metal chair and lifted it high above his head, slamming it toward me. I threw my shoulder into his unguarded chest and tackled him to the floor. He was bigger than I was, so I quickly shifted into an armlock and snapped his right elbow without hesitation. He yelled out in pain as I jumped to my feet and ran toward Claire, Sam, and Tony, who were watching me as they stumbled toward the back of the club.

We headed for the back door, but before we reached it, a guy jumped at me with a sawed-off shotgun in his hands. I knocked the weapon from his grasp just before he could pull the trigger, grabbed him by his shirt, and threw him face-first into a metal table that collapsed from the force of the blow.

The four of us stormed out the exit and hustled to my truck. A few groups of people were smoking, and the big guy at the door yelled at me as we rushed by, bellowing that if I ever returned, he'd shove my face into the pavement.

Tony sat shotgun, and Claire and Sam were in the back. Just as I stuck the key into the ignition and twisted it, a hand appeared through my door's window and pressed a .44 Magnum against my chest. It was the bald guy. His face was contorted as he tried to hide the pain I knew was burning from his right elbow, which I'd recently fractured. Now that we were out of the dark club and I was able to see the man under the light of the alleyway, I instantly noticed a tattoo of two black snakes slithering around his left wrist.

"Get your ass out of the truck," he growled.

I contemplated stealing the gun right out of his hand but didn't want to risk a stray bullet accidentally hitting one of the others. Doing as he said, I opened the door and stepped out. He shifted past me and glared at the three still in the truck.

"Any of you move so much as a fucking muscle, and I'll blow you all to pieces."

The man winced as he slid a shaky right hand into his pocket and pulled out a cellphone. Just as the screen lit up, I forcefully slapped his gun to the side, then slammed my elbow into the side of his head. Grabbing his wrists, I smashed his hands against a lamppost, and his Magnum fell onto the blacktop. He swung at me with his left fist, but I was able to block it and counter with two quick punches to the center of his face.

His nose cracked, and blood flowed out across his face. A final kick sent him to the ground, causing him to writhe back and forth, unable to get back up. I grabbed his pistol, emptied the six rounds onto the ground, then threw it into a nearby dumpster and hopped back into the driver's seat.

As I drove us out from the alley and onto the main street, I heard sirens approaching the club from all directions. A few police cars were already parked outside the main entrance, their red and blue lights flashing and illuminating the darkened streets.

TWENTY-THREE

I drove the truck down Duval Street, trying my best to fit in with the other cars on the road. Claire was crying and delirious in the back seat, and Sam held her close, consoling her as best as she could. I handed Tony a first-aid kit, and he bandaged up his and Sam's wounds. After just a few minutes of driving through the crowded Duval, I turned onto Olivia Street, which had far fewer people walking the sidewalks and crosswalks.

After two blocks, I pulled up to the curb beside the cemetery, stopped the truck, and killed the lights. Holding my Sig in hand, I checked my mirrors. When I was confident no one was following us, I pulled back onto the road, and a few minutes later, I reached their small bed and breakfast and parked the truck up against an old railroad tie right behind their unit.

I helped Sam carry a passed-out Claire around the stone walkway to their patio, which was right over the

218

sand and overlooking the ocean. Tony opened the sliding glass door, and we all stepped inside. I did a quick scan of the room, making sure we were alone, then helped carry Claire to her bedroom.

After she was in her bed, I walked back out into the living room. "Sure was a bad idea going out to a club like that alone," I said to Tony as he grabbed a container of aspirin and swallowed a few of the white pills.

"I'm sorry, Logan. She'd been asking me to go see the nightlife with her for days." He held his hand up to his head and closed his eyes. There was a bruise on his forehead from where the thug had hit him.

"You might have a concussion. You should get it looked at."

He tried to walk across the room but lost his balance and almost stumbled to the floor.

"Here," I said, holding out my hand. "You should rest." I helped him into his room, then walked back to the kitchen, filled a glass of water, and sat on the sofa. For the first time since the fight at the club, I realized my knuckles were bleeding. Over the years, I'd been in many fistfights, so I knew that bloody knuckles were unavoidable. At least those guys back at the club made out a hell of a lot worse than I did.

After chugging the glass of water, I headed back to my truck and unlocked the silver toolbox in the bed. The hinges creaked as I opened it up, and I reached inside and pulled out an MP5 submachine gun, an extra magazine, and a night-vision monocular.

I hopped into the driver's seat and pulled the truck around the front of the rental unit. I was pretty sure I wasn't allowed to park there, but it would be more out of sight from the main road than in the actual parking spot. I locked her up and headed back to the B and B, carrying the submachine gun and night-vision monocular. When I opened the door, Sam was standing in the kitchen next to the counter.

"I thought you'd left."

"No. Just had to move the truck. I'm staying here tonight to make sure nothing happens to the three of you." I set the gun and monocular on a table. "In the morning, I'm driving you, Claire, and Tony out of the Keys. We'll take US-1 up to Homestead, then the three of you will continue northwest back to your home."

Sam approached me and wrapped her arms around my torso. I pulled her in close, holding her tightly. Her heart rate was still high, and I could tell she was having a hard time coping with what happened.

I kissed her cheek. "It's going to be okay, Sam. I'm gonna get you out of here."

She paused for a moment, then loosened her grip on me and looked into my eyes. "But what about you? What are you going to do?"

"I'm gonna come back here, and I'm gonna track these guys down. They won't get a doubloon of that treasure so long as I'm alive."

"But they're dangerous men, Logan. What if something happens to you?"

I wanted to tell her that I'd been in situations like this many times over the past fourteen years, but I figured it wouldn't make her feel any better about it. "I'll be careful, all right? Besides, I've got a friend flying in tomorrow morning. He was in the SEALs with me. Plus, I also have Jack. There's no trouble the three of us can't handle."

If my words made her feel any better about the situation, she didn't show it. "What's that?" she asked, pointing at the table beside us.

"It's a night-vision monocular. Look, you should really try and get some rest. It's gonna be a long day tomorrow."

She frowned. "You're not coming to bed?"

"I'll be in later. I'm gonna have a look around the property just to make sure we're safe tonight. Just do me a favor and make sure all of the lights are out once you're in bed. We need to be on the road before sunrise in the morning. We'll leave at zero six hundred."

She nodded, then, after kissing me passionately on the lips, turned and walked into her bedroom. When the door shut behind her, I turned off all the lights, gave my eyes a minute to adjust to the darkness, then grabbed the monocular and my Sig.

My watch showed that it was just after midnight. I stepped out the door and shut it quietly behind me. The grounds were exceptionally quiet compared to the rip-roaring party that was downtown. In fact, there were no sounds at all aside from the ocean waves and the strong breeze swaying a few palm branches and a wind chime on the patio. I moved slowly, sticking to the shadows and keeping my wits sharp. I was confident that we'd made a solid escape, but deep down, I had an eerie feeling that I was being watched. My father had always taught me that instincts are there for a reason, and I expected an enemy to pop out from a corner at any second as I surveyed the grounds.

After patrolling the beach, I migrated back up along the rental unit. Just as my feet left the sand, I heard shuffling in a bush at my six. The instant my brain processed the noise, I dropped, whirled around, and took aim toward the shrub. With my finger on the trigger, I watched as a chicken stumbled around a fan of palm leaves and eyed me stupidly. I sighed, released the tension from my body, and lowered my weapon.

After another ten minutes of scanning the property, I concluded that the place was clear and that it would be almost impossible for someone passing by on the main road to see my truck.

I headed back inside, locked the door behind me, and crawled into bed beside Sam. I kept my Sig and the monocular on the nightstand beside me and set my cellphone alarm for five. Sliding over, I moved in close to Sam, and she curled into me, placing one of her arms over my chest.

TWENTY-FOUR

At zero five hundred, I woke up to my alarm and rolled out of bed, a little groggy from the night before. Sam was still asleep, so I grabbed a quick shower and changed into a spare set of shorts, a T-shirt, and tennis shoes I kept in the cab of my truck. Before waking the others, I sent off a quick text to both Jack and Scott, letting them know what I was doing and informing them that Black Venom had infested Key West.

By zero five forty-five, everyone was awake, packed, and ready to head out. We would have to take both vehicles since I would need a way to get back to Key West after reaching Homestead. Tony and Claire took the Pathfinder, and Sam and I rode in my Tacoma.

They took the lead in the Pathfinder as we rolled out of the bed-and-breakfast parking lot onto the main road. I told Tony, who was driving the Pathfinder,

223

that when we reached US-1, I wanted us to keep five hundred feet of distance between us so I could cover them in the event something went wrong. We drove that way out of Key West, past the Key West Golf Club on Stock Island, then past the Naval Air Station on Boca Chica Key. The drive was mostly silent, and I was sure Sam was still going over the events of the previous night. I know I was.

It wasn't until we were leaving Big Pine Key and entering the Seven Mile Bridge that I suspected we were being followed. A large, blacked-out Suburban was getting bigger in my rearview mirror with each passing second. We were traveling ten miles an hour over the forty-five limit, which meant that whoever was driving the Suburban was either in a terrible hurry at zero six hundred on a Sunday morning . . . or we were being followed.

I continued watching my rearview mirror.

"What is it?" Sam asked. She turned around and stared out the back window. The Suburban was now only a few hundred feet behind us, but I noticed it had slowed a little. "You think it's the guys from last night?"

"I sure as hell hope not." I grabbed my Sig from the center console and placed it on my lap. "But I like to assume the worst."

I watched the Suburban intently for a few minutes as it kept its distance to a hundred feet behind us. Ten minutes later, we drove through Bahia Honda Key and entered the longest stretch of bridge in the Keys without land. I kept an eye on the Suburban, and right when we were about to hit the midpoint between Bahia Honda and Marathon, it sped up in a hurry.

"Shit," I said, grabbing my Sig and hitting the gas. "Call Tony and tell him to floor it!" I looked at Sam, who was obviously shocked by the loud and intense tone of my voice. "Sam! Tell him to get the hell out of here. That guy's about to ram us."

Sam took a quick glance behind us, then grabbed her phone, tapped the screen, and held it up to the side of her head. After she relayed my message to Tony, he floored the Pathfinder in front of us. I watched as the speedometer on my Tacoma rose quickly past eighty, then ninety miles per hour. The concrete walls that lined both sides of the bridge flew past us in a blur, along with the turquoise water surrounding us, which had just recently become visible in the morning light. The blacked-out Suburban was still gaining on us and was now no more than fifty feet behind. I did a double-take as I watched a guy lean out of the passenger-side window, his hands clutching a stockless AK-47.

"Logan!" Sam yelled frantically.

She was pointing through the windshield, and when I drew my gaze from the rearview mirror to the road in front of us, I saw a semitruck heading our way. It had already passed the Pathfinder using the oncoming lane and had now turned into our lane and was cruising straight for us. The moment before we were about to collide head-on, I turned the wheel sharply to the left and then back to the right. The Tacoma made the first turn, then went into a sideways skid right around the semi as I turned back to the right. The colossal truck tried to maneuver into us but was too slow and just missed hitting the front right bumper.

Keeping my eyes forward, I realized that there was more than one semitruck. The second one, which had been cruising closely behind the first and had remained hidden, was now about to collide with us. Sliding out of the skid, I tried to turn, but the tires on the Tacoma failed to gain enough traction, and the semi clipped the back right bumper. The Tacoma spun a few times before flipping over onto its side, jerking both Sam and me into our seat belts. The Suburban slammed into us from behind as we collided with the wall on the other side of the road, forcing the Tacoma to flip onto its back and spin out of control. Both airbags exploded in our faces as our bodies rattled side to side. Glass shattered, and my head slammed against the side paneling, causing blood to drip down my forehead. After what felt like an eternity of screeching metal and violent shaking, our upside-down bodies went limp as the Tacoma finally slowed to a stop against the concrete barrier.

My mind a delirious mess, I looked over at Sam and saw what seemed to be her lifeless body. I reached overhead and pressed a hand against the top of the truck, then unbuckled my seat belt. Catching myself and shifting onto my knees, I crawled over to Sam and was relieved to feel a heartbeat pulsing at the base of her neck. I wrapped my arms around her and clicked her seatbelt free, as well, bringing her down softly.

Blood slid down the side of her head as I tried to wake her up. I spoke to her, saying her name over and over, until finally, her eyes opened. She looked scared and confused as I told her everything was going to be okay. Tears filled her eyes, and I had trouble believing my own words.

She glanced through the shattered window behind me, and I heard footsteps approaching our position. I searched the cab quickly and reached for my Sig, which had slid down to the floor under the gas pedal. Grabbing ahold of it, I shifted my body to try and kick open the driver's-side door so we could escape, but before I could, men surrounded the truck.

"Drop the fucking gun!" a guy yelled, pointing his rifle through the broken window.

There were at least five men, and they had us surrounded. There was nothing I could do. I dropped my Sig and told Sam one more time that everything was going to be okay. A moment later, the man behind me slammed the butt of his rifle into the back of my head.

TWENTY-FIVE

I woke up in a small, dark room and had one hell of a headache pounding deep inside my skull. My legs and arms were tied to a heavy metal chair, and a chain was latched around my neck with the rest of it coiled up beside me. The room was almost empty, though it was difficult to see anything. The only light in the room came from a round glass window cut into the door ten feet in front of me. For a few minutes, I tried to move around, but the weight of the chair, along with the chain around my neck, made even the smallest movements incredibly difficult.

A bright light flashed through the window, and I saw the outline of a man staring at me through the glass. The light vanished and was followed a moment later by the door screeching open on its rusty hinges. The large man in the doorway walked with heavy footsteps to the side of the room and then turned on a high-powered construction lamp. The room brightened in an instant, and I had to look away as the asshole angled the light right into my face.

He took a step toward me and kicked my left shin, causing pain to radiate up my leg. "Sit your ass up," he growled. "Boss is on the way." Then he disappeared into the shadows.

My eyes still hadn't adjusted yet when a second set of footsteps approached my position. Squinting, I saw another man walk through the doorway.

He lit up a cigarette and stood in front of me as he took a few drags, hovering over me and observing me from head to toe. "So, you're the scumbag who's been giving my men trouble," he said in a strong Spanish accent. He kept away from the light so I couldn't see his face, but judging by his voice, I pegged him to be in his late thirties or early forties. He took in two more long, deep inhalations of his cigarette, then blew a cloud of smoke into my face. "My name is Marco, as you've probably realized by now. I did a little research on you, Mr. Dodge. Your background in the military and as a mercenary made for some interesting reading. I wonder, how is it that you learned about the Aztec treasure's possible whereabouts?"

I kept my eyes, which had almost fully adjusted to the light, drawn to the ground.

Marco sighed. "I expected as much from a trained military professional like yourself. But in my line of work, we specialize and take pride in our ability to make people say what we want them to say." He moved closer to me, though not close enough to see his face, then flicked his cigarette into the corner of the room.

"I'm not a patient man, Mr. Dodge. I'm also not one to easily forget events that resulted in the death of my men, and more importantly, made me look foolish." He bent down close, staring at me with his dark eyes. A scar across his left eyebrow looked like it had come from a knife wound. "Where's the treasure, Mr. Dodge?"

I answered only by looking away.

"Very well. Have it your way, then."

He stepped back and motioned to the guy standing in the corner, who I realized was the big Hispanic dude I'd knocked out at the club the previous night. He snarled at me, hulked his way toward me, then without hesitation, hit me with a hard right to the side of my face. He hit me again, this time in the shoulder, then again on the other side. I fell down a few times, and each time he lifted me back up with ease before continuing to punch me at various points across my body. Blood trickled down my face, and pain surged from all parts of my body at once. After a strong blow to my jaw, my head flailed backward, and I almost lost consciousness.

"Stop!" Marco said.

The massive guy growled at me, then walked away.

Marco grabbed me by my shirt collar and shook me violently. "Where is it? Where the fuck is it?" He pushed me back, and my chair slammed against the floor, rattling the chain around my neck.

Blood spewed from my mouth and formed a pool of dark red as I lay on the cold metal floor. The guy lifted my chair up, and Marco moved in close again.

I spat a wad of blood in his face. "Go fuck yourself."

He lifted a rag and wiped it casually away. "Have it your way, Mr. Dodge." Marco stepped back, and a moment later, the big guy and two other guys I hadn't previously seen, grabbed me.

Marco moved swiftly for the door as the guys lifted me and the coiled-up chain clasped around my neck.

Marco opened the door, then smirked at me before stepping through the doorway. "I'm certain Miss Flores will be more agreeable."

"You son of a bitch!" I yelled before the door shut.

I struggled to break free, but it was no use. The knots were tight around my arms and legs, and the chain around my neck was clipped on with a large carabiner that would be impossible to unclasp with my hands tied. The three men turned me around, then carried me out a back door.

"Let's hurry up and waste this fool," one man said as they carried me up a narrow set of metal stairs.

It was obvious from the gentle sway of the floor that we were on a boat, and sure enough, they opened a door and carried me out onto the deck of an old shrimp trawler. We were tied off to a pier beside a run-down warehouse. All the nearby structures were old and falling apart, and there seemed to be nobody but us for miles. I wondered where in the Keys we could be, but I didn't have time to wonder long. Out over the channel, which was flanked by thick mangroves, I saw a distant sun dropping below the horizon and was amazed that I'd been unconscious so long. Clouds filled most of the sky, and a strong

231

breeze blew against my face.

The three men dropped me on the edge of the deck.

The Hispanic said, "You're going over, tough guy."

Making quick work of the knots, they freed my legs, then untied the chair from my hands, which were still tied behind my back. With the heavy chain clasped around my neck, they lifted me out of the chair, then dropped me against the railing. One of the guys pressed the tip of a bowie knife against my back.

"Just kick his ass in," the other growled.

I swiveled my head to look at the guy holding the bowie knife against my back. He was much smaller than the Hispanic, but he was muscular and covered in tattoos. His face contorted into a smile as he pressed the tip of the blade harder into my back.

Obviously frustrated, the big guy drew his leg back in preparation to kick me overboard. Just as his leg was about to meet my back, he screamed in pain and fell to the deck, wrapping his hands around his leg and rolling onto his side. "What the fuck!" he yelled.

The other men looked at him and then at each other in confusion. A second later, the shorter guy fell to the ground, clutching his chest. The last guy standing reached for an Uzi lodged in his cargo shorts. With my legs no longer tied to the chair, I reared back and struck him with a powerful side kick into his abdomen. The force of the blow made him drop the weapon as he fell to the deck. He stumbled, then tried to stand back up and retrieve his Uzi, which had slid down the deck thirty feet.

A figure appeared from the cockpit of the trawler wearing a bulletproof vest and aiming a silenced pistol. He wore sunglasses, gloves, and a black headband over his head, but from his movements, I instantly recognized that it was Scott. He fired two rounds into the guy going after his Uzi, causing him to go limp in his tracks. Scott slid a knife out from his side, stepped behind me, and made quick work of the rope tied around my hands.

I smiled as he freed my hands and I unclasped the chain around my neck. "The hell took you so long, Scott?"

"You know how traffic can get down here." He cocked his head toward the large Hispanic guy still squirming in pain on the deck. "What are we gonna do with him?"

"We need answers. And my guess is tubby here has at least one." I walked over to the guy and kicked him onto his back.

Scott pressed his Glock to the guy's chest. "If you don't start talking, you'll end up just like your buddies."

The man gave Scott the middle finger, then tried to break free of my grasp. Holding his arms back, I shoved my knee between his shoulder blades, keeping him immobilized. When it was clear we weren't getting anything out of him, I grabbed the bowie knife and slammed the handle into his temple, knocking him unconscious.

We searched the guys' clothes and found a cellphone and leather wallet on the skinny guy. We then did a quick search of the boat, each knowing what we were looking for: anything that would help us find where these guys were keeping Sam and what they were planning to do next. The old boat that looked like it hadn't seen open water in years was empty aside from damaged nets and other rusted shrimping gear. It was obvious these guys only used this location because it was off the beaten path.

We climbed over the side of the trawler and onto a sorry excuse for a dock that had more broken planks than non-broken ones. As we moved down the dock, we kept our eyes peeled for any sign of others.

"Did you see anyone leave the trawler?" I asked as I climbed over an old levee and into bushes and palm trees.

"No. There were a few guys in the parking lot, but that was it. I did hear a large outboard as I approached, but it was far in the distance."

"Damn."

"Why?"

We reached a cracked slab of concrete covered in old pilings and a rusted chain-link fence, and on the other side was a black Dodge Charger parked in the shade of a gumbo-limbo tree. Scott remote-started the car from fifty feet away, and we moved toward it quickly.

"That was Marco," I said.

We hopped inside, Scott in the driver seat, and myself in the passenger seat.

"What? *The* Marco?"

"Yeah. The same one from Mexico."

Scott put the manual transmission in gear, then spun out the tires as he floored the sports car, weaving in and out of old junk as he picked up speed. He drifted onto an old dirt road, blazing through overhanging banyan branches before popping through a patch of bromeliads and onto a two-lane road. There were a few other cars, but none appeared suspicious as we drove toward the city of Marathon.

"How in the hell did you find me anyway?"

Scott pointed at my watch. "I installed a tracking device during the flight to Miami."

I shook my head. Scott never did like leaving anything up to chance, a facet of his character that had saved me and others many times before.

We drove over the Seven Mile Bridge, heading southwest.

I thumbed through the history on the skinny cartel guy's cellphone, starting with messages, then moving to recent phone calls. I called the first three most recent numbers and received the same message for each—a robotic female voice informing me that the number I'd dialed was no longer in service. When I called the fourth number, a woman answered on the second ring.

"Good evening. La Playa Bonita at Key West, this is Cindy speaking. How may I help you?"

As the woman spoke, I scrambled for the man's driver's license in his wallet. "Yes, I'm calling to speak with one of your guests. Ruben Castillo. Can you connect me, please?"

"No problem, sir. May I ask who's calling?"

"Yeah, tell him it's his friend, Marco."

"Okay, one moment, sir."

A second later, I heard the sound of the phone ringing again as she transferred my call. After three rings, a man's voice came over the other end of the phone. Before he could finish saying hello, I hung up.

"What is it?" Scott asked.

"They're at the Playa Bonita Resort. Not sure how many are there, but if we're gonna find Sam, that's our best option. I doubt they'd keep her at a public place like a resort, but I'm sure we can find answers."

"You want to go there now?" Scott raised his eyebrows. "You're crazy. You were just beaten half to death. You need medical care. Look at yourself." He pulled down the visor above my seat and flipped out the mirror.

My face was covered in blood and cuts, and my shirt and pants were ripped and covered in dirt.

"They'll never even let you past the lobby looking like that."

I flipped the visor back up. "Look, it might hurt as bad as it looks, but I don't care. I need to find Sam."

TWENTY-SIX

In less than an hour, we were back in Key West and pulling the Charger into the Conch Harbor parking lot. I'd relented and agreed to stop by the Baia to clean and care for my wounds before heading over to the resort. The truth was, I'd wanted to stop by my boat anyway in order to saddle up for the upcoming confrontation that was likely to take place. We rushed down the dock, and when we reached the Baia, I did a thorough check of the security system, which included a state-of-the-art sonar sweep of the hull and the water below it. When I saw that there were no discrepancies, we climbed aboard, and I went straight for the head. I hopped into the shower, and using more hot water than I had the entire previous week combined, soaked my body and washed away the dried-up blood from my face and upper body.

I wiped the condensation from the mirror as I dried off. The cuts were still visible, and though I decided a few might scar, it didn't appear as though I needed stitches. Instead, I grabbed a first -aid kit and rubbed antiseptic on the wounds, then wrapped bandages over the gashes in my shoulder. When I finished, I moved into the main stateroom, dressed in a pair of jeans, then slid on a bulletproof vest under a T-shirt. Like the vest Scott wore, it was thin, and though it offered little defense against high-caliber rifles, I would be protected from smaller arms and knives. I unlocked and opened my safe, pulled out my spare Sig, and slid it in the back of my jeans. I also grabbed a duffle bag, then moved into the saloon, where Scott sat at the table using my laptop.

"You find anything on those guys?"

Scott shook his head. "Coming up dry on all three. I'll contact my guy at the agency and see what he can do."

I locked up the Baia and carried my duffle bag as I stepped onto the dock alongside Scott. The sky had darkened even more, and it had started to rain. We climbed back into his Charger, and he hit the gas, taking us to the resort.

It was well past nineteen hundred as we cruised down the main streets of Key West, soon seeing the big white building with rows of large windows and balconies that marked the Playa Bonita Resort. We pulled into one of the side lots and parked in a guest spot near the back of the site, where the palm trees met the white sandy beach. Just as Scott killed the engine and we were both formulating a strike plan, a brown El Camino pulled up beside us, and two guys hopped out. I didn't recognize the first guy, but the second was the skinny guy who'd come at me with the sawed-off shotgun in the club the previous night.

Scott and I opened our doors and stepped out in perfect synchronization. We followed the two men in through the side entrance of the resort, past palm trees and patches of green grass. Once inside, we casually shortened the gap between us as we followed them around a hallway with marble floors and white walls covered in beautiful paintings.

They reached the elevators, pressed the button, and waited. The light came on, followed by a ding, and the doors opened. Inside the elevator, the sound of the Beatles' "Polythene Pam" playing faintly through speakers reached our ears. We rushed the doors, and before they could shut, stepped through into the elevator. Just as one of the guys looked up from his cellphone, I shoved him into the back wall. He collapsed to the floor, and the skinny guy swung at me with a right hook. I maneuvered around the blow and punched him square in the jaw. Grabbing him by his shirt collar, I pulled him down forcefully and struck my knee into his forehead. As the first guy crawled toward me, Scott kicked him in the face, whiplashing his head and knocking him out. Within seconds of our entering the elevator, the two guys were on the ground and wouldn't be getting up under their own strength anytime soon.

We saw that we were just about to reach the eighth floor, so we searched their pockets and pulled out a plastic card key in a paper sleeve with the number 406 written on it. I pulled out two silencers from my duffle bag, and we tightened them to the end of our pistols. When the doors opened on the fourth floor of the resort, we stepped out, not bothering to try and hide the bodies. Somebody would stumble upon them and call the police, but we would be long gone by the time they arrived.

We headed down the hallway and stopped in front of the door with 406 etched into a metal nameplate. I slid the card into the lock, then pulled it out when the light turned green. Turning the handle, I pushed open the door, and we stepped inside with our pistols raised to chest height.

One man was in the kitchen, reaching into the refrigerator, and two others were sitting on the couch watching television and holding their phones in front of them. As soon as the guy in the kitchen saw us, he reached for a revolver on his left hip, cross draw. Before he could grip the handle, I fired off two quick shots into his chest, splattering blood over the granite countertops beside him. The two other guys dove for cover behind the couch and a recliner. Scott hit one of the men before he could disappear from view, but the third guy made it to cover unscathed. I ran for his position behind the recliner, and as he raised an Uzi in my direction, I kicked it into the wall. I bashed a nearby lamp onto the top of his head, shattering the ceramic and knocking him out.

Once we were certain all three guys were down, we searched the unit for any sign of Sam. The place was a mess, with dirty clothes strewn over the bedroom floor and empty pizza boxes and beer cans in the living room and patio. On the table in the living room were recently killed cigarettes, white powder residue, and a few used blunts. After a quick search, it was clear that the unit was empty, and unfortunately, we didn't find Sam tied up anywhere like we'd been hoping.

A door in the living room leading to an adjoining unit wasn't shut all the way, so I twisted the handle and pulled. The door on the other side was wide open, and the adjoining unit was also trashed to hell. We stepped through the doorway with our pistols raised.

"The bedroom," Scott whispered.

Quiet sounds came from the room, hinting that someone was inside. As we cautiously approached, we heard the distinct sound of shuffling feet just on the other side of the door. We glanced at each other, nodded, then barged through. As the door swung open, a man wearing a black sweatshirt with the hood covering most of his head turned our way and stared at us like a deer caught in headlights. We yelled at him to freeze, but the idiot reached for something and turned to run out toward the bedroom patio. He grabbed a pistol and fired off a round into the drywall across from us before we took him down with a few well-placed shots to his chest. He fell to the deck beside the sliding glass door, blood pouring out of his limp body.

We searched the rest of the room, but like the first one, it was empty aside from trash left over from a party. We felt somewhat dejected that neither Sam nor Marco were in either of the rooms. As we were about to give up searching and get the hell out of the resort ahead of the police, I noticed something under the king-sized bed, right next to where the black sweatshirt guy had gone down. Kneeling and lifting up the white silk sheet, I laid eyes on five rows of C-4 explosives, enough charges to engulf half of the resort in flames. My heart skipped a beat as I realized that the bombs were rigged to a central control timer that was counting down from forty-three seconds.

TWENTY-SEVEN

My eyes remained locked on the timer as the numbers flashed closer to a fiery doom. Clearly, the guy in the sweatshirt had armed the bomb as a last-ditch effort to kill Scott and me before breaking for the patio. I blinked, forced myself to remain calm, and went to work.

Carefully, I slid the black plastic box with the timer on it out from under the bed. I slipped a multi-tool I kept in a small case attached to my wallet and went to work on the screws holding the casing in place.

"Shit," Scott gasped as he appeared behind me just as the final screw came loose. Like me, Scott had dealt with explosives many times before, but being an officer, he didn't possess the extensive hands-on experience I did.

My heart shifted up a gear as ten seconds appeared on the LED screen. With no time to lose, I removed the outer shell of the black box, revealing a tangle of various colored wires. I sifted through the wires, found the two that connected the power source to the blasting cap, and withdrew my dive knife. With the timer at two seconds, I sliced the wires with the titanium edge, severing the connection. The timer flashed to zero, but the bomb didn't go off.

I let out a deep breath and relaxed.

Scott placed a hand on my shoulder. "Try and cut it a little closer next time, Dodge." He patted me on the back, then knelt to help me deal with the explosives. "Nice to see you still got it."

Scott and I pulled out all of the C-4 from under the bed. I checked all of the bundles for a backup ignition mechanism but found nothing. It was a relatively simple bomb, and in my experience, those are generally the most effective. Though it was easy to disarm by someone who knew what they were doing, I had no doubt that that bomb would've gone off without a hitch and would've made national news with the death toll and damage done.

"Damn, that's a lot of boom," Scott said. "These guys weren't just trying to cover their tracks."

I shook my head. "No. They were trying to send a message. And it's obvious they knew we were coming."

I grabbed a roller suitcase from the closet beside us and emptied out the clothes inside. We loaded the C-4, then zipped up the main compartment of the bag. We then gave the room a quick search, looking in every nook and cranny, making sure there weren't any more bombs. When we were confident the rooms were clear, we headed out the door and down the hallway toward a different set of elevators. We kept our pistols holstered out of sight and walked quickly but casually past two maids who were running frantically down the hall. When we reached the elevator, we pressed the button and didn't have to wait long for the doors to open in front of us.

On the bottom floor, we used the emergency exit in the back of the building, which caused the fire alarm to go off as we walked down the concrete pathway toward Scott's rental car. We kept our eyes peeled for more bad guys but didn't see anyone else as we unlocked the Charger and climbed in after dropping the roller bag of C-4 and my duffle bag in the trunk. Just as the police cars arrived, we peeled out of the parking lot and headed back over to the marina.

Scott turned onto Whitehead Street, and as we were passing the Ernest Hemingway House, he gazed into the rearview mirror. "I think we got a tail," he said.

I turned around and got a good look at a blacked-out Escalade two cars behind us. "It's one of the same SUVs that followed me this morning and rammed us off the road on the Seven Mile Bridge."

We drove west three more blocks, then I told Scott to turn into a narrow alleyway between a liquor store and a scooter rental shack that was currently closed for the night.

When he rounded a sharp corner, I said, "Stop here."

Scott pulled the Charger against a brick wall and put it in neutral. "I'm tired of playing around with these assholes."

Scott cut the lights and killed the engine, and we hopped out.

I kept my Sig at the ready as we peeked around the corner and surveyed the alleyway. Once we saw that it was clear, we moved in toward the road. The Escalade was parked beside a row of chained-up scooters. The lights were on, and the engine was running.

We approached the vehicle slowly, then we jumped out from the alley, and I threw open the passenger door as we aimed our pistols. But the Escalade was empty. I looked at Scott, shrugged, then scanned the streets and sidewalks.

Back in the alley, I heard the distinct sound of footsteps coming from an adjoining walkway. Out from the shadows appeared a man walking straight for us. We crouched behind a corner and listened as his footsteps grew louder. When he came around the corner, I jumped out from my hiding place, grabbed his shirt collar, and forced him to the wet ground.

I pinned him down with my knee in his chest, right below his neck. "You're dead in two seconds if you don't start talking," I said. With his face now under the glow bleeding into the alley from the streetlights, I realized that I recognized him. It was the young man from Sierra Gorda who I'd pulled off the boat and dragged deep into the water. A member of Black Venom.

I gripped him tighter and started to count down angrily.

"Please, please don't hurt me," he said, panting for air. "I'm not here to hurt you."

I saw the terror deep within his eyes as he pleaded

frantically, but I didn't loosen my grip.

"My name is Daniel. I'm here to warn you, Mr. Dodge."

"Warn me? About what?"

He struggled to catch his breath, and his heart rate was well over a hundred beats per minute.

"About the others. About what they plan to do."

"Why in the hell should I believe you?"

"I want to help you. I want to escape this life. They . . . they killed my family." Tears filled his eyes. "I just want to escape."

I loosened my grip but kept my Sig aimed at him, ready to take him out at a moment's notice if he came at me.

He let out a sigh. "I'm sorry, Mr. Dodge. I'm sorry for trying to hunt you down before." He sat up and stared down at the concrete, his shoulders hunched. "I'm sorry for ever being a part of all of this. I just want out. I . . . I can't do this anymore."

Scott appeared from around a corner, shaking his head, indicating that the young man was alone.

"What are you here to warn me about?" I asked.

Daniel collected himself. "They know where the treasure is. That woman you were with told them its location. I was listening in the next room as they talked to her." He cleared his throat. "They're going there tomorrow morning, and they're gonna blow up the reef and take all of the gold."

"And Sam?" I said with a stone-cold expression. I already knew what his answer was going to be, but I still asked anyway.

"They're gonna take her with them to make sure her info's good. Then once they have the treasure,

247

they'll probably toss her to the sharks." His gaze drifted to the pavement once more. "I've seen it happen many times before."

Instinctively, my grip tightened on my Sig, which was no longer aimed at Daniel. "Any idea what time they're heading out in the morning?"

Daniel thought it over for a moment. "Marco's an arrogant and powerful man, but I'm sure even *he* won't go out there and start blowing shit up in the middle of the afternoon. I'd wager he'll have all of their yachts on the water before sunrise. All I know for certain, though, is that he told us all not to go out tonight—that it would be an early one in the morning, and he'd have someone call to wake us up."

Scott was still standing over us, impatiently looking around the alley and at Daniel's idling truck. "How many men does Black Venom have here in Key West?"

"I think around fifty."

Scott and I looked at each other, surprised to hear such a large number come out of his mouth.

"Since the new drug-trafficking prevention laws passed, they've had a hard time getting drugs out of Mexico," Daniel said. "The higher-ups of Venom have put a lot into this endeavor."

I saw a slight grin materialize on Scott's face. As a senator in Florida, he'd worked closely with the Mexican government to combat the drug trade. Now, he was seeing the rewards of his efforts as the drug cartels scrambled to make up for their losses. He knew firsthand how businesses, large organizations, and big governments worked, and when you get down to the books of it all, it's about the inflow and outflow of cash. When the outflow starts to exceed the inflow, then either changes must be made to the organization, or new streams of income must be found. Black Venom was no different.

I reached out my hand and helped Daniel to his feet.

We peered down the alley, making sure no one was watching us, then I turned back to Daniel. "Thanks for the tip."

"It's the least I could do to repay you for sparing my life in the lake, and also for tonight."

"When this is all over, you take as much cash as you can get from those guys, and you run. You hear me? Start a new life on the other side of the world. I'll do whatever I can to help you."

He smiled as he made his way toward his SUV.

Scott and I turned on our heels and headed back to Scott's rental, still parked around the corner. We climbed inside the Charger, and Scott drove us out of the alley and back onto Whitehead Street, heading toward the marina.

"So, what's the plan?" Scott asked, keeping his eyes on the road.

Words shot out of my mouth uncontrollably. "Tomorrow, you and I will sneak up on their boats, underwater. We'll find Sam, and then we'll give Black Venom back their bomb."

TWENTY-EIGHT

The rain had died off a bit, and through the water trickling down my passenger window, I watched as a few tourists walked the streets in brightly colored ponchos. We reached the marina in under five minutes, and as we pulled into the parking lot, I saw Angelina's red Camaro parked in front of the wooden dock railing. Scott parked a few spots down from her, and we both had a quick look around to make sure we hadn't been followed again. A moment later, we stepped out, grabbed the roller and duffle bags from the back, and walked down the steps to the dock. I felt a lot better knowing that Angelina was somewhere nearby. I'd worked with her hundreds of times all over the world and trusted her with my life as much as anyone.

We started toward the Baia, then spotted both Angelina and Jack on the *Calypso*. They were sitting in the cockpit and waved us over.

Jack leapt over the transom and rushed down the dock as we approached. "What the hell happened, bro?" He moved in close and patted me on the shoulder. "Sheriff said your truck was in an accident on the Seven Mile Bridge but that no one from the wreck was found. That Tony guy called a few times and said you'd been chased down by drug smugglers."

"So, he and Claire made it out of the Keys safely?"

Jack nodded. "Been staying in a hotel in Homestead and working with the police to help find Sam. You all right, bro? Your knuckles are bleeding, and your face looks like hell."

I looked down and saw that only my right hand was bleeding, and just a little. It must have been from decking that guy in the elevator.

"Thanks. But it would be a hell of a lot worse if Scott hadn't arrived."

"Black Venom?"

I nodded. "The bastards rammed us into the wall and flipped my truck over. Then they took us both and beat the crap out of me to get me to talk while I was tied to a chair. If Scott hadn't arrived when he did, I'd be a permanent resident of deep six right now."

We climbed aboard the *Calypso* and sat in the cockpit. Jack set two mugs in front of Scott and me and filled them with hot coffee.

"We tracked them down to the Playa Bonita Resort," Scott said.

"Any idea where they're going next?" Angelina asked.

I took a sip of the coffee, savoring the warmth and

flavor. After the couple of days I'd had, a good dose of caffeine was just what I needed.

"I may have a lead on that," I said, "but it isn't going to be easy. I've been informed that Black Venom has over fifty guys here in the Keys. That's a lot of tangos with Uzis for just the four of us."

Angelina set her mug on the table in front of her. "That's why I'm here. Nazari wants to meet you, Logan."

"Why would he want to meet me? And don't tell me he's just looking to get information about the treasure."

"No, it's not that. He wants to help. You see, he's also had trouble with Black Venom. After all, it was his men whose boat blew up at the ledge a few days ago."

I thought back to that day and how we'd watched the boat explode, then were chased by those who had done it. Nazari's men had died without being able to fight back as their boat was engulfed in an inferno of flames right before our eyes.

I downed the rest of my coffee and rose to my feet. "Having a guy like Nazari on our side might not be such a bad idea." I looked Angelina dead in the eye. "Do you trust him?"

She took a sip, then nodded.

"Okay, then. It's time I paid a visit to this man I've heard so much about."

After Jack locked up the *Calypso*, the four of us headed toward the Baia. I brought the roller bag with the C-4 inside with me and locked it inside the Baia before continuing alongside Angelina. Scott and Jack decided to stay to keep a lookout.

"What was in the bag?" Angelina asked as we walked down the dock.

"It's a gift from Black Venom," I replied nonchalantly, and her eyebrows shot to the top of her head. "Don't worry," I said. "I disarmed it."

We walked along the waterfront to the Key West Yacht Club next door, then stepped onto the dock and climbed aboard a Zodiac tied off near two other dinghies. Angelina fired up the outboard and piloted the small inflatable boat over the calm water toward Nazari's yacht. As we approached the yacht, I realized it was even larger and more luxurious than I'd originally thought. I gauged it to be over three hundred feet long, with a sleek steel hull, a helicopter pad on the bow, a swimming pool back aft, and five levels of sundecks. I'd never seen a yacht like it before in my life.

Angelina maneuvered the Zodiac alongside the yacht, and we idled for a second before a large rectangular section of the yacht's hull hinged outward, then opened up, revealing a large storage bay with a boat inside. It was a speedboat that matched the yacht and was probably about as long as the Baia. Turning the Zodiac and starting up the prop, Angelina accelerated us onto a padded platform, oriented us right in the middle, then killed the engine. The platform lifted us out of the water and then set the Zodiac down right beside the other boat. We climbed out, and Angelina led me through a door and into a luxurious hallway lined with fancy paintings.

We used an elevator to reach the main deck, where Angelina said Nazari was waiting for us. When we entered, he was sitting on a white leather couch, overlooking a row of windows that displayed 180-degree views of the ocean and the islands surrounding Key West. He was reading on a tablet but set it aside as we approached. I recognized his dark complexion and thinning white hair instantly from the few pictures I'd seen of him in the tabloids over the years. He looked to be in his early sixties, though if I remembered correctly, he was actually significantly older than that.

When Nazari stood, he smoothed his crisp white dress shirt and held out his hand, first to Angelina. "Angelina, my girl." He embraced her and kissed her cheek, then with a friendly gaze, held out his hand to me. "You must be Mr. Dodge. My name is Arian Nazari. It is a great pleasure to welcome you to my boat. Miss Fox has told me a lot about you. Please, make yourself at home."

I accepted his hand, then returned his smile. "Just Logan is fine, sir. And thank you for your hospitality."

"And you may call me Arian. Would either of you care for a drink? The tequila is from Jalisco. It's some of the best I've ever had." He pointed to the rusty liquid that half-filled a sparkling glass on the mahogany table in front of him.

"Sounds great," I replied, never one to turn down great liquor.

"Ah, very good." He grabbed his tablet. "Would you two please come with me to the lounge?"

Arian led us out a sliding glass door, where two rows of white leather couches sat beneath an upper deck overlooking the ocean. I was surprised to see three glasses already filled with ice and tequila situated on a marble table. Arian motioned for us to sit down across from him. I gripped one of the glasses and pushed back a sip, surprised at how strong yet smooth it was.

"Well?" Arian said, eyeing me questionably.

"Very good. Some of the best I've ever had, as well."

Arian smiled. "It's from Don Hector Martinez's private reserves. He gave me a few bottles as a gift just before he passed. He was a good man and a good friend." He set his glass on the table and cleared his throat. "But I did not invite you here to talk about tequila."

"No, I didn't think so."

Arian leaned back into the couch cushion. "As I'm sure you are well aware, I am an avid collector of ancient artifacts. My home in Dubai features some of my findings over the years. It is a passion of mine. So, naturally, I've always been interested in the story of Montezuma's gold. And my interest was amplified when I learned that a certain piece, that was once mine, was originally found off the coast of the Florida Keys. An Aztec medallion. You, of course, know the piece I speak of."

Though I'd only known him for a few minutes, Arian was nothing like how I'd expected him to be. I'd always taken pride in my ability to read people and judge their character. Based on my impression of him, and Angelina's recommendation, I decided to trust him. From my pocket I pulled out the gold medallion I'd found on the reef years before and set it on the table in front of Arian. "Scott told me—"

He waved me off. "I'm not upset about what

happened with Mr. Cooper. He won the relic fair and square." He grabbed the medallion and examined it, admiring its finely etched details. "It's magnificent."

"Yes, it is," I replied, then took another sip. "The rest of them are, as well."

Arian's eyebrows shot up, and his eyes darted to meet mine. "Are you telling me that you found the rest, Logan?"

I grinned. "Yes, I found the treasure with a professor friend of mine. But she's been taken, and now the guys who took her are gonna try and make off with all of the gold."

Arian paused a moment. "Black Venom."

I nodded.

He said, "I've had trouble with them before. One of my farms in Mexico was raided by Black Venom and burned to the ground three years ago. They murdered hundreds of workers and their families. And the poor people in that region would have starved to death had I not been able to send hundreds of trucks full of supplies. They are a wretched bunch, Logan. But judging by what I've read about you and what Angelina has told me, you are a man used to dealing with such people."

"I guess you could say I have a strong dislike of bullies. Always have."

Arian took another sip of tequila, then leaned back on the couch. "I like you, Logan. Tell me, what do you plan to do about Black Venom?"

"Tomorrow morning, we're going out to the ledge where we found the treasure. Black Venom has at least two yachts here in Key West and probably a salvage vessel by now, as well. We're gonna sneak up on them underwater, climb aboard, find Sam and get her to safety, then take them all out. It won't be pretty or easy, but it's all we have. I have two rebreathers we can use to swim undetected to their yachts. We plan to keep the Baia, which is my boat, and Jack's boat, the *Calypso*, far enough away from the ledge so they won't be spotted."

"How do you know they will be at the ledge tomorrow morning?"

"A young member of Black Venom told us. He's renounced them, and he's trying to escape that life."

"And you trust this stranger?"

"Yes, I do. When faced with death, a man's true character is revealed. I've seen him on the brink of death twice now, and I can tell you that he's not one of them. I'm gonna do everything I can to help him start a new life."

Arian listened intently to every word I said. He leaned forward, placed the tips of his fingers together, and rested his forearms against the table. "What can I do to help?"

"For starters, I'm assuming a man of your means has access to some advanced satellites. I need you to track the movements of Black Venom's boats tomorrow and have that information relayed to me. And"—I glanced at Angelina—"do you have a sniper rifle aboard?"

"The weapons locker is fully stocked," Angelina said, meaning that Arian not only had sniper rifles, but some of the most lethal ones in the world.

"Good. Ange can use that to provide cover. That way, you can keep your distance with this yacht. Anything under a quarter mile, and you'd probably draw too much attention and provoke Black Venom to attack."

"Are you certain that is all? I have sixteen highly trained professionals here in Key West. They can help you and Mr. Cooper."

"No, surprise is key. If too many go, we'll be spotted for sure. I'm not willing to risk so much, especially when we already know they have weapons like RPGs aboard."

"Very well, Logan. I shall do as you have requested."

"Thank you, Arian." I rose to my feet and set my empty glass on the table. "I appreciate you requesting to meet with me and your willingness to help us."

Arian walked with us out of the lounge and down the hall toward the elevator. A young guy wearing a tuxedo without the jacket and carrying two large plastic cases approached us. He handed the cases to Arian, then gave a quick bow of his head before turning and walking away.

Arian held the cases out to me. "These will help you in the morning, Logan."

I grabbed one and then the other, surprised by how heavy they were.

The elevator took Angelina and me down to the level where we'd left the Zodiac.

Once again, the side of the yacht opened up smoothly, and we eased the Zodiac into the water, then hopped aboard, setting the cases in between the two front bench seats.

Angelina started up the outboard, and when we were about halfway to shore, she turned to look at me. "You sure about this, Logan? We could always contact the authorities and see if they could help out."

"I'm not doing that." I didn't want the police or the Coast Guard to get involved, and it wasn't just because I hated dealing with the government. "I don't want to put their lives at risk," I said.

Seeing that I couldn't be persuaded, Angelina dropped the subject, and we didn't say a word to each other until we were back at the dock. She pulled up just down from the Baia and dropped me off.

"We'll be in contact in the morning," she said. "We'll use Arian's satellites to track them, and I'll relay their positions to you. Once you're at the site, I'll be ready with my sniper to provide cover. Just don't do anything stupid, Logan . . . like get yourself killed."

I gave her a kiss on the cheek before she fired up the engine and disappeared around the entrance to the harbor. My dive watch showed that it was just past twenty-two hundred. The dock was mostly quiet as I approached the Baia, aside from a few distant neighbors enjoying the calm night air and listening to Pirate Radio.

Jack and Scott were sitting in the cockpit of my boat. They had the grill fired up, and I could smell the fresh fish and corn on the cob.

"How'd it go?" Scott asked.

"Good. Anyone come near the boat?"

Scott was cleaning his Glock, and Jack was holding a pair of tongs and rotating the fish as he dabbed Swamp Sauce over it.

They both shook their heads.

"No one at all," Scott replied. "What's in the cases?"

I headed for the steps down into the saloon. "Do me a favor and kill the flames and shut the grill for a minute, will you, Jack? We gotta talk about the plan for the morning."

Jack plated the food but kept it covered beneath a metal lid so it would stay warm, then they followed me down into the saloon. I set the two cases on the deck beside the dining table. Grabbing a chart of Key West and its surrounding islands, I unrolled it and spread it out over the table, using a few mugs and a lamp to hold it in place. After briefly looking it over, I looked up at Scott and Jack, who were eyeing me skeptically.

I grabbed one of the cases and smiled after unclasping the hinges and lifting up the lid. "Looks like Nazari just made this a hell of a lot easier," I said, eyeing a brand-new, top-of-the-line Aquanaut Pro Seascooter.

"Damn," Jack said. "That's an X Series. She'll pull you through the water at seven knots, bro. And this model has the expanded battery, so you're looking at well over an hour of operating time."

"The other one's for you," I said to Scott, who was eyeing the other case on the deck. "Using these, we'll be able to sneak up on Black Venom from a few miles away."

I moved into the main cabin, opened my closet, and pulled out two Draeger rebreathers. Back in the saloon, I set them on one of the padded seats beside the table. "I ordered these a while back, and they just arrived yesterday. They're military-grade, almost identical to the ones we used back in the SEALs."

The closed-circuit breathing systems meant no

noisy bubbles, which would give us the best chance of reaching Black Venom's boats undetected.

"That kid said Black Venom had more than fifty guys here in Key West," Scott said. "It's a safe bet that most of them will be at the ledge in the morning, and they'll be spread out over multiple boats. Even if we do reach them without being seen, there's no way we can engage that many on our own. Even the two of us."

"We'll have backup," I said. "Ange will be providing cover from Nazari's yacht."

"And I can be close by, bro," Jack said. "I'll take the Baia. She's faster than anything else cruising the Keys. If you need backup, I could be there within minutes, armed and ready."

"We also need to remember that this is more of a rescue mission than anything else. Once we find Sam and get her off whichever boat she's on, we can just blow all of their boats to pieces." I grabbed the black roller bag resting against the kitchen counter. Opening the flap revealed the stacks of C-4 Black Venom had rigged to blow up in the Playa Bonita Resort. "These assholes have already given us just what we need to send them and their boats burning into the drink."

I grabbed the stacks of C-4 and set them on the table, along with the firing mechanism. I knew it wouldn't be difficult to separate the one bomb they'd rigged into three separate smaller bombs. That way, we'd be able to destroy multiple boats at the same time. Fortunately, Black Venom had decided to use C-4, which is waterproof, so Scott and I would be able to swim them over and attach them to the hulls, no problem.

We spent five more minutes talking about our plan for the following morning, using the chart spread out over the table to plot out exactly how we were going to approach Neptune's Table. Then we migrated back out to the cockpit, where we lounged and enjoyed the food Jack had prepared, along with a few cold ones to take the edge off. I polished off two Coronas with lime and downed three plates of fish, not realizing how hungry I was after not eating all day.

When we finished eating, we went back into the saloon, and I worked on disassembling the bomb while Scott checked our equipment and Jack perused the chart and a handheld GPS.

In less than an hour, I'd finished and had three separate bombs, all with their own firing mechanisms that would be triggered using a common switch. When it comes to bombs, it's always best to keep it simple. Each of the bombs would be set off by a simple battery in a waterproof housing, which, when activated, would initiate the blasting cap and detonate the C-4.

Unable to head to a store for extra parts, I took apart a few of the less useful components from the cockpit control console, including a toggle switch, complete with its waterproof housing. What I especially liked about the switch was that it had a plastic cover, which would prevent me from accidentally setting off the bombs while Scott and I swam them through the water. I planned to simply replace the switch in the future when I had a little more time on my side.

In order to attach the C-4 to the hulls of Black

Venom's boats, Jack said he had an idea and headed over to the *Calypso*, appearing a few minutes later with a plastic box in his hands. It contained rubber suction cups with plastic handles that he'd used before to stabilize himself underwater while cleaning grime off the *Calypso*'s hull. When pulled back, the suction created a vacuum that held them in place to a flat surface. We pulled a MacGyver and attached one suction cup to each of the bombs, then stowed them inside a black duffle bag.

Before hitting the sack, we set all of our equipment aside, including the masks, fins, dive knives, snorkels, flashlights, and small tanks of Spare Air. Scott gave the okay on the rebreathers, saying they looked to be in perfect order, and we both tested the sea scooters and made sure they were both fully charged. We knew we wouldn't have much time in the morning to prepare, so we did everything we could the night before. In my experience, when it comes to warfare, there's no such thing as overpreparation. Planning out and being ready for the worst had saved my life countless times, and it was a habit I couldn't shake even if I wanted to.

It was just past eleven when I turned off the cockpit lights and turned on the security system. We didn't know when we'd leave in the morning, but we knew it would probably be before sunrise. Despite wanting to get as much sleep as we could, we decided it was best that we stationed a lookout just in case Black Venom tried anything in the middle of the night.

I took the first one from twenty-three thirty until zero one thirty, while Jack and Scott hit the sack in

263

the Baia's two guest beds. I brewed some coffee and sat on the sunbed with my Sig in hand, watching the goings-on at the marina. Gus had most of the dock lights shut off at twenty-one hundred every night, so I used my night-vision monocular to scan the docks and look over the parking lot. By midnight, it was quiet enough that all I could hear was the slow shifting of the docks and the ripples from the occasional fish snacking on bugs.

At zero one twenty, I heard footsteps coming from inside the Baia, then watched as the door swung open and Scott appeared holding a mug of steaming liquid in one hand and his Glock in the other. He looked like he'd been up for hours, showing no signs of grogginess—a trait that forms after spending years doing what we did while in the SEALs on little or no sleep. He stood beside the sunbed and took a long look around before taking a sip of his coffee.

"All quiet on the western front," I said.

He sat down beside me. "Looks like there's a storm blowing in."

The sky above the open ocean was darker in some parts than in others, indicating patches of rolling clouds.

"Good thing you don't believe in omens," I said.

"Right."

"Here." I handed him the night-vision monocular. "I'll see you bright and early in the morning."

I stepped down into the saloon, shutting the door behind me, then made my way into the main cabin. With my Sig and cellphone on the nightstand beside me, I sprawled out on the bed and fell instantly asleep.

TWENTY-NINE

I woke up the following morning to the sound of my phone, and tilting the screen toward me, saw that I'd received a message from Angelina. She informed me that Black Venom had a yacht, a large salvage vessel, and three smaller boats on the move out of a private marina on Stock Island, just east of Key West. She wrote that they had left at zero four hundred and were making wake for the ledge. It was almost zero five hundred, which meant their small fleet would soon be reaching Neptune's Table.

I stepped into the saloon and heard the unmistakable sounds of raindrops splashing on the topside of the Baia. I grabbed a rain slicker from the closet, slid it over my shirt, and zipped it up before stepping out into the cockpit.

Jack was hunkered down on one of the white-cushioned seats, his body hunched back, and his eyes gazing out over the marina. He held a Navy coffee mug in one hand and his compact Desert Eagle in the other. "Storm's gonna get worse. Gonna be hell out there on the water all day."

"Did you see anything?"

He shook his head, then set the mug on a cork coaster resting on the table.

I gazed out over the marina, watching the rain fall from the black clouds swarming overhead. The wind had picked up, blowing in gusts, rattling deck lines, and flapping the loose sails of the catamaran moored beside us.

"It's time to go," I said before heading back below deck.

Scott was already up and filling his mug with coffee when I entered. I told both him and Jack what Angelina had said in her message, and we made quick preparations to get the Baia underway.

I started up the engine while Jack untied the lines, disconnected the shore power cables, and removed and capped the water lines. The rain picked up as we cruised out of the marina and toward the heart of the dark clouds above. When we were about to reach the end of the no-wake zone, I noticed an unusually large white buoy floating directly in front of us. As I motored closer to it, I saw black letters painted on its side.

"What the hell is that?" Scott said, peering through the rain-splattered windscreen. He grabbed the pair of binos from the locker beside the console.

"You're not allowed to drop pots here," Jack said. "Must be a mainlander."

Scott shook his head, then eased the binos down to

his side. "I don't think it's a crab pot." He looked at me gravely and handed me the binos.

I eased back on the throttles as we got within a few hundred feet of the buoy, then took a look. Written clearly on the side of the buoy in what looked like black spray paint was a name. My name. I stared at it in awe for a moment, wondering what it could mean, then I noticed something metallic in the water below it.

"Take the wheel, will you, Jack?" After he grabbed it with one hand, I stepped around the cockpit, climbing up onto the bow. "Ease her beside the buoy."

Jack brought the bow right up to the buoy, and I peered over the starboard side, into the water below. The heavy rain and the choppy surface made it difficult to see, but I could tell there was something down there. I looked up and saw that Scott had climbed onto the bow and was looking down, as well. "Toss me a mask," I said while I slid off my rain slicker and dropped it in the cockpit.

Jack threw me a clear Cressi dive mask. I pulled off my T-shirt, strapped the mask over my eyes and nose, then hurled my body over the side, splashing into the water headfirst. As soon as I broke through the surface, I saw the body of a man anchored to the bottom by a metal chain. I dove down a few strokes, and upon seeing the man's face clearly, realized that it was Daniel. I didn't know how long he'd been there, but judging from the condition of his body, it hadn't been more than a couple of hours. The chains were shackled around his ankles so tight that there was no way I'd be getting them loose. I let out a little air and kicked for the surface.

Rain and choppy water returned as I broke up from under the ocean. Scott was standing at the bow, leaning over the side and staring at me while Jack kept the Baia as steady as possible.

"What is it?" Scott asked, no doubt noticing the grim look on my face.

I stroked over to the swim platform, then climbed onto the deck. "You remember that guy from the alley last night? Well, he's dead now."

"The one who told you guys where Black Venom would be this morning?" Jack asked.

I nodded while grabbing a towel and drying off. "Great. So, now they know we're coming."

"We're just gonna have to start even farther away, that's all." I moved over to the table, opened my laptop, and brought up satellite imagery of the water around Neptune's Table.

Scott stepped down, standing beside me as I continued.

"They'll be on the lookout for us. Hell, they might even have a few of their boats doing tours around them, so we're gonna have to move quickly." I reviewed the map for a moment, then pointed at the location I knew would be best. "Here."

Jack left the engine in neutral and stepped over to the table. "Mooney Harbor Key? That's over six miles from the table, bro."

"It's our best bet. You can pull us up to the windward side of the island, using it as cover as we dive into the water, then you can cruise away."

"We've got at least three hours on the rebreathers," Scott said, "and the sea scooters have an hour of battery charge when operating full speed. At that speed, we should reach the bank in well under an hour, though."

A boom of thunder roared over the surface of the water, followed by a flash of lightning. The rain had picked up even more and was now a full-fledged tropical storm.

I moved back over to the cockpit and gripped the wheel, then eased the throttle forward.

Jack's eyes were wide, and he glanced at the buoy. "You're just gonna leave him down there?"

"We have no choice right now," I said. "He's dead, and if we don't get to that treasure soon, they're going to kill Sam, as well."

Since we were now a good two hundred feet clear of the entrance into the harbor and the no-wake zone, I pushed the throttles forward, roaring the engines to life and accelerating us like a racing boat over the water. Within a few seconds, I had her up on plane, and even with the whitecaps on the surface, I was able to keep her steady at thirty knots.

The wind howled past the boat, and sheets of rain slammed into the windscreen. Looking down at my phone, which was resting in a dashboard compartment, I saw that I'd received two messages from Angelina. The first said that Black Venom had reached the table, and I saw that she'd sent it twelve minutes earlier. The second message said that based on satellite images they had of its movement, they believed Sam was being kept on the yacht. Though with the storm, Angelina said they were only able to get a quick look at the boat before it vanished behind black clouds, so they weren't a hundred percent certain she was there.

I took us into the Gulf through the Northwest Channel, keeping north to avoid Black Venom and then approach them from a distance. Forty-five minutes after pulling out of the harbor in Key West, I eased the throttles as we approached the eight islands that formed the Marquesas Keys.

"I got it," Jack said, taking the wheel. "You guys gear up."

Scott and Jack had already brought all the gear we would need out onto the deck. I grabbed the binoculars and took a quick look around.

After seeing we were the only ones nearby, I slid into my thin, 3mm wetsuit and strapped my dive knife around my leg, then secured my holster and Sig around my hip and slipped into my booties. After bringing my fins and the duffle bag with the bombs inside over to the swim platform, I donned the rebreather gear. Scott handed me a tank of Spare Air and a waterproof walkie-talkie. I unzipped a pocket in my rebreather and set them both inside, right next to the detonator switch. Jack killed the throttles when we were within a few hundred feet from the shore of Mooney Harbor Key.

I looked over the stern of the boat and could see shallow reefs beside us. "Jack, send a message to Angelina. My phone's on the dash. Let her know when we're in the water, and tell her we're approximately forty-five minutes out. Keep your radio close. We'll call you if we need backup."

Jack nodded as he helped Scott with his gear, then checked both of us over, making sure we hadn't messed anything up when donning our equipment and verifying that we were properly weighted. He gave us a thumbs-up, and I rinsed my mask so it wouldn't fog, and then strapped it over my face.

Turning to Scott, I said, "Ange said they think Sam's on the yacht. That's where we're heading first."

We grabbed each other's forearms and let out a loud hooyah, taking us back to our days in the Navy. I returned Jack's gesture, giving him a thumbs-up, then pumped my fist as I took a big step into the white-capped water.

The tropical storm with its heavy rains, roaring thunder, and howling winds went silent in an instant as I broke through the thrashing surface. I rose back up for a moment, grabbing hold of the sea scooter Jack handed me and the duffle bag, then gave the all-good signal and descended toward the bottom of the ocean.

Scott followed closely behind, and we met up under the bow of the Baia, about fifteen feet down beside a shallow reef. Scott held out a waterproof GPS in front of him and indicated where the bank was in relation to our current location. I was confident enough in my knowledge of the area around Mooney Harbor Key, and the water between it and Neptune's Table, but I was still glad Scott had brought it just in case.

I drew my gaze forward, planning out the first stage of our course toward the ledge, then glanced over at Scott as I clipped the sea scooter's tether to my chest and switched it on. He fired his up, and we both leveled out our bodies and held our sea scooter in front of us while engaging the propellers. I was surprised by the power and acceleration as we shot through the water faster than Michael Phelps freestyling toward a gold medal on the final lap.

The reefs and marine life went past us in a colorful blur as we made quick work around Mooney Harbor Key, using occasional kicks of our fins and smooth rotations of the scooter to ease around shallower underwater features. It was then a straight shot south to the table, and I told Jack that judging by our speed of about seven and a half knots with the kicks of our fins, we would reach it in less than the forty-five minutes.

Gazing toward the surface, I saw that the rains hadn't let up. I heard what I thought was a distant roar of thunder, but as we drew nearer to our destination, I realized it wasn't thunder. I eased back on the throttle, and Scott did the same. The loud rumbling sound hadn't come from above us; it had come from in front of us. Judging by the look on Scott's face, which I could see even behind his mask, he'd heard it, too. Holding his right hand up in the water between us, he curled it into a tight fist, then spread out his fingers rapidly. It wasn't an official diving signal, but I instantly knew what he meant. There were explosions coming from underwater near Neptune's Table. Black Venom was trying to blow their way to the treasure.

THIRTY

Scott and I slowed our pace, stopping every couple hundred feet until we were within a quarter mile of the shelf. We took cover behind a patch of coral the size of a school bus and waited for another explosion. After five minutes, we felt it—a powerful pressure change followed by a distant rumble that shook the seafloor around us. We stuck to our cover to avoid the brunt of the blast wave, knowing that underwater explosions can wreak havoc on the human body. When the force from the blast dissipated, I glanced over at Scott, who gave me a thumbs-up.

We pushed onward cautiously, sticking to cover as best as we could. Before we'd traveled a hundred feet toward the table from our hiding place, Scott pointed up at the surface and slowed his scooter to a stop. I looked to where he was pointing and saw the dark hull of a small boat cruising quickly overhead. We pressed up against an edge of dark Staghorn coral and kept perfectly still. The hull was in and out of sight in an instant, leaving behind only a long-spreading wake. I glanced at my dive watch and saw that we were only twenty-three feet below the surface. If it had been a clear day and lighter outside, they would've been able to spot us pretty easily. Turned out, we were right about them having at least one of their boats on patrol around the site.

Scott pointed forward, and I started up my propeller. Within just a few short minutes, we spotted more hulls floating on the surface three hundred feet in front of us. Two were massive, which meant they were the yacht and the salvage vessel Angelina had messaged me about. The third hull, and the only other one in sight, was much smaller, roughly the same size as the one that had cruised over our heads a few minutes prior.

We noticed movement beneath the waves, as well, and upon moving closer, we realized they had divers in the water descending toward the ledge. We spotted two of them and saw that they were using regular scuba equipment, making it easy to spot their large tanks and their exhalations bubbling up to the surface. Scott and I moved in slowly, keeping between the reefs that circled around the shelf. We left the sea scooters under a large spread of lettuce coral. They operated quietly, but we no longer needed to travel a long distance, and we didn't want to risk the sound of the propellers giving away our position as we snuck up on the two unsuspecting divers.

There was still a cloudy haze of sediment in the water surrounding the site from the explosions. It made the visibility worse than it would usually be, but also provided us with ample cover as we moved in closer. The table had been severely disfigured, now having a large crater right in its center. Pieces of rock lay spread out around it, like the aftermath of a volcanic eruption. What just hours prior had been one of the most pristine and untouched marine life habitats in all of the Keys, now resembled a battlefield barraged by artillery fire. There was no movement anywhere aside from the two divers. All marine life had vanished from the area, either being killed or scared off by the rapid changes in pressure.

As we moved within a hundred feet of the ledge, I looked down and saw a gold artifact resting on the seafloor. After examining it for a moment, I saw that it was a cuff bracelet with markings etched along its surface. I held it out for Scott to look at, but he just pointed in front of us at the sediment clearing around us. Hundreds of pieces of gold Aztec jewelry rested in the sand and on pieces of coral. They'd used too many explosives, and as a result, launched a good portion of the treasure out of the cave.

We kept hidden in the shadows as the two divers lowered a metal container into the crater in the center of the shelf. It was being lowered by a chain that rose up to the surface at the stern of the salvage vessel. When the two divers disappeared from view, Scott and I moved in. We left the bag of C-4 near the rim of the bank and swam stealthily toward the divers.

The closest diver spotted me just as I was about to grab him. He reached for the speargun strapped to his hip, but I gave two quick kicks of my fins, propelling myself into him and pushing the speargun out of his hand. Forcing the large man around, I grabbed hold of him from behind and locked my arm around his neck.

The other diver froze when he glanced up at me, then let out a mass of bubbles from his regulator and reached for the dive knife strapped to his leg. Scott pounced on him from behind, grabbing him in a strong sleeper hold and pulling his body back. I tightened my grip on the guy locked in my arms and ripped out his second-stage as he tried to struggle free. After about ten seconds, he lost consciousness, and his body went limp. My initial instinct was to finish the guy with my dive knife, but I knew that a cloud of blood could let the others know they were under attack. Also, blood in the water would attract every shark within a mile, like an old triangle bell signaling that dinner was ready.

With both of the divers down for the count, we vented all of the air from their BCDs and left their bodies inside the cave. Then we swam quickly to the top of the shelf, grabbed the duffle bag, and kicked toward the bottom of the boats. Keeping an eye out for any other divers, we attached the explosives to the hulls using the suction cups we'd rigged the night before. We attached one to the yacht and two to the salvage vessel, which was larger and had a much stronger hull than the yacht. We made sure to attach them to the middle of the keels, where the most damage could be done. In naval warfare, when a torpedo is fired at an enemy vessel, its target is the middle of the keel so that the explosion acts like a hinge and the ship cracks due to its own weight. With a ship's hull cracked in two, it doesn't take long for it to sink to a watery grave.

Once the explosives were secure, we finned back

to the seafloor, took in a deep breath, then slipped out of our rebreather gear and stashed it and our fins under a large growth of elkhorn coral. I grabbed the detonator from the rebreather pocket along with the waterproof radio. We didn't know how long it would be before the guys topside sent another diver down to investigate what was happening, so we kicked to the surface in a hurry, breathing out as we ascended.

Since Angelina was confident Sam was being kept on the yacht, we swam to its hull and surfaced along its port side. Poking our heads out of the water just enough for our masks to break the choppy surface, we took a quick look around before inhaling and dropping back down beneath the waves. The rain had died off, leaving only a soft drizzle, but the wind was still hollering with the same intensity. I counted eight guys topside on the salvage vessel just a hundred feet off the bow of the yacht. Two were donning scuba gear and looking over the railing toward the table below. The third and smaller boat was out of our view, cruising on the other side of the yacht.

Once back underwater, we kicked for the stern, Scott toward the starboard side and me toward the port side. Rising out of the water, we saw two guys standing on the swim platform. One of them was puffing on a cigarette and wearing a Hawaiian-style button-up that revealed the tattoos on his chest and arms. The other wore a white polo shirt and was staring intently at the screen of his smartphone. Both had pistols holstered to their waists, which was unfortunate for them. If they'd had them in their hands, they'd have at least had a small fighting chance.

Seeing no one on the deck above looking down and that the smaller boat was out of view, Scott and I rose out of the water in unison. I lunged for Hawaiian shirt guy, who didn't realize what was happening until I had him flat on the deck. I bashed my elbow into his temple, knocking him unconscious. Scott had Polo shirt down for the count, as well.

We bounded up the steps toward an open patio, then took cover on the outboard as I reached for the radio in my pocket. I informed Jack that we were on the yacht and told him to relay our position to Angelina so she could provide cover if necessary. Just as I stashed the radio back on my hip, a guy in dark sunglasses and a black cut-off shirt moved toward our position. He held a stockless AK-47 in his hands, and upon seeing us, started to raise it to shoulder height. Before he could level it, I slid my dive knife from its sheath and threw a frozen rope. The blade stabbed right through the guy's neck, causing him to gag as he twisted and fell facedown onto the fiberglass.

We darted to his position, making sure he was done for, and looked around for others. A glass door in front of us led into a beautiful lounge, but we didn't see any movement inside. Hearing footsteps coming from the level above us, we hit the staircase leading up the port side of the yacht. Before reaching the top step, I unholstered my Sig and screwed the silencer onto the end of the barrel. Glancing back at Scott, I saw that he'd done the same.

We moved in. Three guys were sitting around a table on the upper-level patio. They were glued to laptop monitors and barking orders over their radios, most likely to the guys on the salvage vessel. It was clear they knew something was going on since they'd lost contact with their divers. Uzis and revolvers rested on the table in between the laptops.

Rising from our positions, we put a few rounds through each of their chests, sending them to the deck before they knew what was happening. We moved toward the sliding glass door leading into another lounge, but before we could sneak in, we were caught off guard by the sound of automatic bullets rattling against the side of the yacht beside us. Dropping flat onto the deck, we rolled behind a nearby hot tub for cover and tried to get our bearings on where the rounds were coming from.

I peeked over the side of the yacht and saw the center-console had pulled up alongside the starboard side. Two guys were standing alongside the guy manning the helm, eyeing our position, and aiming two submachine guns our way. The large outboards roared to life as the boat cruised around the stern of the yacht, then turned to head straight for the port side. Scott and I waited for them to stop firing, then stood up in unison, aimed our handguns, and rained hot lead down on the three men. The pilot fell forward, his hand slipping against the throttles and pushing them all the way up. The huge engines screamed, launching the center-console through the water like a dragster at the starting line. It crashed into the port side of the yacht, causing the deck to rumble beneath our feet as the screeching collision of the two fiberglass hulls resounded in the air.

Scott and I struggled to get to our feet as the yacht swayed back and forth. We strode back toward the inside lounge, but before we passed the table, a

Samoan guy with his arms and half of his face covered in artistic tattoos cut us off. He'd sprinted up the stairs from the deck below, and before I could aim my Sig at him, he tackled me to the ground, knocking my pistol out of my hand. Every trace of air exploded from my lungs in an instant as the giant hulk of a man fell on top of me. It felt like I'd been hit by a freight train, and glimmering stars soared around my head as the guy threw a hard right square into my face. My vision a blurry haze, I barely made out Scott behind the guy on top of me, fighting off a second adversary I hadn't seen before.

Bringing myself back into the moment and taking a split second to get my bearings, I diverted Samoan guy's fist as he tried to throw a second punch. His fist slammed into the deck with a loud crack less than an inch from my ear, and I retaliated by shoving my right palm as hard as I could up into his nose. There was a loud crunch as I broke the fragile bones and blood flowed from his nostrils like a river. Using all of my strength, I dug my heels into the deck and pushed my hands into his huge chest, forcing the three-hundred-pound man off of me.

He rolled onto the deck but swiftly jumped to his feet. I squared off about ten feet away from him as he growled, wiped the blood from his face, and spat a spray of dark red over his shoulder. He lunged toward me and reared back his fist, preparing to hit me with a strong hook. I rolled to the side and kicked him in the shin, causing him to tumble and collapse onto the deck beside the glass door. I glanced over at Scott and watched as he grabbed his man by the collar of his gray rain slicker and threw him over the side of the yacht, his body slamming into the deck below, then splashing into the water. I turned back to Samoan Guy and darted toward him as he rose sluggishly to his feet. Leaping high into the air, I grabbed ahold of the eave over my head and swung my body, striking my heels into the center of his chest. His body flew backward, crashing through the door and sending shards of broken glass in all directions.

Grabbing my Sig from the deck, I moved into the upper-level saloon alongside Scott, stepping over Samoan guy as he lay unconscious in a pool of blood and broken glass. The saloon was empty and quiet, but we could hear yelling and the shuffling of feet coming from other levels.

A steaming mug of coffee was sitting on the dash in front of the captain's chair, indicating that someone had been there recently. I froze as I heard the unmistakable sound of a woman screaming for help, her voice rising above the howling wind and rain outside.

It was Sam.

THIRTY-ONE

Before I could look to Scott, a massive black guy appeared out of nowhere, swinging an ax toward my face. I flexed my body backward, whipping my head back in a move from *The Matrix* as the steel blade cut through the air just inches from my face. It struck one of the large monitors with a loud crash, causing sparks to fly as the glass cracked to pieces. Using one hand, the man ripped the ax free in a quick jerk.

Scott fired off one 9mm round into his chest before being grabbed and thrown back to the deck by a second guy. It barely affected the big guy, who snapped a roundhouse into my side. It knocked me into the control panel, and he grabbed my wrist and jammed my right hand into the dashboard, causing my Sig to slide up against the windscreen. He hurled his fists into the side of my head, then grabbed me in a sleeper hold. I hit him with my elbows and jerked my head back into his face, but nothing loosened his grip around my neck.

Forcing my chin into my chest, I protected my windpipe as best as I could, but I could still feel consciousness slipping away. Through the windscreen, I saw two figures walking forward to the end of the foredeck. Although rain danced down the glass, I knew it was Sam, and she was being led by Marco, who had a pistol pressed against her back. The guy's grip tightened even more around my neck, and I knew I only had a few seconds left.

I searched frantically for my Sig, but it was just out of my reach. Reaching behind me, I felt a wooden handle and gripped the ax with all my strength. In one quick motion, I reared it back and muscled it down, flicking my wrist and stabbing the blade into the guy's back. He let out a loud moan and loosened his grip just enough for me to thrust his forearms aside and slip free.

Turning around, I hit him with a strong uppercut square into his jaw, which caused his muscular body to fly backward into the control chair. I snapped my head sideways as two more men ran into the cockpit from the lounge, one carrying an Uzi and the other a large revolver. On the other side of the cockpit, Scott was finishing off his man, unaware of the two approaching guys. I stretched out over the dashboard and grabbed my Sig with my fingertips, clasped it with my palm, whipped my body around, and fired off round after round into the two guys just as they were about to make Scott a human cheese grater.

When they were down, I took aim at the burly black guy, who was now barreling toward me and yelling wildly. I only managed to fire off one round before he plowed into me like an NFL linebacker, tackling me backward and sending us both hurtling through the windscreen. It shattered as we broke through the glass and tumbled toward the bow, rain drizzling over us and making the bow slippery as hell. Just as we were about to reach the deck, I ripped free of his grasp and kicked him in the face as hard as I could. His body flew backward, and he lost balance. His calves slammed into the bow rail, and his momentum forced his body to somersault over the edge. All I saw was his shoes before he disappeared into the gray and splashed into the water below.

I tumbled a few more times, then reached for my Sig, which was sliding down the slick fiberglass beside me. Gripping it in my left hand, I landed on the deck feetfirst and took aim toward the forward end of the yacht. Marco was standing at the end of the bow, his Luger pressed against Sam's neck. His arms were wrapped around her body, holding her so tight that her every breath appeared to be a struggle. Tears flooded her eyes, and her black hair ruffled in the wind as she stared at me.

"Drop the fucking gun!" Marco said, his breathing quick and erratic.

Sam shook her head, trying to get me to hold on to the only bargaining chip I had. I thought about taking the shot, but Marco had Sam positioned directly in front of him, giving me only a few inches to work with. I only had one round left in the chamber, and I wouldn't have been able to deliver a fatal shot, which meant he'd send a bullet through Sam's head without skipping a beat.

Staring at Marco, I loosened my grip, and my Sig

slid out of my hand, rattling onto the deck at my feet.

"You should never have fucked with me," Marco said. Pulling the Luger away from Sam's neck, he aimed it straight at me with a shaking hand. "You and that asshole brought this upon yourselves. I told you that you had no idea who you were messing with. And now you will see what Black Venom is capable of." He glared at me, pulled Sam in tighter, then took a step toward the bow rail. I noticed a cut above his left eye and a trail of blood flowing down his cheek, indicating Sam must have landed an elbow while he was moving her.

I gritted my teeth. "Let her go."

Marco shook his head. "You don't get it, do you? She's dead, Logan. Along with you, Scott, and all of your little friends here in the Keys." He glanced over at the salvage vessel, where three men stood holding rifles against their shoulders and staring straight at us. "Once we've smuggled this gold out of here, there's gonna be a bloodbath in the Keys. Anyone you've ever associated with will be murdered. It's a pity you won't be able to live with that on your conscience."

Gripping the Luger tighter, he suddenly pulled the trigger, sending a surge of hot lead through the side of my chest. I yelled out violently as pain radiated through my body. Placing my hand against the wound, I dropped down to one knee and winced as I felt the bullet lodged under my skin. Blood trickled out from the hole in my wetsuit, dripping onto the white deck at my feet.

Marco wore an evil grin as he kept the Luger aimed at my head. Sam struggled to break free, but he gripped her even tighter. Time slowed down, and I was about to make a last-ditch effort and reach for my Sig, when Marco's head suddenly exploded in a gory plume of blood.

A loud crack echoed across the water as Marco's body collapsed to the deck. I sprang forth from my position before the report of the high-caliber rifle died, ignoring the pain in my chest, and launching my body toward Sam and wrapping my arms around her. My momentum hurled us both over the side of the yacht, and we spun in a freefall toward the white-capped ocean.

As we splashed through the surface, I held on tight to Sam, kicking as hard as I could and forcing us deeper as bullets torpedoed from the surface, breaking apart before making contact with our bodies. I swam for the elkhorn coral, reached underneath it, and retrieved the Spare Air from the rebreather for Sam. She grabbed it frantically, let out all of the air from her lungs, and took in a few deep breaths before calming down.

Sam handed the Spare Air back to me and gave me a thumbs-up just as Scott broke through the surface over our heads. He was swimming for the bottom as fast as he could. When he reached Sam and me, we kicked a few hundred feet away from the yacht and took cover inside the crater in the middle of the ledge. I pulled the detonator from my pocket, flipped open the plastic cover, and flicked the switch. Three deafening booms rumbled from overhead, and we heard the sounds of both the yacht and the salvage vessel's hulls cracking into pieces. Flames consumed both boats, and they sank to the bottom of the ocean within minutes.

I handed the Spare Air back to Sam, and she took another deep breath as her eyes met mine. Wrapping my arms around her, I brought her body in close, holding her tight as we floated beside the colorful reefs and the underwater shelf littered with gold Aztec artifacts.

EPILOGUE

Key West
One Week Later

"You don't look so bad anymore, bro," Jack said, smiling at me as he surveyed my face. He held out a glass of sparkling champagne. "Have a drink. It's from Nazari's cellar, and boy, is it delicious."

"Thanks," I said, grabbing the glass from his hand.

My body still felt like hell, even a week after the 9mm bullet had been lodged into the side of my chest. I had bruises all over my body and a ringing in my left ear from the Samoan's punch to my head. But my body was healing itself, and I knew that in a few more weeks I'd be feeling right as rain. I'd gone to the hospital after the incident, just to take care of the gunshot wound and to get a quick MRI. I'd never liked hospitals much, and I'd spent enough time injured in the middle of nowhere to tend to my own

288

wounds well enough, but Sam, stubborn as she was, had insisted that I go.

I walked alongside Jack through the sliding glass doors on the second level of Salty Pete's. The outside patio was decorated with white lights, and the cedar-planked deck was covered with tables and chairs. A large group of locals had assembled, dressed in their finest island clothing, and the sound of the Marshall Tucker Band's "Can't You See?" filled the establishment. Scott joined us, and we moved toward the center of the patio, where everyone was gathered around Nazari, who was dressed to the nines, as he stood in front of an object covered with a blue sheet.

"Logan," he said as he wrapped an arm around me. "You have arrived just in time. I was just discussing with Scottie the particulars about what we plan to do with the treasure." Raising his voice, he spoke to the entire group. "The treasure will be returned to the people of Mexico." He gave a slight bow of his head. "It is, after all, rightfully theirs. And such a vast sum will do a great deal to combat their poverty. I have no doubt that millions of impoverished people will have their lives changed for the better by this money, and they all have you to thank for it." He motioned toward the group as he lifted his glass high into the air. "To the Aztec treasure. And to those who made sure it never fell into the wrong hands."

I raised my glass, then chimed it against the glasses of those standing around me before taking a sip. I quickly threw back half of the champagne, savoring the flavor. With Scott's help, Nazari lifted the sheet covering the object in the middle of the cluster of people, revealing a solid gold statue of

Montezuma. The group cheered and took more drinks of champagne while admiring the immaculate piece of art.

"Look who's finally on his feet," Angelina said as she approached me from the other side of the gold statue. "I thought you weren't about hospitals."

"I'm not." I raised my glass and chimed it against hers. "To a hell of a shot."

Angelina had shot Marco in the head with a rifle from three hundred yards away while lying on the bow of Nazari's yacht. Given the conditions of the sea, the time of day, and the fact that she and her target were on separate yachts, it was the most impressive shot I'd ever witnessed. Then there was the fact that, with Sam being held in the way, she'd only had a target a few inches wide. Once Marco was down, it wasn't hard for Angelina to pick off a few more cartel while we jumped into the water. After the explosions took out both boats, Jack had moved in with the Baia to pick us up and take out the few cartel who were still alive.

We took a sip of our champagne, and I heard her phone vibrating in her pocket. She checked the screen, then slid it back where it was.

"Leaving so soon?" I said.

"You know I'd love to stay and party, but I have some very important business to take care of."

"Oh, really?" I said, my interest piqued. "Anyone I know?"

"I'd tell you, but then I'd have to kill you, Captain Dodge. What about you? I'm sure you've been offered that gig in North Africa."

"I think I'm gonna stay and try out the conch

290

lifestyle a little longer. See how it fits."

She chuckled, then downed the rest of her champagne. Moving in close enough for me to smell her intoxicating perfume, she kissed me on the cheek. "You know who to call if you're ever looking for excitement. Just don't get too soft living here." She patted my stomach. "Your stock will go down like that." She snapped her fingers to emphasize her words, then smirked, batted her eyes, and walked inside.

A moment later, Pete appeared, carrying a platter of fresh fish straight from the grill. I ate alongside Scott, Jack, and Nazari, and we talked about everything from the legend of the Aztec treasure to the attack Scott and I had made on the cartel at Neptune's Table.

"I've always been curious, Arian," I said, glancing over at Scott, "just how Scott here managed to take that medallion off your hands."

They both grinned at each other, then Arian said, "Let me just say, Logan, that the next time Scott is in Dubai, I will challenge him to a rematch. I'd never lost a trap-shooting challenge before."

They both laughed as they recounted their match and how Scott had barely snuck away with the win on his last shot. While I was walking up to one of the tables, my taste buds craving a second helping, a hand grazed against mine. Soft fingers clasped into mine from behind, and I turned around to see Sam. She looked beautiful in a dark red dress and heels, and her sexy smile made it impossible for me not to bring her in close, wrap my arms around her, and taste her cherry-red lips.

When the fresh seafood meal was finished, Sam and I made our way to the dock and set off on the Baia, racing the sunset west. The sky lit up shades of red, yellow, and orange over the blue waters of the Gulf. I tuned my stereo to Pirate Radio and blared "Burning Love" through the speakers, loud enough to be heard over the roar of the engines and the splashing of the propellers through the water. Sam stepped up from the saloon, wearing a white bikini and holding two drinks in her hands. Sitting on my lap, she handed me a fresh mojito and set another in the cup holder beside the wheel. I took a few swigs, relishing the taste of my favorite drink before handing it back to her.

With one hand on the wheel, I reached into my pocket and pulled out the gold Aztec medallion I'd found years before. It shone brightly in the light of the dying sun, and looking out over the endless ocean off the Keys, I wondered what else hid beneath its waves, waiting to be discovered.

Sam and I smiled at each other, then kissed until the sun dropped well below the horizon. Perhaps I'd found a good career change after all.

THE END

LOGAN DODGE ADVENTURES

Gold in the Keys
Hunted in the Keys
Revenge in the Keys
Betrayed in the Keys
Redemption in the Keys
Corruption in the Keys
Predator in the Keys
Legend in the Keys
Abducted in the Keys
Showdown in the Keys
Avenged in the Keys
Broken in the Keys
Payback in the Keys

JASON WAKE NOVELS

Caribbean Wake
Surging Wake
Relentless Wake

Join the Adventure!
Sign up for my newsletter to receive updates on
upcoming books on my website:

matthewrief.com

About the Author

Matthew has a deep-rooted love for adventure and the ocean. He loves traveling, diving, rock climbing and writing adventure novels. Though he grew up in the Pacific Northwest, he currently lives in Virginia Beach with his wife, Jenny.

Made in United States
North Haven, CT
02 April 2023

34893295R00176